ADVANCE
BOOK 6
BY BOUNDS

ALASKAN SECURITY-TEAM ROGUE

Jemma
WESTBROOK

CHAPTER 1

"I'M GONNA MISS this." Elise's pale green eyes were fixed on the mirrors as she took her turn on the leg press machine.

"I know." Lennie eyed Gentry, the lead for Beta, as he ran on the treadmill, his long hair tied up on top of his head. "I heard they're all shipping out tomorrow."

"Not all." Elise's gaze went to the treadmills. "But definitely a lot of the good ones."

"I'm not sure how I feel about the man-bun." Lennie tilted her head. "Sometimes I love it and sometimes I don't."

"You use it like a handle." Elise made a gripping motion with her hand. "Make sure they go where you want them to go." Her fisted hand went down, making it clear she had a pretty specific location in mind.

"Do men like that? Women just shoving their face down there?" It was hard to imagine doing that not knowing how a guy would react.

He might be horrified. Totally put off by the demand.

Totally put off by the woman doing it.

Elise snorted. "Uh, yeah." She pressed up on the platform, extending her legs. "They like it when you sit on their face too."

"That seems dangerous."

"They don't care. They want to die." Elise locked the machine in place and stood up. "Your turn."

Elise clearly didn't understand what she meant by dangerous. Her thoughts weren't on suffocation. They were on rejection.

And the embarrassment that would follow.

Lennie settled into Elise's vacated seat. "I think I need to practice being more assertive with men." Just the thought of it made her sick to her stomach.

"I think you missed your golden opportunity on that one. You could have practiced on a new man every day for months." Elise shot Gentry a smile when he caught her staring in the mirror.

There was no shame in Elise's game. She and Heidi were friends for a reason.

They were kindred spirits, with one major difference.

Elise was a social butterfly. She loved going out. Planning parties. Meeting for lunches. Any chance to get out and have fun.

Not that there was much of an opportunity for that here. Not with the way things had been.

"I feel like we went from slim pickings to an overwhelming number of options." Lennie released the catch on the exercise equipment and huffed through her presses.

Unlike Elise, she was actually here to work out.

"I know." Elise smiled wide. "It's freaking great."

"But how do you pick when there's so many options?" Lennie glanced up in the mirror as a few members of Rogue walked out of the locker room and into the gym.

"Who says you have to pick?" Elise's smile held as she turned it toward where Tyson, Abe, and Shawn were crossing the rubber-floored room. "I think you're due a hoe phase."

"That's one of those things that sounds fun in theory, but I'm not sure I'd be able to put it into practice." Lennie finished her reps then locked the machine. "I think I'm just a serial monogamist." Find one man, fumble through the learning phase of the relationship and then settle in for whatever came next.

Happiness maybe?

So far she'd never made it past phase one, with every relationship she'd been in ending because she couldn't figure out how to settle in. How to feel comfortable.

Elise finally turned her way, offering a little shrug. "No one's perfect."

"I'll just live vicariously through you." Lennie stood, grabbing her bottle of water and twisting the cap free. "Who are you going to make fall in love with you first?"

"That's the way it always goes, isn't it?" Elise crossed her arms and let out a sigh. "Men act like they don't want anything serious, but the minute you just want sex they get all weird."

"Guess you'll have to reverse-psychology them." Lennie grinned at Elise. "Go in guns blazing. Talk about babies and weddings and commitment."

"That's not a bad idea." Elise tapped one finger where it rested against her bicep. "Use them and then trick them into ditching you."

"Otherwise you'll end up getting proposed to again."

"And no one wants that." Elise scanned the space. "You done here?"

Lennie took a step, her legs wobbling enough to make it clear their trip to the gym was a success. "Only if I want to walk tomorrow."

"I'd like to not be able to walk tomorrow." Elise lifted a brow as Zeke, the lead for Shadow, came in from the open door to the hall and went straight to where Gentry was still on the treadmill. "I wonder if I can convince two of them I'm in love at the same time."

"Pretty sure they'd compare notes and figure out you were messing with both of them." Lennie grabbed her towel and slapped it over one shoulder.

Elise gave her a wicked smile. "I literally meant both of them at once."

Keeping her eyeballs from falling on the floor was nearly impossible. "At once?" She nearly choked trying to swallow. "Have you done that before?"

"No. It's on my bucket list, though." Elise snagged her untouched water and headed for the door, hips swaying more than usual as she peeked toward where Tyson was spotting Abe. She shot him a wink when he looked her way.

"You're going to get Abe killed." Lennie glanced back to catch Tyson staring at Elise like a deer in the headlights.

"That would be a shame." Elise smirked as they walked out of the gym and down the hall toward the main building at Alaskan Security. "He's making me think I might have a thing for older men."

"It's the voice." Abe had the deepest voice she'd ever heard. It was rough and low and probably made most women shiver in their shoes.

"Can you imagine what that sounds like in your ear when—"

A broad figure came rushing around the corner, moving so fast that neither of them had time to react or dodge the collision. Not her and not the dark-haired man whose body hit hers straight on.

Rico's hands immediately grabbed Lennie as she started to tip back toward the floor, her jello legs doing nothing to keep her upright. His dark eyes fixed on her face as he settled her back on her already unsteady feet. "You okay, Loba?"

"I'm good." Lennie worked hard to keep her eyes on his.

Because while Elise was busy building her imaginary harem, Lennie was struggling not to trip over her tongue every time one single man's gaze rested on her.

And now here he was. Close enough to touch.

Close enough to smell.

Good God what made a man smell like he did?

It was spicy and clean and rich.

"Where are you going in such a hurry?" Elise eyed the stretch of Rico's black shirt across his broad chest, her eyes trailing over his shoulders.

But Rico's eyes stayed right where they were, locked onto Lennie. "I need to talk to Shawn."

"He's in the gym." Lennie managed to get the words out in a way that sounded mostly normal.

"That where you've been, Loba?" Rico's fingers flexed where they still held her biceps. "Trying to bulk up?"

"Maybe." Lennie put all her energy into lifting one eyebrow at him. "Someone around here has to be in shape."

Rico's face split into a wide smile. "Be careful with that. We'll put you in gear and send you out in the field."

"Only if Mona's on my team." Of everyone at Alaskan Security, Mona was the one she related to the most.

And it gave her hope.

Hope that she'd be able to come out of her shell at least a little. Figure out how to be the kind of woman who goes after what she wants.

Like Elise.

"Smart move." Rico still held her arms. "Mona's a threat no one sees coming." His chocolate eyes

10

drifted over her face. "Makes her a dangerous woman."

"Rico." Shawn's voice carried down the hall.

Rico slowly pulled his gaze from her face. "I'll be there in a minute." His eyes dragged back her way, voice lowering. "Almost as dangerous as you are, Loba." His hands eased away and Rico straightened to his full height. "Enjoy the rest of your day, ladies."

Lennie watched as Rico sauntered his way to the gym door.

"That man has swagger in spades." Elise shook her head. "You better watch out."

Lennie turned to her friend. "For what?"

Elise's lips pulled into a slow smile. "For him."

"You think?" Lennie chewed her lower lip. "I kinda thought he was like a big teddy bear."

Elise snorted. "Yeah. No. Definitely not." She shook her head. "That's the kind of man who makes your legs forget how to work."

Lennie turned away from the door. "I'm not familiar with that particular problem."

"That's a shame." Elise walked beside her as they went toward the front of the building where the finishing touches were being put on the entryway's repair. "But I'd say if you keep hanging around Rico you might find out real quick."

"I'm not *hanging out* with Rico." So far Lennie had only spoken to him a handful of times, and each one was wickedly awkward and terrifying. "He just happens to work at the same place I work."

"That sounded awfully defensive." Elise paused outside the door to her office.

Lennie pressed her lips together. Anything else she said would only make Elise's suspicions worse, so she shoved on a smile. "Go back to work."

"Elise." Pierce strode from his office. "Have we heard back from the property manager in Cincinnati?"

"He promised to let me know by this afternoon." Elise snapped into work mode immediately. "If I don't hear from him by 1:00 I will follow up."

Pierce tipped his head in a nod. "Excellent." He spun on one heel and disappeared back into his office.

"Cincinnati?" Lennie lifted her brows at Elise in question.

"Our old building. Pierce is trying to negotiate an early termination of the lease." Elise backed into her office. "Thanks for accompanying me to the meat market." She gave Lennie a wink as she closed the door.

"Meat market?" Harlow, one of the two in-house hackers, stood just behind her, a giant cup of coffee gripped in one hand.

Lennie fell into step beside Harlow. "It's what Elise calls the gym."

Harlow snorted out a laugh as they walked through the doors of Team Intel's office. "That's amazing."

Lennie went to her desk and eased into her chair, using the arm rests to give her wobbly legs a helping hand.

Mona eyed her from where she sat. "You're gonna feel that tomorrow."

"Remind me of this next time I want to tone up." Lennie shifted in her seat turning toward her friend and former boss. "How's Eva?"

"Grumpy." Mona moved around the line of papers across her desk. "She doesn't like feeling bad."

"At least she feels bad for a reason." Lennie flipped through the file she'd been working on before leaving for her scheduled gym trip. "Better than the flu, where you barf for nothing."

"Dutch is sure I'm never having a kid now." Harlow spun in her chair to join the conversation. "And he might not be wrong."

"Yeah. The only one selling it is Heidi." Mona glanced up as Heidi strutted in through the door. "Speak of the devil.

Heidi made a show of looking Mona up and down. "Dang, Monster. That tan is holding strong."

After her wedding to Pierce, the owner of Alaskan Security, Mona was whisked away by her new husband to an extended honeymoon in Hawaii. It was the break they both needed after a long and terrifying winter.

Heidi went to her chair and dropped into it before spinning toward Lennie, grinning.

"What? Why are you looking at me like that?"

"I heard you had a run in just a little bit ago." Heidi's smile widened. "With Rico."

"I literally bumped into him in the hall." She turned her attention to the papers she should be working on. "That's all."

Alpha Team was shipping out tomorrow, and she was assigned to the task of researching each of their clients. Making sure they knew everything there was to know before walking onto the job. This was her final file, and it was turning out to be a mess of tabloid articles and paparazzi photos.

Dutch strode in with Roman, Isaac, and Alec, his contemporaries on each of the other teams. The men were deep in conversation about the logistics of the transition that would take two of the teams from headquarters and spread them around the world on assignment. Everyone at Alaskan Security had been working on the plan for months, and it was finally time to put it into motion.

Seth came into the room, immediately walking her way. "Hey, Lennie. You done with Twyla's file yet? I gotta get it to Silas so he can run through it on the plane."

"She's something else, isn't she?" Lennie flipped the file closed and passed it off to the team lead for Alpha. "Silas's going to have his hands full with her."

"They're all a handful." Seth flipped through her research. "Damn. She's good-looking too."

"You say that like it's a bad thing."

Seth shot her a dimpled smile. "Don't take it personally." He held up the file. "Thanks for working so hard on these."

"It's my job." Lennie turned a little in her chair, scanning her empty desk as she tapped her fingers on the surface.

Now what?

She came to Alaska thinking it would be the push she needed.

A career that would force her into areas she usually avoided.

Excitement. Adventure.

And at the beginning it was.

Nothing like the possibility of imminent death to spice up your life.

But once things calmed down, it became pretty clear this work wasn't going to be much different from what she did in Ohio at Investigative Resources, the company Mona and Eva owned along with a third partner who turned out to be a bigger piece of crap than they already knew.

And at least in Ohio she had other things to do.

Not all of them good.

Which was what made her so willing to come here in the first place. In spite of her fear of flying.

In spite of her fear of change.

In spite of how long her family begged her to stay and keep living the same life she was stuck in.

Mona turned her way. "You okay?"

Lennie forced a smile. "Yeah." She pushed the smile higher. "I'm good."

Mona lifted a brow.

She'd spent almost three years working at Investigative Resources for Mona and Eva. They were great bosses and even better friends.

And watching how this place changed Mona from a passive person into a woman who took the world on headfirst was the only reason she was still here.

Still hanging onto the hope that Alaska might be able to help her too.

But she couldn't expect it to happen all by itself. She was going to have to give it a hand to get the ball rolling.

Lennie grabbed a pad of paper from one drawer and started a list, writing the title in neat letters.

Shit that scares me.

And there was one thing that belonged at the top of that list.

Rico.

"Loba."

Lennie kept her eyes on the paper as her stomach hit the floor. "*Si, señor.*"

She caught Rico coming her way in her peripheral vision as she slid her hand to cover the two lines she'd managed to write.

"So formal." He stopped at the edge of her desk.

"Not all of us drip with charm." She lifted her eyes and nearly passed out when she found his locked onto her face.

Rico's lips twitched. "So you think I'm charming."

Flirting was not her strong suit. Never had been. Every time she went out with her friends Lennie was the one sitting alone, awkwardly holding her drink as she struggled to find a way into a conversation with the opposite sex.

"You know you're charming."

Rico leaned closer. "I'm more interested in what *you* think, Loba."

And here was where she shut down. Ran out of courage and steam.

Lost her nerve.

"I don't know what I think." It was about as lame of a response as you could get.

But Rico didn't walk away, which is what usually happened right about now.

His eyes stayed on her. "I would be happy to help you figure that out, Loba."

There was no stopping the widening of her eyes.

The drop of her jaw.

Rico's head tilted just a hair as his eyes moved over her face.

"Hey, Rico." Roman leaned back in his seat. "Have you filed the flight plan for tomorrow?"

Rico straightened, gaze holding her pinned in place a second longer, before dropping to her desk as he turned to where Roman sat with the rest of the technical coordinators. "Sent it over first thing this morning."

"Good." Roman turned to his computer. "It'll be a long day. Get a good night's sleep."

"It'll be two long days." Alec tipped his head Roman's way. "Beta's heading out the day after Alpha."

"It's time for us to get back to business." Pierce strode in, heading straight for Mona's desk. He perched on the edge. "We've been out of the game for too long as it is. We need to reestablish."

"We didn't have trouble filling every availability we have." Mona's tone was strong and solid as she focused on Pierce. "The company is fine."

Pierce softly smiled. "As always, I will choose to believe you're correct."

"Because I am." Mona poked him with the end of her ink pen. "Now go back to work."

Pierce leaned to whisper something in her ear.

Something that made Mona's fair skin flush almost immediately.

No one ever whispered things like that in her ear.

Certainly not in public.

Probably because she wasn't the kind of woman men went crazy over. The kind of woman they struggled to keep their hands off.

The kind of woman they pursued.

Pierce stood, smoothing down the front of his expensive suit before turning to Rico. "Come run over the flight plans with me."

Rico tipped his head in a nod before falling in behind Pierce. He was almost at the door when his eyes came her way.

Catching Lennie red-handed as she watched him go.

Lennie immediately looked away, jerking her eyes to the pad of paper on her desk.

Her heart stopped.

The hand she'd so carefully placed was not where it used to be, leaving her words uncovered for anyone to see.

Not just anyone could have seen them, though.

Only one person was close enough to read the lines she'd damned herself with.

The same person who was on the list.

Rico.

CHAPTER 2

"YOU OKAY TODAY?" Shawn eyed him from his spot in the cockpit.

Rico kept his focus on the panel in front of him. "I'm fine."

He'd been hoping today would offer a distraction. Keep his disappointment at bay for at least a little while.

So far it wasn't turning out that way.

Shawn lifted his brows, settling back in his seat. "Whatever you say."

They were at the end of a long-ass day of shuttling the members of Alpha around, dropping pairs off at the airports closest to their new assignments. It was something he used to do all the time, and after months of being mostly grounded due to the constant threats against Alaskan Security, Rico was itching to get back to business as usual.

Especially since things weren't shaking out the way he hoped they would at headquarters.

"How's Heidi doing?" The best option was to shift the conversation. Move it somewhere Shawn would be happy to stay.

"Good. She loves being pregnant." Shawn almost smiled. "But I can't keep enough cheese in the fridge."

"Gotta keep her fed. She's growing your babies."

"She makes that very clear." Shawn was the last person Rico expected to end up in love and starting a family.

To be fair, he hadn't expected most of the men he worked with to end up there, but the number seemed to be growing every day.

"She want to get married?" Rico scanned the instruments, keeping an eye on everything as they made their final leg of the day's journey.

"She's apparently not in any hurry." Shawn's disappointment was obvious.

"Not going to make an honest man out of you?"

"Heidi says she doesn't need a piece of paper to be happy." Shawn slumped down a little.

"What about you?" In the past six months he'd somehow managed to become the resident therapist for the men falling for the women he kept flying in.

Maybe that was because he was the only one of them with experience in the marriage department.

Not that he'd been successful at it.

"Do *you* need a piece of paper to be happy?" It was a fair question. One many men thought they couldn't consider.

Shawn shrugged. "I just want her to be happy."

"You can't just worry about her happiness, *Amigo*. You've got to be happy too, otherwise it won't work." It was a fact Rico was quite familiar with.

It was why he'd spent the past five years chasing whatever made him happy.

It was also why he'd considered chasing the sweet new face that joined Intel.

Up until yesterday, that is.

Shawn went silent. Rico had known him long enough to know that meant his friend was thinking.

Maybe obsessing was a better term.

But the seed was planted, and that was all he could do.

By the time they were in Alaska Shawn was dozing in the seat beside him, headset askew. He stirred as ATC communications came through the radio, assisting their landing. Shawn straightened in his seat as the plane eased toward the airport and their elevation dipped.

It was late enough they would each manage less than five hours of sleep before they had to be back up and out again to take Beta to their stations, but it would be worth it to have things back to normal.

As normal as life at Alaskan Security ever was.

They unloaded, greeting the men in charge of refueling the largest of Alaskan Security's jets, making sure it was flight ready in the morning. Rico pulled the keys to the Rover they drove to the airport from his pocket and unlocked the doors. By the time he tossed his bag in the back Shawn was already on the phone, checking in with Heidi, letting her know he was on his way.

"Everything okay?" Rico pulled out of the airport and headed toward the main campus of the largest private security company in the United States.

"She said she's just sore." Shawn tucked the phone into his bag.

"I can't imagine all that stretching feels very good." Heidi was carrying twins and even though she was plenty tall, two babies took up a lot of space.

"Probably not." Shawn's lips turned down in a frown. "I wish it was one at a time."

"Didn't she want twins?" When Heidi found out she was pregnant everyone got to hear all about it.

Whether they wanted to or not.

Usually more than once.

"Yup." Shawn scratched at the growth of hair on his jaw. "How in the hell do you juggle two babies at once?"

"Luckily you got a lot of hands around here to help."

Shawn glanced his way. "That mean you're going to come change diapers?"

"I will pass on that, my friend." Rico shook his head. "I will wear one around in one of those chest packs, though."

Shawn barked out an unexpected laugh. "I can only imagine how the women would chase you if you had a baby strapped to your chest." He snorted. "You'd be beating them off with a stick."

"What makes you think I don't do that now?" Rico turned into the commercial park that sat in front of the entrance to headquarters.

"You forget we've all been up each other's asses for six months. I haven't seen a woman come anywhere close to you." Shawn eyed him. "Except for Lennie."

"In case you missed it," Rico rolled down the window and punched his code into the newly-replaced gate, "we had more important things to deal with."

"I like how you ignored the second part of what I said." Shawn smirked at him.

"Lennie isn't my type."

"Why not? She's breathing."

"Ouch." Rico pulled through the gate and down the long lane leading to the main building.

"I don't mean that in a bad way." Shawn sounded apologetic. "I'm just saying you're an equal opportunity appreciator of the female species."

"Maybe I've gotten more discerning." It wasn't a lie. He'd spent almost six months like everyone else, powering through the chaos breaking out around them at every step, planning what he would do the second it was all over.

The answer was always the same.

He'd go find some companionship of the female variety.

24

But once the time came he'd found every reason to put it off.

And it all came down to the dark-haired woman who intrigued him in a way no other had.

Until yesterday.

"Lennie is too sweet for me."

"Still sticking with the bad girls then?"

"They're not bad girls." Rico preferred his women to be just as experienced as he was. It made for one hell of a good time for everyone involved.

And for a minute he thought Lennie might fit that bill.

"Let me rephrase that." Shawn's hand was on the handle as Rico pulled into their designated parking space. "You're sticking with girls looking for something just as shallow as you are."

"Oh, it's not shallow, *Amigo*." Rico shot him a wink.

"I really didn't need that visual in my head." Shawn was out of the SUV the second it was in park, pulling his bag from the floorboard at his feet.

"You figure out where you and Heidi are going yet?" While Alpha and Beta teams were spread out, Rogue and Shadow would be staying closer to home, and a few of the men were looking into off-campus living.

"She's been looking at houses every night." Shawn walked alongside Rico as they went to the new main entrance. When the man threatening all of their lives remotely crashed a van through the front of the building Pierce took the opportunity to rework the whole thing.

Make it bigger. More impressive.

Now it stood two stories tall, the full height of the main office building. The entire front wall was glass, letting in any bit of light Alaska had to offer.

But the entrance wasn't the only thing that had changed since a man from Pierce's past tried to take them all down.

Now there were plants everywhere. Scented candles lit on desks and tables.

The campus was huge. Sleek. Modern.

And the addition of a team of women made it something it had never been before.

Comfortable.

It's probably why so many of his teammates managed to find themselves getting even more cozy with the members of Intel.

"Hopefully she finds something while the weather is still decent." They were in the most mild of the seasons Alaska had to offer, and while moving wasn't impossible in the winter, it sure as hell wasn't fun.

"She'll have to if she wants to be in before the babies come." Shawn swiped his badge through the security system before punching in his own code. As soon as the locks clicked open he was through the door and headed straight for the walkway that connected to the rooming building where most members of Shadow, Rogue, and Intel lived.

"She might just decide to drag her feet so she'll have help." Rico opened the door to the glassed-in hall leading to the other building, holding it as Shawn went though.

"Not sure how much help there will be to go around with Bess and Eva pregnant too." Shawn shook his head. "There must be something in the water around here."

"I'll keep that in mind."

"Thought Lennie wasn't your type." Shawn pulled the next door open, letting Rico go first.

"Didn't say it had anything to do with Lenn—" Her name died in his throat.

Lennie stood in the central kitchen of the rooming building, a forkful of cake hovering in front of her parted lips. Her wide eyes fixed on him, making it perfectly clear she'd heard every bit of what he said.

And what he didn't.

Heidi smiled from where she stood next to Lennie. "What doesn't have anything to do with Lennie?"

"Lenton." Shawn went straight to where Heidi was holding her own piece of cake, wrapping one arm around her widening waist and pulling her close. "It was one of the airports we stopped at today." The wink he gave Heidi revealed his lie.

Luckily Lennie was now staring at her plate, completely focused on her fork as she moved around the crumbs and icing.

Shawn spread one hand across Heidi's barely-rounded belly. "How's it going, Kitten?"

"Fantastic." Heidi smiled as she took another bite of what appeared to be chocolate cake. "Brock made cake."

"At eleven at night?" Shawn shook his head as she held a forkful out for him.

"Eva thought it sounded good." Heidi ate the cake Shawn rejected. "Apparently it only sounded good until he started baking it. Then the smell made her puke."

"Her loss." Harlow sat on the counter between where Heidi and Lennie stood, eating her own slice of cake.

Elise came around the corner. She scoffed when she saw the women lined up across the kitchen. "You couldn't wait for me?"

"You take forever in the shower." Heidi held out a plate. "And I was hungry."

"You're lucky you're pregnant or my feelings would be hurt." Elise took the plate and turned toward him. "Hey there, Rico."

Elise was the woman he should have set his sights on. She was warm and clearly enjoyed flirting as much as he did.

The problem was, every time he saw her Lennie wasn't far behind, and she pulled his attention like a fucking magnet.

He struggled not to get closer.

Not to try his hand at reeling her in.

"How was the flight?" Heidi leaned toward Lennie, stealing a forkful of the icing Lennie shoved to one side.

"Long." Shawn backed toward the hall leading to the private rooms. "And tomorrow's going to be just as long." He tipped his head toward Rico. "I'm gonna go shower and turn in."

"In that case." Heidi dropped her paper plate into the trash. "Goodnight, ladies."

Shawn wrapped one arm around her as they walked out of the kitchen and headed to their suite.

"I should go too." Harlow jumped off the counter. "Dutch is helping Alec tomorrow and I'll probably end up getting up when he does."

"I'll walk you up." Elise rushed to Harlow's side, peeking back Lennie's way as she rounded the corner.

Lennie stood in the kitchen alone, looking like she wasn't sure how to escape the situation her friends left her in.

He could help her out with that. "I should turn in too." Rico looked at the hall that led to his single room. "Gotta get up early."

"Have a good night." Lennie gripped her paper plate in her hands, her eyes still glued to it.

He should go. Leave the woman who was scared enough of him to make a whole damn list about it.

But it bothered him.

Made him want to prove there was nothing about him to be scared of. Not the way she thought anyway.

"You don't like frosting?"

"What?" Lennie stared at him.

He pointed to the pile of icing she'd scraped from the cake. "You didn't eat the frosting."

"Oh." Lennie looked down at the plate. "Um. Yeah. It's too sweet for me."

His next words were impossible to censor. "I doubt that."

"You probably shouldn't." Lennie dumped the plate in the trash before loading her fork into the dishwasher.

Rico went to the fridge for a bottle of water he didn't need. "And why is that, Loba?"

"Lots of reasons." Lennie backed against the counter as he came closer, her spine curving in a way that probably made her feel like there was more space between them than there was.

"I'm going to have to say those reasons are all wrong, Loba." He eased in a little more, teasing himself with the scent of her skin. "Because you are definitely sweet."

It should have been the reminder he needed to keep his distance. Instead it pulled him closer.

Lennie's eyes darted down his front, skimming the length of his body with a look that was pure curiosity. "Then why do you call me a wolf?"

"You can be sweet and dangerous at the same time, Loba." Rico leaned into her ear, daring to brush his lips against it with his next words. "And that's definitely what you are."

Most women he spent time with would toss their head back and laugh at that. A deep rich sound that would shoot straight to his dick.

That's not what Lennie did.

She gasped. Soft and short.

And he was hard in a second.

Half a second if he was being an honest man.

And that was why he needed to get the fuck away from her.

"Goodnight, Loba." He straightened away from Lennie, stealing one last lungful of the soft

30

sweetness of her skin before backing toward his room.

Her eyes stayed on him as he went. Unfortunately, they weren't filled with desire or anything else that might make him want to change his mind about what he had to do.

Lennie's dark eyes were wide and filled with shock.

Like an animal staring at a bright light, held in place even though they knew they should run.

So he'd do the running for her.

Rico flipped on the lights in his room as the door closed behind him. After tossing his bag on the chair in the corner he went to switch on the shower, turning it as hot as it would go before stripping down, systematically taking off his gear and lining it down the dresser before peeling off his clothes and stepping under the spray.

His dick ached with the need for release. He grabbed the soap and went to work scrubbing, doing his best to ignore the lingering effects of Lennie's soft gasp.

He could imagine her making that same sound a million fucking times for a million fucking reasons.

Each one of them because of something he could do to her.

But if Lennie was scared of him with clothes between them then she'd be terrified without them, and a terrified woman was not anything he ever wanted to take to his bed.

A man would have to be patient with a woman like her.

Show her how to give him what he wanted.

How to take what she wanted.

It was a thought Rico never should have allowed in his mind because it was immediately accompanied by the image of Lennie over him, taking what she wanted while he tried to fight his way free of the ties holding him in place.

He gripped his dick, trying to soothe the desperation making it burn.

It was a rule he refused to break. No matter how tempting it was.

No jacking off to women unless they know he's doing it.

Even better if they're the one making him do it.

Rico flipped the faucet in the opposite direction. Freezing water pelted his skin, making it burn as it tightened from the chill.

It took too many minutes to kill the bite still lingering from being close to her. To force his body and mind back into safer territory. When it finally happened it had more to do with exhaustion than the freeze of his skin.

Rico shut off the water, flipped a towel around his body, and went to the bed, falling against the mattress.

Thank God he'd be gone tomorrow.

He might have to make it happen the next day too.

Whatever it took to put some distance back between him and Lenore Bates.

Before the woman made him want to break more than one of the rules he'd made for himself.

CHAPTER 3

"SO WHAT HAPPENED after I left last night?" Elise wiggled her brows. "Anything exciting?"

"No." Lennie grabbed a mug and filled it with some coffee from the pot on the counter in the open kitchen of the rooming building. "I went to bed."

Mostly.

Elise's lower lip pushed out in a pout. "Alone?"

"Uh, yeah." Lennie tipped a little bit of the sweet cream creamer she loved into the coffee before stirring it with a stick. "I keep trying to tell you, I'm not the girl men try to coerce into their bed." She tossed the strip of wood in the trash before taking a tentative sip.

"Men are stupid."

"I thought you loved men." Lennie peeked at the line of breakfast items stretched across the counter.

"It's more of a love-hate relationship." Elise snagged a small Danish with a dot of cherry filling in the center and took a bite. "Aren't they supposed to be after one thing?"

Lennie laughed a little as she picked up an English muffin and headed for the toaster. "I think that ship sailed after twenty-two for most of them."

Elise frowned down at her breakfast. "Great."

Lennie split her muffin over the sink before dropping it in to brown. She turned her back to the counter, leaning against it while she waited. "Now they want five hundred different things, and none of them are what they have."

"That was just what one man wanted. Kyle was a prick." Elise moved in beside her, wrapping one arm around Lennie's shoulders. "He's going to kick himself for letting you go."

"I doubt that." Lennie offered up as much of a smile as she could manage. "I'm sure he's quite happy with his life choices." The toaster popped up, giving her an excuse to turn away from a conversation she didn't really want to have.

It's why she came to Alaska in the first place.

To get away.

And maybe to start fresh.

Unfortunately, it wasn't turning out to be as easy as she was hoping.

Lennie spread a little peanut butter across each side of the toasted muffin before grabbing her coffee and turning back to Elise. "Ready?"

"I guess." Elise snagged another Danish as they passed, Lennie leading the way.

The halls were much less crowded than they were when she first came here, and the place seemed almost empty in spite of the fact that there were still at least thirty people in residence.

"It's really going to be weird when Shadow and Stealth are out of town." Lennie balanced her coffee and paper plate as she opened the door at the end of the hall connecting the rooming building to the main office building.

"The pickings are getting slimmer and slimmer." Elise huffed out a sigh. "I really thought this would be it."

"It? I thought you were shooting for multiple its." Lennie slowed as they got close to Elise's office.

Elise lifted one shoulder and let it drop. "Whatever."

Lennie bumped her with one hip. "Don't give up." She gave her a grin. "I'm sure you'll find someone to service your needs."

"You wouldn't think it'd be this hard."

"That's what she said." Lennie snorted as she cackled at her own joke.

"I think I know why you don't get hit on."

"Shut up." She stuck her tongue out at Elise. "You know that was funny."

Elise waved her toward the office at the end of the hall. "Go to work. I've got to figure out the new amounts of food to order now that we're down almost twenty big strong men."

Lennie lifted the plate in her hand. "Keep ordering these." She turned then doubled back. "And those yogurt cups with the toppings on the other side."

Elise lifted a brow. "Any other requests?"

"No, thank you." Lennie shot Elise a smile. "Thank you. Love your face."

Elise was already half in her office. "You better."

Lennie headed for Intel's office, her steps light since she didn't have to worry about running into a certain someone.

For today at least.

Tomorrow was a different story.

But hopefully by then Rico will have forgotten how she made an ass out of herself last night.

Hell, he probably already forgot.

Because she was definitely forgettable. Most men couldn't remember her name by the end of whatever little amount of conversation they managed to have with her while looking for another, better option.

The technical coordinators for the five teams at Alaskan Security were already in place at their desks spanning the front of the room, working their teams through the day. Dutch was assisting Alec as he learned the ropes. Alec actually came to Alaska the same time she did, but her former coworker quickly put his technical skills to good use filling the vacancy on Beta's team. He was well-suited for the position and it kept Intel an all woman team.

Which shouldn't please her as much as it did.

Mona and Bess were already at their desks. Bess was one of the few members of Intel that didn't previously work at Investigative Resources, but what Bess lacked in the investigative arena, she made up for with wicked problem-solving skills.

Lennie smiled as they both looked her way. "Good morning."

Bess had a mess of papers across her desk. "I'm not sure we can call it good."

"What's wrong?" Lennie sat her plate and coffee down beside the pictures lined across her desk.

Bess rubbed her temples. "I'm trying to completely untangle this mess we just dealt with. Pierce wants to be sure we know exactly what happened." She turned to the wall they'd scribbled a messy web of names across in their quest to figure out the convoluted plot to take Alaskan Security down.

The unsuccessful, convoluted plot.

"He may not ever know exactly what happened." Mona sighed. "And he'll just have to learn to deal with it."

"Morning, girls." Heidi came into the room carrying her bag and the giant cup of water that never left her side. She plopped down in her seat. "I've got to go to GHOST headquarters today. Anyone want to come help me give Vincent hell?"

Lennie shook her head. "I'm taking a hard pass on that one. Vincent scares the crap out of me."

Vincent was the commander of a team in charge of maintaining 'global and homeland operational security'.

Whatever that actually meant.

At any rate, his dealings leaned into a grey area the government preferred not to touch directly, so he did it for them.

"What are you going to GHOST for?" Mona leaned to look at the papers Bess was scanning.

"Vincent's trying to do the same thing we're trying to do." Heidi pointed at Bessie's desk. "Figure out exactly what happened."

"It'll give him a migraine." Bess relaxed back in her chair, resting both hands on her largely-pregnant belly.

"That's probably just the threat of impending childbirth." Mona glanced at the door as Eva came into the room, her expression softening. "Hey. How are you feeling?"

"Like death." Eva eased into her seat. She shot Heidi a look. "I just want to be clear how much I hate you right now."

"I would puke for you if I could."

"I'm not even really puking." Eva blew out a slow breath. "I just feel like I might every second of every hour of every day."

"It's probably a boy then." Heidi sipped at her drink. "All those extra hormones fucking you all up."

"Boys'll do that to you." Elise came through the door, a few papers stacked in one hand. "Looks like Pierce managed to negotiate the early termination of the lease on the building in Cincinnati." She passed the papers to Eva. "Which means now we have to get it cleaned out by the end of next week."

"I didn't think he could do it." Mona stood and went to Eva's desk, leaning over her shoulder to scan the documents Elise passed off.

"I won't tell him you doubted him. It'll hurt his feelings." Elise turned to scan the row of men at the front of the room before looking Lennie's way and lifting her brows.

Lennie shrugged.

She and Elise hadn't been particularly close before coming to Alaska. They worked at the same company, but not side by side. Elise and Heidi were best friends, but now Heidi had other things to do.

Mostly Shawn.

Which was how she ended up pregnant with twins. To be fair he probably just looked at her and it happened.

"Who's going to go get it cleaned out?" Heidi spun a little in her chair as she waited for Mona and Eva to answer.

"It can't be me." Eva burped, covering her mouth with one hand as she did. Her eyes lifted to Mona. "And Pierce won't let you go anywhere without him."

"He can't leave right now. There's too much happening with Alpha and Beta taking their new assignments this week." Mona looked at Elise. "You know everything that's there. Is that something you'd be interested in handling?"

"Sure." Elise smiled. "Especially if I can sneak some nightlife in while I'm there." Her eyes came to Lennie. "Can I take someone with me?"

"You should. It's a big job." Mona slid the papers around. "I think we should send a couple guys with you too."

"That sounds like a great idea." Elise slowly walked Lennie's way. "Is there anyone in particular you think should go?" She rested one hip against the desk between them.

Mona turned toward Lennie. Her eyes went to the line of frames down her desk. "Would you like to go see your family?"

"Um." Lennie pressed her lips together. "We would be driving so we could bring everything back, right?"

"Pierce wants to ship it all back." Elise wiggled her brows. "We'd be flying."

Lennie's stomach dropped.

Getting on that damn plane was hard enough last time, and that was when she had anger on her side. "I should probably stay here in case Alpha needs any information."

Mona turned to fully face her. "If you really don't want to go we won't make you."

Shit.

She did want to see her niece and nephews.

"I'm sure Eli could give you something to get you through the flight." Elise lifted her brows. "And we could have some fun while we're there."

She should be ashamed at how hard she had to think about this. "Maybe."

"Excellent." Elise stood. "I'll go tell Pierce we've got it covered." She paused at the door, turning to Lennie. "Could you let Rico know we need him to fly us out there?"

Hell and damnation.

The thought of flying sent her brain scrambling so much she hadn't really taken the whole scenario much farther.

"Thanks, Len." Elise shot her a wide grin as she spun and walked out the door.

The room was a little quiet.

Instead of looking around to see how many sets of eyes were on her, Lennie stared at her computer, pretending she was actually seeing what was there.

How could she back out of this now? Flying was one thing. One big thing.

Rico was something else all together.

Something she wasn't even capable of explaining at this point.

"Thank you for doing this, Lennie." Eva leaned back in her chair and let out a slow breath. "I'm glad you'll be there to help Elise organize everything."

Was she really going to tell her sickly pregnant former boss there was no way she could get over herself enough to fly on a plane with Rico?

No.

No she wasn't. Because that would be a dick move, and while she might be a chicken who was scared of just about everything, she was not a dick.

Lennie spent the rest of the afternoon working through the background of a new potential client. Everyone who hired Alaskan Security did so knowing they would be fully investigated beforehand, which made her job here slightly less interesting than the one she had before. More often than not these people laid it out for her, putting any of their questionable activities front and center.

Because they wanted Alaskan Security to take them on. And she couldn't blame them. Their power was far reaching.

Farther than most people even knew.

When Heidi and Mona came back from the meeting with GHOST both were frowning. Lennie pushed her work to one side. "What's wrong?"

"We missed something." Mona sat down at her desk, fingers immediately going to the keyboard.

"We missed *someone*." Heidi turned to scan the wall. "There's one more person with their fingers in the cookie jar." At one point Vincent attempted to lure Heidi away from Alaskan Security, but when that didn't work he and Pierce negotiated terms that allowed Vincent to request Heidi's expertise in exchange for certain liberties.

Liberties that are what made Alaskan Security unparalleled in their field.

Lennie eyed the wall lined with the names of the people they'd identified as being involved in the group trying to funnel drugs from the United States into Canada, with a side goal of taking Alaskan Security down in the process. "Does Vincent know who it is?"

"If he did he wouldn't have called me." Heidi twisted in her chair. "He wants this cleaned up as much as Pierce does. These guys were able to find way too much information and it makes him hella nervous."

"What kind of information?" Lennie fell into her career by accident. She never intended to be a de facto private investigator, but after spending time working for a collection agency tracking down missing vehicles and jet skis she discovered a knack for digging up dirt.

It was a challenge and something she could do from the comfort and safety of her desk.

A way to live a pseudo exciting life without really taking any risk at all.

"I'm not entirely sure." Heidi rolled her head from side to side before laying her fingers to the keys of her computer. "I'm going to see if I can find it in GHOST's system."

"Vincent's going to get tired of you hacking into his stuff." Mona didn't look away from her own computer.

"Then he'll start telling me what I want to know from the beginning." Heidi tucked a tiny wireless headphone into each ear and fell silent as she worked.

Lennie finished the last of what she needed to get done for Alpha before packing up her things. "I'm going to head out for the night, unless someone needs something else from me."

Mona was already gone, leaving just Heidi and Harlow and the tech guys in the room.

Heidi shook her head. "See you tomorrow."

Lennie paused in front of Heidi's desk. "You should probably get some rest too."

"I'm finding this information tonight to prove a point." She lifted her eyes from the screen. "And Shawn won't be back for a couple hours anyway."

In that case, Lennie was going to take full advantage of the next two hours. She hurried to her room where she dropped her bag on the chair in the corner and went to take a quick shower before pulling on a pair of shorts and a t-shirt.

Then she added a hooded sweatshirt, tucking her phone into the front pocket. Even in the summer the place was still not quite warm enough.

She made her way to the kitchen in the common area of the building. At some point she would have to figure out exactly what her future plans were. If she was staying here. If she was going back to Ohio.

Living out of a glorified hotel room was fun for a few weeks, but she was going on six months without a kitchen of her own, and it was getting really old.

As Lennie reached the end of the hall her phone buzzed in her pocket. She pulled it free, swiping open the text from Elise as she went into the kitchen.

Don't forget to tell Rico he's flying us to Ohio.

Yeah. She was going to go ahead and forget to do that.

Lennie opened the fridge as she responded with one thumb.

K

It was about all the effort she could put into dealing with that right now.

She pulled out a container of chicken salad and turned toward the island that sat between the kitchen and the media space.

And ran straight into a wall of chest.

A familiar wall of chest.

"Are you hungry, Loba?"

How could a handful of words make her shiver and consider throwing up at the same time?

"Um." Lennie kept her head down as she sidestepped Rico's wide frame. "Seems like." She dared a peek his way as she continued collecting the food that no longer held the appeal it did a few seconds ago. "I thought you weren't coming back for a couple more hours."

"The wind was on our side." Rico was still awfully close.

Maybe closer than he was last time she looked his way.

Lennie struggled to slice into one of the bakery rolls tucked into a bag on the counter.

"You can't saw at it, Loba. It's not a man who's wronged you." Rico took the bread and knife from her hands, his fingers lingering on her skin longer than seemed necessary. "You have to commit." He slid the point of the knife deep into the roll before working it to one side in a neat slice. "It's so soft if you keep at it like that you won't do anything but crush it." He laid the perfectly split roll on the counter in front of her.

"Thank you." Lennie risked another glance his way, her heart racing. She wanted him to go away, but felt obligated to at least offer him some of the food she was preparing.

That's all it was. Obligation. "Do you want a sandwich?"

Rico eased a little closer. "Are you inviting me to dinner, Loba?"

CHAPTER 4

HE SHOULD NOT be here.

He should have walked right past when he saw Lennie in the kitchen, oblivious to what was going on around her, leaving her to murder the sandwich roll in peace.

"I was just trying to be polite." She forked some chicken salad onto the roll he'd sliced for her.

"If we're being polite, then I will accept your invitation." Rico reached for a second roll and went to work cutting it in half. He'd been gone since the sun came up, busting his ass to get everyone where they needed to go, which meant he hadn't had much time to eat.

It was the reason he gave himself for following her into the kitchen.

Hunger.

"What do you like on top, Loba?"

Her eyes snapped his way. "What?"

His brain didn't need any help being dragged into places it had no business going when she was concerned. "On your sandwich. What do you like on top of your sandwich? Lettuce? Tomato?" Rico backed to the fridge, putting distance between them.

Distance he probably needed more than she did.

"Oh." Lennie's voice was soft. "Both."

"A woman after my own heart." He pulled a head of romaine from the fridge and snagged a tomato off the counter. This was probably where their mutual tastes ended, especially since his leaned toward the adventurous side.

And this woman was definitely not the adventurous type.

Lennie peeked his way from the corner of her eye. "So your flight was good?"

"The weather was clear. The wind was low. It was perfect."

"That's good." Lennie's shoulders relaxed a little.

"How was your day?"

"Good. Fine." She smashed some chicken onto the bun he'd cut for himself, shifting on her feet as her lips rolled inward.

"Do you have more to say, Loba?"

"Um." Her dark brows came together. "I was just wondering how you got into flying."

Rico sliced into the tomato. "I wanted to make my mother proud."

She smiled softly. "And is she?"

"She was very proud."

"Oh." Lennie's face fell a little, lower lip tucking between her teeth.

"What about you? How did you get into hunting people down over the internet?" Rico laid a few slices of tomato on each sandwich before topping them with lettuce.

"It was an accident." She laid the other halves of the rolls on top of the finished sandwiches. "My college degree is not as useful as I thought it would be, so I ended up at what I thought was a dead-end job."

Rico picked up both plates and went to one of the small tables situated around the space.

Lennie hesitated. He felt it as much as he saw it.

One more thing he should pay attention to. Another reminder he should keep his distance.

Finally her feet started in his direction, bringing her to the table he chose in front of one of the large windows overlooking the property. Rico waited for her to sit before taking the seat across from her. "Do you like Alaska?"

"It's not really turning out the way I expected it would." She took a bite of her sandwich.

"What you have seen is not normal for us, Loba." He wanted to reassure her. Let Lennie know the chaos of the past six months wasn't normal, even for them. "It will be much calmer now."

Lennie swallowed her bite. She was quiet for a minute. "That's part of the problem."

Rico's sandwich hovered in front of his mouth. "The calm is the problem?"

"Sort of." Lennie shrugged. "I came here because I thought it would be exciting."

Rico set his sandwich down. "You came here because you thought it would be exciting?"

She stared across the table at him. "That's what I just said."

"I wanted to be sure I heard you right." Rico rested his arms on the table and leaned in closer. "So you came to Alaska looking for excitement?"

Lennie gave him a little nod. "That's right."

Interesting.

And problematic.

"What exactly were you expecting?"

Lennie sighed. "I don't know." She took another bite of her sandwich. "Bad guys. Car chases. Shooting." She huffed around the food in her mouth. "But I just sit at a desk all day. Exactly like I did before."

"You're not excited by hunting bad guys down through your computer screen?" Rico studied the woman across from him.

He thought he'd figured her out.

Thought he knew who Lenore Bates was.

Maybe he'd jumped to conclusions.

"I bet things get a little more interesting soon." Rico finally dug into his sandwich.

"Maybe." Lennie was quiet as they finished eating. It wasn't awkward. Wasn't strange.

The silence was oddly comfortable.

And it was something he wasn't used to.

Usually silence bothered him. Made him try to fill it with conversation.

But Lennie's silence was different.

It was peaceful.

And God knew he could use a little more peace in his life.

So he took advantage of it.

When she was done, Lennie shifted in her seat. "Thanks for the conversation." She smiled a little. "I usually eat alone."

"I'm happy to eat with you anytime, Loba."

She stood, snagging her plate off the table. "Bye."

Rico waited for her to walk almost back to the hall. "Lennie."

She stopped, barely turning his way.

"Goodnight."

Her eyes dipped. "Goodnight."

He watched until she was out of sight.

Lennie might be more complicated than he initially thought.

She was soft and quiet. A little shy.

But there were times where the tiniest bit of defiance peeked through to tease him. Make him want to think she might be the kind of woman he could take to his bed.

And that was before he knew she wanted excitement.

He knew excitement.

Thrived on it. It's what led him to the sky and to Alaskan Security.

The thrill.

And tomorrow he was going to give Lennie a taste of what she was looking for.

****

PIERCE SAT ON the other side of the desk, fingers steepled in front of his mouth. "It's not a bad idea."

"I hope there's no reason for it, but I don't think we can be too careful." Rico went to Pierce's office first thing, a little too eager to start a plan he should not be crafting.

"I don't disagree." It was clear Pierce was already on board, but Rico wanted the owner of Alaskan Security to pull the trigger now.

Today.

Pierce straightened in his seat. "However, we have a certain number of participants who are not in a physical place where it would be safe for them to be trained."

"That's why now would be a great time to get the ball rolling. We can work with the team members who are ready and then pick up the rest when they're no longer—" Rico tried to come up with a word that explained the situation.

"Pregnant."

He nodded at Pierce. "Right."

"That means Bess, Heidi, and Eva are out for now." Pierce leaned back, crossing one leg over the other. "We could start with Harlow. See how she handles it and go from there."

"I was thinking Lennie might be the best to start with. She's calmer than Harlow. Less likely to take out someone who cuts her off."

Pierce's brows lifted a little and his mouth turned in an appraising line. "Fair point." He tipped his head. "Fine. Lennie is where we start." He picked up his phone. "Ms. Bates, could you come to my office for a minute?" He hung up. "We should probably also consider reinstating the weapons and defense training with Shadow."

51

Pierce picked up a pen and scratched across the notepad in front of him.

"I thought Shadow was busy with GHOST?" He shouldn't care that Shadow was training Intel.

It should be fine.

And for the most part it was.

Pierce's eyes lifted to him. "Shadow's main focus is Alaskan Security." He straightened, eyes shrewd as they held Rico's. "They are the most suited to train Intel."

"I don't know that I'd say most suited." Irritation pricked Rico's skin at the inference that Shadow was capable of something that he wasn't.

"If one of them wants to learn to fly a plane I should send her to you, correct?"

"Are you insinuating that I'm as capable of hand to hand combat as everyone else is of flying a fucking plane?"

"Oh." Lennie skidded to a quick stop in the doorway. "I thought you meant to come now."

Rico and Pierce stood.

Pierce motioned to the chair at Rico's side. "I did. Please come sit."

Lennie's eyes darted Rico's way for a second before going to the chair. She pressed her lips together as she walked into the room and lowered to the seat, sitting at the edge, back perfectly straight.

"It has come to my attention that it would benefit all of us if every employee at Alaskan Security was able to handle certain situations."

Lennie stared at Pierce. "Okay."

"Since we are currently experiencing our first down time in nearly a year, I think now would be a perfect time to begin this training."

Her brows came together. "What training?"

"Defensive driving."

"You want me to learn defensive driving?" She didn't seem thrilled. Maybe this was not as exciting of an idea as he thought it would be.

"If there is ever a situation where you are required to outrun or outmaneuver a threat, I would like to know you are capable of handling it." Pierce eased back into his chair.

"Is there something else going on?" Lennie glanced at Rico before turning her attention back to Pierce. "If there is we should know about it."

"There is no current threat that I'm aware of."

Her dark brows lifted. "That you're aware of?"

"There is always the possibility that someone wishes one or all of us harm, Ms. Bates. We deal with dangerous and powerful people." Pierce's head dipped as he held Lennie's eyes. "That is why I think this is a worthwhile endeavor."

Lennie rubbed her palms down the front of her dress pants. "Oh." She rocked a little in her seat. "Okay. That's fine then, I guess."

Pierce smiled. "Good."

"So do you want me to go tell the rest of the team?" Lennie thumbed over one shoulder.

"Actually, you are going to be the first one to attempt this training."

Lennie's chin tucked. "Me?" She blinked a few times. "When?"

"Today."

Lennie stared at Pierce for a second. "Today?"

"Yes." He lifted a brow. "Is that a problem?"

"No." Another swipe of her hands down the front of her pants. "I just wasn't really expecting it. That's all."

Pierce barely smiled. "You should probably be ready to expect the unexpected if you plan to stay with us." He stood.

Lennie's eyes followed him. "I'll keep that in mind."

"Gather anything you need." Pierce held one hand Rico's way. "When you're ready Rico will take you for training."

Lennie sat motionless. "Okay." She blinked a few times before her mouth spread in a tight smile. "That's fine." One hand tucked a bit of long dark hair behind her ear. "I guess I'm ready now."

"Excellent." Pierce slid the second button of his suit into place. "I'm sure you will perform fantastically."

"You clearly haven't seen me drive." Lennie eyed Rico as she turned toward the door. "You might decide to rethink who gets to go first."

Rico tipped his head Pierce's way as he followed Lennie out of the room.

His boss couldn't have handled that better.

"So where is this training happening? Some sort of simulation or something?" Lennie rolled her shoulders a little and shook out her arms.

"You warming up, Loba?" Rico opened the door leading to the underground tunnels that ran beneath the buildings.

"Something like that." Lennie chewed her lower lip as they made their way to the corridor leading to the garage situated at the back of the main building. "Do you really think there's the possibility someone might try to come after one of us?"

Did she sound almost hopeful?

"There's always the chance. You work with high-level intelligence in a company that deals with the worst of the worst. Someone could realize how valuable you are at any time." The thought of it made him walk a little faster.

Even though the original reason for this was to give Lennie a bit of the excitement she claimed to want, the more Pierce talked the more it made him realize it was something they should have considered long ago.

Rico opened the door to the stairs leading to the garage entrance, holding it as Lennie walked past him, the scent of warm amber tickling his nose.

It was one of the many things about her that intrigued him.

She looked like the kind of woman who would wear perfume that smelled like cookies. Sweet and innocent.

But the rich, decadent, slightly exotic notes that clung to her skin were nothing anyone would call sweet.

Or innocent.

She smelled like sin and seduction.

Two of his favorite things.

Lennie swiped her badge at the top of the stairs, unlocking the next door before pulling it open. The garage was huge and lined with the many vehicles it took to keep a company like Alaskan Security functioning.

Rico headed straight for the easy-to-drive SUVs. "Pick your poison, Loba."

Lennie's eyes went along the row of Rovers and Jeeps. She slowly walked down the lineup before stopping at the last vehicle. "I guess this one's fine."

"Fine is what we're after right now." Rico went to the cabinet where each set of keys dangled from their designated hooks, snagging the set for the black Jeep she selected. "Today I just want to get a feel for you."

Lennie's eyes barely widened and a slow flush crept across her skin.

He fought to ignore her reaction and her ability to drag him down without saying a word. "For how you drive." Rico held the keys out to her.

"I'll be on my best behavior then." Lennie took the keys and went to the driver's door.

"I want you to drive like you normally do, Loba. I need to see what I'm working with." Rico settled into the seat beside her, waiting while she adjusted the mirrors and seats, spending a surprising amount of time on the side mirrors.

By the time she finally started the engine he was fairly certain Lennie would gain more than just the excitement he hoped to give her from this exercise.

She turned to him. "Ready to go?"

"I'm always ready to go." Yet another thing that sounded more suggestive than it should.

Old habits.

Or maybe it was her reaction to him earlier that spurred him on. Made him try to make it happen again.

Lennie's lips pressed together as she turned away, eyes going to the windshield as she pulled out of the parking space and headed toward the exit.

At about two miles an hour.

"You can drive a little faster in here." Rico stretched his legs out as she pushed the gas a little more.

Taking them up to four miles an hour.

"Everyone knows to watch their step in here, Loba. You don't have to worry about hitting anyone." He clicked the opener, lifting the garage door as she approached it.

Lennie pulled out of the building and slowly made her way to the front gate. She stopped.

"How do we get out?"

"Roll down your window."

She pressed the button as Rico leaned in close, keeping his eyes on hers as he reached across to scan his badge and punch in the code he used to come and go.

Lennie sat perfectly still. She might not have even been breathing, but she held his gaze, eyes steady. "You could have just told me the code."

"You're right." The gate in front of them slid open, forcing Rico back into his seat and away from her. "I could have."

Lennie cleared her throat a little as she gripped the wheel and pulled off Alaskan Security property. "Where are we going?"

"Let's go to Steese Highway."

"I don't know how to get there." She glanced at the screen in the center of the dash. "Does that thing have GPS in it?"

"That thing has everything in it." Rico put in the address to GHOST headquarters. It was a decent drive that would give him plenty of time with her.

Plenty of time to try to figure out exactly why Lenore Bates put him at the top of her list of fears.

Lennie followed the directions the GPS laid out perfectly, sticking to the speed limit like glue. She merged onto the highway and stayed in the right lane.

Her fingers tapped the wheel as she stayed behind a truck going ten miles under the speed limit. After a couple minutes she huffed out a breath and switched on her turn signal to change lanes.

As she moved the truck in front of her moved too, essentially cutting off her attempt to get around him.

The right-hand lane was now empty, so she attempted to ease back that direction.

The truck cut her off again.

Lennie's hands gripped the wheel and her eyes narrowed as they snapped to the rearview and side mirrors.

A heartbeat later she cut to the left, crossing two lanes of traffic at once, sliding between two semis in the process, before hitting the left lane and flooring the accelerator to jump into the flow of traffic.

Rico straightened in his seat.

Lennie gave him a little smile. "Sorry. That guy pissed me off."

Before he could respond her expression turned to a glare. "Son of a—"

CHAPTER 5

LENNIE JERKED THE wheel hard to the right as she whipped around the truck that had cut her off three times now.

Prick.

"Who the fuck does this guy think he is?" She hit the gas, racing up one side of the truck before cutting back in front of him, leaving less than a foot between the back of the Jeep and the front of the truck as she did.

Rico spun to look behind them. His eyes were sharp as they stayed out the back window. "Get out of this lane, Loba. Now."

There wasn't enough room for her to get out of the lane.

But that was just a technicality.

She watched in the rearview as the truck edged closer. At the last possible second Lennie hit the brakes.

Rico didn't flinch as the truck behind them fishtailed, tires squealing against the blacktop as they tried to stop.

The second she could, Lennie jerked the wheel to the side, jumping back across the lanes and straight onto an exit ramp, leaving the truck stuck on the interstate.

Her heart was racing and her chest was burning, but she stayed focused on what she was doing. If she messed this up Pierce would never let her do anything else again.

And she might want to do this again. Once she recovered.

Lennie ran the red light at the bottom of the ramp, taking the turn so fast her body leaned toward the door.

Rico punched at the display screen in the dash, pulling up the menu. "Slow down."

"Are you sure?" She scanned all the mirrors, looking to see if there were any more suspicious vehicles around.

"I'm positive." He punched Dutch's name as it popped up on the screen.

"I figured you might call me." Dutch's voice carried a smile.

Rico was not smiling.

He looked like he might murder someone.

Which did nothing to help her racing heart.

"Where's Luca?"

"Pretty sure you know where Luca is."

Rico's already deep voice dropped as he leaned toward the screen, teeth clenched tight. "Tell him I'm kicking his ass the next time I see him."

"My ass is the one you should be threatening to kick." Pierce's voice cut through the line. "I'm the one who sent Luca out."

"She could have killed herself."

Lennie scoffed.

Rico's head snapped her way, his eyes dark and dangerous.

And a little scary.

It's why he ended up at the top of her list.

He punched the knob on the dash and the screen went black. "Pull into that lot."

"Why?"

"Because I'm driving home."

"No." She felt a little sick and might have almost passed out, but now that it was over, the euphoria was kicking in and she felt like she could conquer the world.

Or at least her own personal demons.

Rico grabbed the wheel, jerking it hard to the right, taking them into the lot she was planning to pass.

Lennie tried to steal the wheel back but he held firm, taking them straight toward a row of parked cars.

He was really killing her buzz.

Instead of braking, she sped up, glaring at him as the cars came closer.

"Loba." The low rumble of his voice carried a hint of warning.

She looked toward the cars as the Jeep ate up the lot between them.

"If you want excitement this is not the way to get it."

Lennie slammed on the brakes, taking her anger out on the pedal under her feet.

Rico shifted the Jeep into park and switched it off. "Thank you."

"You're not welcome." She shoved open her door and stepped out into the warmish air of the Alaska summer.

She'd gotten a taste of what pushing her comfort zone did. What it felt like after she got past the initial panic and dread.

It was liberating. Proof she wasn't what some dick claimed she was.

She wanted more of that.

Lennie glared Rico's way as he got out of the Jeep, slowly standing to face her down. "Don't be mad."

"Don't tell me what to be." Normally Rico made her panic. Made her worry she would say something stupid.

Or worse, say nothing at all. That she'd just end up standing there staring at him while her tongue played dead.

But right now she wasn't having any of those issues. Adrenaline must fuel bravery. "Why'd you take me out to drive if you're not going to let me drive?"

"Luca will circle back. He will come back for you, Loba. I won't let you risk your life for a little fun."

"You won't *let* me?" All her adult life she'd worried about what she should do.

Could do.

She let people's opinions limit her. Men's opinions.

Stifle her into a woman who wasn't even sure what she was actually capable of.

But it was definitely more than this.

"That's right. I won't *let* you." Rico wasn't budging. Not in plan or in stance.

He stayed put as she rounded the SUV, ready for the first time in her life to do something about yet another man limiting her. "I don't remember making you the boss of me."

One black brow slowly lifted. "I could make you consider it."

Any other time she would have been so flustered by the comment that she would have struggled to put one foot in front of the other, let alone string letters into words, but right now that didn't seem to be a problem. "I'd like to see you try."

It came out as a challenge. One she had no business laying down between them.

She would not like to see him try. All that would happen is she would show Rico just how little sex appeal she actually had. Then she would spend the rest of her days at Alaskan Security dodging him out of embarrassment.

Running from one more man who would think she was cold.

Frigid.

Uptight.

Before Lennie could take it back Rico had her, pushing her against the side of the Jeep, one hand splayed across the center of her stomach, holding her in place. Only one other bit of him touched her, and it was the tip of the index finger pressed under her chin, lifting her eyes to meet his. "I can do more than try, Loba." He leaned close, his head tucking alongside hers until his lips were so close to her ear she could feel the warm brush of his words when he spoke. "Why do you want to drive home, Loba? Didn't that scare you?"

She managed a nod. "Yes." The word had nothing but air behind it.

Rico's head tipped her way, his dark gaze studying her face. "Then why would you want to do it?"

"It's why I came here." She swallowed down the nerves trying to close her throat. "To do things that scare me."

The finger under her chin slid down the front of her neck in a slow drag. "Do I scare you, Loba?"

Lie.

She needed to lie. It was the only way out of this.

But her lips were traitors.

"Yes."

His mouth slowly curved into a wolfish smile. "I wish I could tell you your fears were unfounded." Rico's single finger continued its downward path, sliding over her collarbone. "But they are not."

"Why?"

"I like to push, Loba. I like to be pushed."

Lennie licked her lips, trying to work up a little moisture in her dry mouth. "Like boundaries?"

"Like boundaries." His finger moved down the center of her ribs, between her breasts.

There was no breathing happening. No blinking.

65

Her body was frozen in place.

Her mind, though.

It was running a mile a minute.

Rico's finger reached the waistband of her pants and her heart stopped at the thought of it continuing on.

"What about you, Loba?"

"What about me?" Thank God her mouth didn't betray her twice.

"Do you like to be pushed?" His finger teased along the spot where her blouse skimmed her slacks, tracing the skin of her stomach with a barely-there touch.

"I don't know." She'd been pushed before, but not in the same way she imagined Rico was talking about now.

"Has anyone ever pushed you?"

"I don't know." It was the easiest thing to keep saying. It kept any admissions that might want to escape from working free.

"You would know." Rico's palm flattened against her stomach under the fabric of her shirt. "And I'm not talking about some asshole whining and complaining because you won't do the thing he wants you to do." His lips brushed her ear. "I'm talking about a man pushing you to do the things you are too scared to admit you want."

She was never going to be able to breathe again. Her lungs were going to wither and die before she figured out how to get air back into them.

"Has anyone ever pushed you like that, Lenore?"

Up until this second she'd hated her name. Always felt like it was too old. Antiquated.

As stuffy and uptight as some people thought she was.

But the sound of it on Rico's lips, the barely there tilt to his words, made it sound like it belonged to a woman who was scared of nothing.

A woman who would have most definitely been pushed.

"No."

A low hum that could almost be considered a growl rumbled through his chest. "Have you ever done the pushing?"

Definitely not. "No."

"That's a shame." Rico caught one of her hands in his and lifted it to his mouth.

She was expecting him to maybe kiss the back of her hand. Possibly brush his full lips across her knuckles.

Instead, those same lips wrapped around her finger, pulling it into the heat of his mouth as he sucked it, tongue sliding over her skin.

She couldn't look away as he slowly pulled it free, his teeth raking against her flesh.

"Oh my God." It slipped out. There was no stopping it.

She was in over her head.

But still willing to risk drowning.

"What do you think, Loba?" Rico's lips were back at her ear. "Do you want to be pushed?"

"*Hey.*"

The sharp male voice made her jump and sent Lennie's already racing heart into overdrive.

Rico's nostrils flared as he straightened, turning away from her to face the man who interrupted the single most terrifyingly exhilarating three minutes of her life.

"Everything okay?" The man leaned to one side, the badge pinned to the front of his uniform catching in the light of the sun.

Everything was not okay. She was barely treading water in a pool with no bottom.

Lennie forced on a smile. "Fine."

The police officer's eyes slid to Rico. "You have ID on you?"

"Of course." Rico reached into his pocket and pulled out his wallet. "I'm going to assume you didn't run the plates?"

The cop glanced toward the Jeep. "Am I gonna find out it's stolen?"

Rico barely smiled. "Definitely not."

The cop's eyes narrowed. "Why don't you come over here?"

His tone was unnecessary, and it bothered her.

Lennie stepped out from behind the blockade of Rico's wide body. "Did we do something wrong?"

The cop's eyes scanned her from head to toe. "Well you're blocking a lane, for starters."

"On private property. It's not like you can issue us a ticket for it."

"So this is your car then?" The cop pulled a small notebook from his pocket and clicked the end of the ink pen attached to it.

"No." She glanced to Rico. "It belongs to Alaskan Security."

The pen skidded to a stop as the officer's eyes lifted to Rico.

Rico gave him a wide smile.

The officer flipped his notebook closed and tucked it back into place. "My apologies." He spun on one heel and went toward where his car was parked in one of the spaces near the front of the grocery store adjacent to the lot.

Lennie looked from the retreating cop to Rico. "What just happened?"

Rico turned to the still-open passenger door. "Didn't anyone tell you that you were special, Loba?" He tipped his head toward the Jeep. "Let's get out of here."

"I still can't drive?"

"Not today." Rico leaned close. "But I will be happy to let you be in the driver's seat any other time, Lenore."

She couldn't let her brain consider exactly what he meant by that.

There were too many possibilities.

Distracting ones.

Lennie tucked into the seat and buckled up as Rico shut her door and went around to the driver's side. "Will Luca try anything if he sees it's you driving?"

"Depends on what Pierce told him to do." Rico pulled out of the lot.

"Why did Pierce make him do that to me?" Lennie still didn't really understand the owner of Alaskan Security and his reasons for doing the things he did. "Someone could have gotten hurt."

Rico glanced her way. "I can promise you no one expected you to react the way you did."

"Obviously none of you have ever driven in Cincinnati." Lennie crossed her arms as Rico merged onto the highway.

"You did very well, Loba. Better than I thought."

She tried not to look at him. "Thank you."

"Pierce enjoys helping people live up to their full potential."

Lennie's head turned Rico's way at the abrupt change in conversation. "Why are you telling me this?"

"Because you need to be prepared any time you leave headquarters from now on." Rico smoothly moved between cars as they coasted down the highway. "Pierce will want to see what you can do."

Her stomach dropped. "Why?"

"Why do you sound upset?" Rico met her eyes. "Isn't that what you came here for? To find out just what you were capable of?"

"I came here because I thought it would be exciting."

"Isn't that the same thing?"

"No." Was it? "I just wanted to get a little outside of my comfort zone."

"Only a little?"

Her thighs clenched at the drop of his voice. At the potential the question held. "Only a little."

"It's a slippery slope, Loba. Once you start down it it's difficult to stop."

Her eyes drifted along the tanned line of the arm draped over the top of the steering wheel. "I can stop anytime I want."

"That's true." Rico's fingers wrapped around the leather of the wheel, squeezing it tight. "You *can* stop any time you want." His fist slid along the braided band. "The question is, will you want to?"

Lennie's eyes were so wide they burned as she fought them away from where his hand held the wheel.

Making her think about what it might look like when he held something else.

"What are you thinking, Loba?"

"Nothing."

"Then why is your skin flushed?" Rico leaned her way. "Why are you breathing heavy?"

"I'm not." It was a lie. Plain and simple. One he would hopefully let her get away with.

"I didn't think I'd find your line so soon, Loba." Rico pulled up to the gate at Alaskan Security. He swiped his badge and punched in his code.

"What?" Her brain was struggling to think of anything besides that damn hand and what it might sometimes grip.

"Your lines, Lenore. The ones you stay inside." Rico pulled around the side of the building and into the back garage. "I didn't think I'd run into one so easily."

Frigid.

Uptight.

"You didn't run into a line." Lennie sat a little straighter.

Rico parked the Jeep and switched it off before getting out.

Lennie opened her door and stepped out as he rounded the front. "You didn't run into a line."

Rico was on her before she could take another breath, his big body crowding hers in the confined area. "Prove it." His head lowered, dark eyes pinning her in place as he came closer. "Tell me what made your skin heat." He leaned into her ear. "Tell me what made your heart race, Lenore."

Good God if he kept saying her name that way. "I was just thinking."

"Mm-hmm." His voice was low and rumbly. "What were you thinking about?" The line of his jaw barely scraped the skin of her cheek. "Paint me a picture."

Lennie squeezed her eyes shut as her skin heated for an entirely different reason. "I can't."

"I'm positive you can." Rico's body barely brushed hers. "I'm just not sure you want to."

Neither was she.

"But if you can't do this then there's no way you can handle anything else I can offer you, Loba."

"What are you offering me?"

Rico's head tilted until his eyes met hers. "All the excitement you can handle." He paused. "And then some."

She came here to prove she wasn't all the things a small man called her.

And that's what Kyle was.

A small man.

Not in size.

Just in everything else.

"So what will it be, Loba? Do you pick excitement?" The heat of his breath skimmed over her lips. "Or will you keep your secrets?"

Fire flamed across her cheeks and fear tried to close her lips.

Tie her tongue.

Shut her down. Send her back into the shell she'd always lived in, choosing safety over anything else the world had to offer her.

Lennie's eyes dipped to focus on a single spot at the center of Rico's black shirt.

"I was imagining what you looked like when you touch yourself."

CHAPTER 6

DIOS MIO.

It took everything he had not to react.

Lennie's admission was not what he was expecting.

Not even close.

Rico took a second to regroup. Wrap his head around everything he thought he knew.

Again.

"You keep surprising me, Loba." He reached out to catch a little of her dark hair. "Just when I think I know what to expect, you prove me wrong."

"Really?" The disbelief in her soft voice was clear.

"Why is that difficult for you to believe?" He relaxed, letting his body ease closer to hers. "Does my wolf not know how fierce she is?"

"I'm not fierce." Lennie let out a low laugh as she shook her head.

"You are wrong." He reached out to run one finger down the length of her nose. "And I will prove it."

Her eyes barely narrowed. A sign she didn't trust him quite yet.

And trust was an important thing.

Maybe the most important.

"Come." Rico backed away. "Time to go tell your friends how you scared the shit out of Luca on your first drive."

Lennie's lips twisted into a little smile. "Do you really think I scared him?"

"I am positive you did." Rico led her to the door that connected the garage to the main building. "I can promise you he was not expecting you to drive like you did."

Her smile filled out a little more. "Wait until it's Eva's turn."

"I'll keep that in mind." Rico opened the door and waited for Lennie to pass through. "Anyone else I should look out for?"

"I mean," Lennie's dark eyes came his way, "Heidi, of course."

"That doesn't surprise me." Rico stayed with her as they made their way back toward the offices. When they reached the door to the main corridor he paused, edging close to her again. He'd made her a promise, and he intended to keep it.

"Come to my room tonight."

"Tonight?" She squeaked the word out.

"Yes, Lenore. Tonight." Rico eased in a little more, teasing himself with the temptation of her body. "Seven o'clock." He took one long drag of the air scented by her skin before backing up. "Don't be late."

He opened the door and walked out, leaving her in the stairwell.

Lennie had three hours to think it over.

Decide what she really wanted from her time in Alaska.

And while she did that, he would make sure she was never in a position like she was today again.

Rico went straight to Pierce's office, knocking the door wide as he marched in. "The fuck, Pierce?"

Mona stood in front of Pierce's desk, her arms across her chest as she glared at the owner of Alaskan Security.

Pierce waved Rico off with one hand. "If you're here to complain about Luca then you're late."

"Complain?" Mona's brows went up. "Complaining is something you do when you are unhappy." She leaned both palms against Pierce's desk. "And I'm so much more than unhappy right now."

"She could have gotten hurt." Rico stepped in beside Mona. "Innocent people could have gotten hurt."

"You both know her reaction was not what I was expecting." Pierce turned his attention to Rico. "I was simply hoping to give you an opportunity to see her potential."

Oh, he'd seen her potential.

It was all he would be able to think about.

"You aren't the potential police, Pierce." One of Mona's pale blonde brows lifted. "And I would think you might have learned my team is more likely to surprise you than they are to give you what you expect."

She wasn't wrong.

Pierce's gaze slowly moved to rest on his wife. "I will keep that in mind going forward, Love."

The owner of Alaskan Security had definitely met his match in the tiny woman staring him down.

Mona was small and sneakily fierce. A quiet storm you never saw coming.

Pierce certainly didn't.

"Thank you." Mona straightened. She eyed her husband. "You should probably send her flowers."

"I will be sure to do that."

"Good." Mona's cool blue eyes came to Rico, holding a second as she turned to stride from the office, leaving both he and Pierce staring after her.

Pierce sighed. "What flowers does Ms. Bates prefer?" He picked up a pen.

"How would I know?"

Pierce cocked a brow. "Do you not have an interest in her?"

"She's not my type."

"That's not what I asked." Pierce stood, smoothing down the front of his jacket. "I assumed when you used me to provide an opportunity to have Ms. Bates to yourself, it was because you held an interest in her."

"She needs to be able to take care of herself. Lennie won't always have one of us at her side." Rico turned toward the door as Pierce's question dug under his skin. "And I have no idea what flowers she likes." He marched out of the office before Pierce could find another way to make him question his actual motives.

The real thing he wanted to gain.

Or regain depending on how you looked at things.

He needed to work out. Keep his mind from seizing the opportunity to pull him into the past. Apply it to the now.

Shawn was just getting on the treadmill when Rico got to the in-house gym.

Rico stepped onto the machine beside Rogue's team lead. "Wanna race?"

Shawn eyed him. "Still pissed about Luca?"

"No." Rico punched one finger at the digital display, setting a punishing pace. "Just need to get my run in." He popped his earbuds in as the belt started to move, picking up speed until all he could focus on was keeping his feet moving.

Shawn was always good for motivation and competition in the gym. The head of Rogue was there every day. Sometimes twice. Burning off the aggravation that threatened his level-head.

And his lady provided plenty of aggravation.

Heidi was funny and smarter than anyone he'd ever met. She was also hell on wheels. The woman did exactly as she wanted. Always.

And now she was pregnant with twins.

It was enough to make a calm man lose his cool.

And Shawn wasn't known for his calm which meant this run probably helped him as much as it did Rico.

Eight miles in Rico's body started to give out. The muscles of his legs started to cramp and his sides started to ache.

He tapped out, bending at the waist as he tried to ease the burning in his chest.

Shawn slowed his pace, knocking a headphone off one ear. "You done already?"

Rico stretched one leg, trying to ease the clawing tightness. "I'm fucking miserable."

"That's how it starts." Shawn grinned at him. "And it goes downhill real damn quick." The team lead for Rogue slid the headphone into place and turned back toward the line of mirrors as he pushed the treadmill's speed back up.

Rico grabbed his towel, bag, and water before heading to his room. He was exhausted. Two days of flying must have taken more out of him than he realized.

That's all this was.

He swiped his badge, unlocking the door. The room was the same one he'd slept in since coming to Alaska looking for his own fresh start.

No. That wasn't the truth.

He came here to escape. To forget.

And it worked.

For a while.

But something had changed.

He'd been able to ignore the past here. Pretend it didn't exist.

Until recently.

Rico went into the bathroom and switched on the shower, cranking up the heat. He peeled off his sweat-soaked shirt and shorts, draping them over the edge of the hamper to dry before turning toward the bathroom. His eyes caught the clock on his nightstand.

6:55

He rolled his head to one side, then the other before looking back at the door.

The seconds ticked by.

Finally he snapped his badge off the dresser and went to the door, twisting the levered handle to barely crack it open before sliding the edge of the badge into the gap.

He didn't let himself think about why he did it.

Why he did any of the things he'd done today.

The glass door of the shower snapped closed behind him as he stepped inside. The spray of water was hot enough to steal any thoughts trying to force their way into his mind.

Into his life.

The barely-audible sound of his badge hitting the floor was all it took for his body to react. For his mind to change gears to a more comfortable place.

That was why he let her come. Because it would give him the distraction and relief he needed.

It would get him back on track.

Back to where he needed to be.

It always did.

She didn't call his name like he thought she would.

Her steps were almost silent as she came through the room, moving so slowly he began to ache.

Lennie edged into the open doorway, her softly-curved frame blurred by the steam staining the glass between them.

And still she was silent. No questions.

No requests.

Nothing.

He reached out to slide one hand down the shower wall, knocking away the fog obscuring his view of her.

Lennie barely gasped, taking a half step back as he moved closer to the strip of clarity.

Maybe she would turn. Run away.

Then all this could be done.

Over before it began.

The thought burned him more than the water scalding his back. More than the past that forced him to build a new life on a mountain of regrets.

Rico lifted one hand to the top edge of the shower, wrapping his fingers over the silver trim and holding it as tightly as Lennie's gaze held him.

She didn't look away. Didn't flinch when his other hand fisted around the part of him throbbing with the need for release.

Her lips parted on an inhale as he thrust into the squeeze of his palm. It was a sound he felt. It raced through him, spurring him on.

This was a game he'd played many times before. Nothing about it should be new.

But the droop of her lids and the rise and fall of her chest seemed completely different.

Like nothing he'd ever seen before. Nothing he'd experienced.

Her cheeks flushed, skin pinking up as she slowly eased deeper into the room.

Closer to where he watched her watching him.

Lennie's hair was pulled up, twisted into a knot at the top of her head. A few dark strands had fallen loose and were curling, clinging closer to her skin with every second she spent in the heat of the bathroom.

A thin sheen glistened across her cheeks and nose as she came closer, her eyes dipping to where his dick fucked his hand in long strokes, each one bringing him closer to the relief he'd denied himself for weeks, thinking it would never be.

But she was here.

With him. Proving what he knew to be true.

That Lennie was the problem. She was the reason for the change threatening to turn his whole world upside down.

Her palms came to rest against the glass as she leaned closer, heated gaze moving over him in a way he could handle.

A way he was used to.

Lust was something he was comfortable with. Thrived on.

It smothered out the more problematic emotions. Distracted from their ramifications.

And Lennie's lust was directed solely at him.

He was the object of her desire.

Which meant it was finally okay for her to be his.

She was the problem, but maybe she could also be the solution.

Rico lowered his hand from the top of the shower, sliding it down to where one of hers was pressed against the glass.

Her eyes lifted to his, locking in place as the tip of her tongue slid across the pink fullness of her lower lip.

He could imagine her on her knees, that same tongue sliding across him. Those same pink lips wrapped tight around his cock.

His balls pulled tight immediately, dick swelling as he came, the heat of the water washing away the evidence almost instantly.

Lennie watched the whole time, eyes fixed on where his hand worked out every bit of pleasure he could find. When there was no more to be had he lifted his other hand to the glass, resting it directly in line with hers. Her eyes followed it, hanging for a second where their palms would meet if not for the glass between them.

Suddenly her dark gaze snapped to his.

Her hands pulled away.

Lennie backed up, each step coming faster than the last.

Then she turned and fled, leaving him alone with nothing but the past to keep him company.

****

"YOU'RE UP EARLY." Abe stood at the coffee maker in the kitchen area of the break room in the main building.

"I could say the same thing to you." Rico grabbed a lidded cup and waited his turn.

Abe lifted one shoulder in a shrug. "Couldn't sleep." He angled the carafe Rico's way.

"It happens." Rico held his cup out, keeping it steady as Abe filled it nearly to the edge. "What's the plan for today?"

"Figured you were taking Lennie out for another drive." Abe popped the lid on his own cup before taking a short, loud sip.

"I'm not sure that's a good idea." Rico drank down a healthy gulp, savoring the burn.

"Is your throat made of fucking asbestos?" Abe blew into the hole of his lid. "This shit is hot enough to burn the hide off an elephant."

"Guess I'm used to it." Rico drank some more, letting it set his mouth on fire. The burn dulled everything else. The old emotions he thought he'd escaped.

The new ones threatening to take him down a path he worked hard to avoid.

Rico followed Abe out into the hall. He'd come over early to make sure he could get his assignment for the day and be gone before Lennie came in.

He'd never run from a woman before in his life.

But it looked like there was a first time for everything.

Pierce stepped out of his office, his eyes landing on them immediately. "I was just coming to find you." He turned. "Come."

Thank God. Hopefully Pierce needed something long and involved. Maybe something that would get him the hell away from Alaska and the woman stealing the peace it used to bring him.

Pierce paused, turning as Abe fell back. "Both of you."

Abe lifted his brows at Rico before joining him in Pierce's office.

"Sit." Pierce motioned to the chairs as he rounded his desk. "I was able to secure the early termination of the lease Mona and Eva had on their portion of a commercial building in Cincinnati." He eased into his chair. "However the offices need to be cleared out. I have moving pods ready to be delivered and filled, but I would prefer we be the ones to do the actual packing and moving."

"When?" Rico drank down the rest of his coffee.

"Today." Pierce tipped his head to one side. "I've been told it's not going to be a one-day job, so you should plan to be gone three to four."

"Excellent." Rico stood. "I'll get the flight plan ready and submitted." He turned to Abe. "We can leave as soon as you're ready."

"You can leave as soon as all your passengers are ready." Pierce relaxed back in his chair. "There are two more going."

"How much stuff is there to pack?" He shouldn't be questioning it. He should take the opportunity and run. He'd done it before, and after last night he was sure he should probably do it again.

"A lot." Elise walked into the room, looking all business in a slim dress and heels. She had a folder open across one hand. "Desks. Computers. Chairs. Filing cabinets. The place is still full."

Rico reached for the file but Elise pulled it away. "I'll hang onto this."

"Do you have a copy for us to take with us?"

Elise glanced toward Pierce. "This is the copy going with you."

It took half a second to connect the dots.

All fucking four of them.

Elise turned toward the hall, leaning to peek out the door. "There you are." She smiled. "I was wondering if you changed your mind."

He knew who their fourth was before she even stepped into the doorway.

Lennie didn't look his way as she came in, but the barely-there pink of her cheeks told him all he needed to know.

All that was running through her mind.

"I know flying is not your favorite activity, Ms. Bates." Pierce focused on Lennie. "I'm sure we can find someone to take your place if you wish."

Rico held his breath.

Lennie was terrified of flying. She should stay here.

Far from him.

Lennie shook her head a little, her dark eyes finally coming his way. "I trust Rico." Her gaze didn't waver as she continued. "I'm sure he will keep me perfectly safe."

He stared back at her.

This woman who had no clue what she was talking about.

Lenore's safety was never in question. Nothing would ever happen to her.

He would make sure of it.

His safety was another matter.

CHAPTER 7

IT TOOK EVERYTHING she had to hold his gaze.

Especially after last night.

The sight of him, what he did, wasn't anything she'd be able to get out of her mind. Not ever.

Even now, in a room full of people it was creeping in at the edges, trying to drag her down the tunnel of embarrassment.

But Rico didn't look embarrassed, and if he wasn't then she sure as heck shouldn't be. He was the one who...

Who...

"Ms. Bates."

Lennie snapped her eyes to Pierce. "Yes?"

"I was asking if you were prepared to leave."

Prepared? Definitely not.

She was going anyway.

Lennie glanced Rico's way to find him still watching her. "I am."

"Excellent." Pierce's palms came together. "Please keep me informed of the process and let me know if there is anything additional you need."

She needed something. Lots of things.

Unfortunately none of them were anything Pierce could provide.

So she was just going to have to figure it out herself.

Elise linked her arm through one of Lennie's, pulling her into the hall where their bags were sitting side-by-side. "I am so excited." She leaned closer. "I need to get out and have some fun. These guys up here are not what I was expecting them to be."

She completely understood.

Rico crossed his arms and focused on Elise. "Abe and I need to pack. We'll be back in fifteen minutes. Be ready to go."

"We're already ready to go." Elise lifted a brow at him. "You're the ones not ready."

Rico's eyes slid to Lennie before he turned and walked down the hall toward the enclosed hall leading to the on-site rooms.

Elise slowly turned Lennie's way, her eyes skimming up and down. "What was that about?"

"What was what about?" Lennie grabbed her purse from where it sat on top of her wheeled suitcase.

"Uh," Elise stepped into her line of sight, "the way he just looked at you."

"He looked at you the same way." Lennie pulled out a tube of lip balm and rubbed it on, making a continuous circle around her mouth.

"He definitely did not. He looked at me like I was annoying him." Elise bent closer. "The way he looked at you made me a little hot."

"Everything makes you hot."

"Untrue." Elise's lips lifted in a sly smile. "But that definitely did." She wiggled one finger in the direction of Lennie's face. "And based on how pink your cheeks are right now it made you hot too."

"If you're going to be like this the whole trip I'm not going." The thought of tapping out and running back to her room relieved some of the twist in her belly.

Not going would be so much easier. Just like not going to Rico's room last night would have been easier.

And she almost hadn't.

Lennie shoved the balm back in place and pulled out a stick of gum, shoving it in her mouth in the hopes that it would give her something else to chew on.

Literally and figuratively.

"Gum?" She held a stick out to Elise.

"Thanks." Elise peeled the silver paper off as she looked down the hall. "What do you think of Abe?"

"He's always been nice to me." Lennie was out of things to pull from her purse so she folded the gum wrapper, working it into as small of a square as she could.

"I'm not asking if you think he's nice." Elise chewed down the gum in her mouth, wadding up her own wrapper as she did. "I'm asking if you think he's someone I should consider having sex with."

"Then wouldn't you also want him to be nice?"

"Nice isn't what I'm currently after." Elise rolled the balled-up wrapper between her thumb and pointer. "I'm currently just looking for a sexual interaction."

"I'm sure men love it when you call it an interaction."

"I just don't want a bunch of questions or for them to try to get to know me." Elise huffed out a sigh. "All I want is to do it and move on."

"You know they make things for that."

"I have a vibrator. It's not the same." Elise slumped against the wall, her lips pulling into a little pout. "How can it be this hard to get laid?" She held both arms out. "It's practically raining dicks around here and not a single one lands on me."

Lennie pressed her lips together, trying to keep a straight face. Elise was clearly struggling. Now was not the time to laugh at the thought of a dick smacking her in the forehead as it fell from the sky. "Maybe you're too pretty." Lennie took a breath as she fought through the urge to laugh at the image occupying her brain. "They're probably intimidated by you."

Elise barely shook her head. "That's not the problem. I promise."

"What's the problem then?" Lennie latched onto the conversation. The longer they talked about Elise's issues, the longer it would be before she had to face hers.

Again.

Elise straightened off the wall. "Nothing." She turned to the break room. "I'm going to go get some coffee. You want some?"

"No." Lennie rested one hand on her belly. "It bothers my stomach when I'm nervous."

Elise's head dipped to one side and she gave Lennie a small smile. "Don't be nervous. Rico is good at what he does. You'll be just fine."

And just like that her brain was once again taken over by images of last night.

Elise turned and went to the break room, leaving Lennie to struggle with something she wasn't used to experiencing.

She pressed her fingers into her eyes, trying to push away the visual stuck there. "Shit."

"What's wrong, Loba?"

Double shit.

"Nothing." She almost cringed as she opened her eyes. "Nothing's wrong."

Rico's dark gaze moved over her face. "You don't have to do this."

"I know that." Lennie stood a little straighter. "It will be fine."

"I'm not talking about the flight, Lenore."

Just hearing him say her name was enough to send heat through her belly, burning away the chill of fear she'd been fighting all morning. "I know."

His eyes barely widened. Like she'd surprised him.

The same way she had last night.

He'd been surprised she showed up at his room.

She'd never surprised anyone before. Not like that.

She was always the same. Always did what she should. What was expected.

And Rico rewarded her boldness with something that surprised her back.

"You are blushing, Loba." His voice was quiet.

"Are you going to ask me why?" She was almost ready for it.

Almost hoping he would.

Rico barely shook his head. "Not this time."

The wiggle of excitement she might be learning to like stalled out. "Oh."

"Does that disappoint you, Lenore?"

His words might as well have been a touch. One that coaxed out the truth she was trying so much to embrace. "Yes."

A deep sound rumbled through his chest.

"*Rico*."

His eyes held hers a second longer before moving to look down the hall where Abe stood.

"You ready?"

Rico eased away from her, reaching out to lift the handle of her wheeled suitcase. "Take your purse, Loba."

She didn't even consider arguing with him. Lennie snagged her purse, looping it on as Rico started down the hall toward where Abe stood.

"You sure nothing's going on?"

Elise's voice made her jump.

Lennie rested one hand on her racing heart. "You scared the crap out of me."

"That's 'cause you were so busy checking Rico's ass out." Elise balanced her coffee in one hand as she tried to fight up the handle to her own suitcase.

92

"I got it." Lennie grabbed it and started rolling down the hall.

Elise's brows came together. "Where's yours?"

"Um." Lennie accidentally glanced at Rico.

Elise followed her line of sight, smirking as her eyes rested on Lennie's bag. "And he's carrying your bag?"

"I'm carrying your bag. What does that mean?"

"It means you're going to be disappointed because you're not my type."

Lennie snorted out a little laugh. "And you think Rico's mine?"

"Honey, Rico's every woman's type." Elise eyed Rico as he passed through the entry doors and went straight to the back of a Jeep that looked identical to the one she drove yesterday. "I mean, look at him."

Oh, she had.

All of him.

"Being attractive doesn't make a man my type." She'd known many attractive men and none of them affected her like Rico did. None of them made her sit up and pay attention the way most women seemed to do when a handsome man was around.

"That's right. I forgot." Elise shot her a grin. "You're looking for nice *and* attractive." She rolled her eyes. "You want the fucking unicorn of men."

"There are nice men who are also attractive." Lennie lifted the bag over the bump separating the building from the poured cement outside. "Dutch is nice."

"Dutch is nice to you because he's not trying to fuck you."

"He's nice to Harlow." Lennie dropped her voice as they got closer to where Abe and Rico were loading their bags and hers into the back of the Jeep. "And I'm pretty sure he fu—"

"Come on, Loba." Rico held one hand toward Elise's bag. "We need to get moving."

Last time he gave her an order she just did it. Automatically.

This time…

This time it bothered her.

She wasn't going to come right out and tell him no, but just passing off the bag didn't seem like what she wanted to do either.

So instead she marched straight around him to where Abe stood, giving the other man a wide smile as she passed him Elise's bag. "Here you go." Then she went and opened the back passenger's door.

An odd silence hung in the warm air as she settled into her seat.

Abe lifted Elise's bag into the back before coming up to the front passenger's door.

Elise slid into the seat next to Lennie, eyes wide as Rico slammed the hatch closed. "He did not like that."

Lennie buckled her belt. "There's nothing to not like."

Elise's lips pressed to a tight line as Rico got into the car, his dark eyes immediately coming Lennie's way.

She refused to look at him.

Elise wasn't wrong. Rico was definitely upset about something, and right now she would normally be thinking of every possible reason she was the thing he was upset about.

It was a vicious cycle she'd struggled with since she was young.

Always worried someone was upset with her.

Always worried they would confront her about it. It made her passive.

Worried about everyone else's feelings.

Worried about just about everything if she was honest.

Fear was what she feared most. It's why she was trying so hard to rename it.

Call it by another name.

Excitement.

"I want some barbeque from Eli's." Elise sighed. "That should be the first thing we do when we get there."

"The first thing we're doing when we get there is working." Rico stared straight ahead as he drove toward the airport. "This isn't a vacation."

"Well not with that attitude it's not." Elise crossed her arms over her chest.

Abe made a coughing sound from his seat. Elise's pale green eyes rested on him for a second before darting away.

"We can order from Eli's for dinner." Lennie smiled at her friend. "We have to eat."

Rico gripped the wheel in a move that snagged every bit of attention she had, pulling it to that single spot.

His eyes caught hers in the mirror as one thumb slowly dragged back and forth over the curve of the wheel.

Then it moved a little faster.

And faster.

"Are you hot?" Elise leaned her way. "You're really pink." She leaned between the seats. "I think Lennie's nervous. Can you turn on the air?"

She was not nervous. Not even a little.

What she was might be worse, though. Especially since she had no real idea how to deal with it.

Lennie forced her eyes to the back of Abe's seat and started counting lines in the leather.

Anything to keep from thinking of this new scenario Rico managed to offer her without saying a single word.

By the time they pulled into the airport she was at five-hundred and sixty two lines of leather.

And still thinking of Rico's thumb.

He parked in a spot near the hangar she vaguely remembered from her flight to Alaska. She'd been scared shitless that day, so most of it was a blur.

Today she'd expected to be the same.

But there didn't seem to be much room in her brain for fear right now. It was otherwise occupied.

A set of open stairs was rolled up to the door of a smallish plane.

Abe pointed to the aircraft. "Go ahead and go in. We'll be in as soon as we're ready to go."

Lennie offered him a smile. "Okay."

Elise came to her side and grabbed her hand. "How are you doing?"

"Okay I think." The normal bite of fear hadn't hit her yet.

"Wow." Elise looked down at their linked fingers. "Your hands are warm." She gave her a wide smile. "Good job."

"I'm trying to be better." Lennie reached the bottom of the stairs and went straight up with Elise coming right behind her.

"I'm really proud of you. I know this isn't your favorite thing, and you are handling it like a bad bitch."

"I'm not sure I'd take it that far." Lennie stopped as the interior came into view. "This is really small."

Smaller than the last plane, and it had seemed super small.

"We don't need a big plane for four people." Elise went to one of the leather seats running up the sides of the cabin. "It's really nice."

It was really nice.

The plane might be smaller than the last, but it was definitely more luxurious. By far.

Lennie pulled her purse to her chest and went to sit in the chair right next to Elise.

"Did you ever think you'd be flying in a private jet?"

"I didn't think I'd ever be flying period." Lennie fished around for the seatbelt and fastened it across her lap, pulling it as tight as possible. "I still question my sanity a little."

"It'll be fine." Elise stretched her legs out. "Definitely better than coach."

"I'll take your word for it." Lennie bounced one leg as she waited.

"You should." Elise grinned. "Otherwise you're going to be miserable."

She was probably going to be miserable anyway.

After too many minutes Abe finally came up the stairs and into the plane. Rico was right behind him. The suck of the door into place made her stomach drop.

"I hate this." Lennie gripped the arms of her seat, squeezing them tight.

Rico leaned into Abe's ear. Abe's eyes drifted to Lennie before moving to Elise. A second later Rico went to the cockpit, disappearing from sight.

Abe lingered. "Do you want something to drink?"

Lennie almost gagged. "No."

"I could use a soda or something." Elise gave Abe a sweet smile. "What is there?"

"You'll have to come back and see. Depends on what Pierce stocked."

Elise leaned into Lennie's side. "I'll be right back. Breathe deep." She stood up. "I'll get you a ginger ale just in case."

Lennie couldn't answer. All she could focus on was her breathing. As Elise and Abe went to the back of the plane she closed her eyes.

The air around her shifted and her next slow inhale carried a familiar scent.

Warm fingers slid over the backs of her hands. "Relax, Loba."

"I am relaxing. That's why my eyes are closed."

Rico's fingers traced along her knuckles. "You are about to tear through Pierce's leather seat."

"I'll buy him another one." She couldn't open her eyes but now it had nothing to do with the impending flight.

Rico was close. Close enough she would make a fool of herself if she tried to look him in the eye.

His hands rested on hers and his cheek brushed her jaw, the perpetual five-o'clock shadow there scraping across her skin as he leaned into her ear. "You told Pierce you trusted me, Lenore."

"I do." Even those two words were difficult to get out.

"Trust is an important thing, Loba. Don't claim it if it doesn't exist."

Lennie opened her eyes, peeking his way from under her lashes.

She was still a little embarrassed about last night, and up until this moment she was almost positive Rico regretted it.

Which would make sense considering she literally ran from his room.

"I do trust you."

"I disagree."

"You don't know how I feel." Lennie had to force the statement out. She was trying so hard to be different. Trying to prove what she really was.

What she wasn't.

And what she wasn't, was a woman who let a man tell her how she felt. Not anymore.

"Then tell me."

"Well." Lennie shifted the gum still in her mouth. Emotional honesty wasn't something she was particularly good at, and up until recently she'd been perfectly fine with that fact. "I am scared." Her head turned his way. "But it's not because I don't trust you so don't say that again."

One of Rico's dark brows lifted but he didn't speak.

"It's because you don't control the whole world. All sorts of things could happen that you wouldn't be able to do anything about."

Birds in engines.

Mechanical malfunction.

Spontaneous combustion.

Maybe not that last one.

"I see." Rico's dark eyes held hers for a minute. "No one controls everything, Loba. If you are only going to live a life with no risk then you will live a life with no reward."

"That's why I'm here in the first place." She narrowed her eyes at him. "Because I'm tired of no rewards."

Rico's lips pulled into a slow, seductive smile. "Is that what you're expecting, Lenore? Rewards?"

"I don't *expect* them." She'd gotten on a plane to get what she wanted. Twice. "I'm willing to earn them."

"It's not about earning, Loba." Rico leaned away just enough so his face was in line with hers. "It's about taking what's yours."

CHAPTER 8

"HOW'S SHE DOING?" Abe settled into the seat beside him in the cockpit.

"She will be fine." Rico kept the answer short and simple.

Something needed to be simple right now.

Because he couldn't seem to stop complicating things when Lenore Bates was involved.

"Good." Abe put on his headset. He'd been working on his own license so they could have two pilots on site in case there was ever a need to have more than one plane out at a time.

And now that Alaskan Security was back to being spread across the country that was a very real possibility.

"I think Elise will do her best to help." Abe watched as Rico worked through the checklist, making sure everything was in order. "She seemed pretty worried about her."

He took a little more time than normal, double checking where he usually wouldn't.

Just to be sure.

When everything was in order Rico let the tower know they were set to go. The small airport was usually quiet, and today was no exception. They were able to immediately taxi to the runway.

Rico clicked on the speaker so he would be heard above the engine. "We're taking off, ladies."

The weather was perfect and the takeoff was textbook. As smooth and steady as he could possibly make it. Once they leveled out Rico glanced at Abe.

Abe immediately knew what he was thinking. "Want me to go check on her?"

"Make sure she's okay." Rico usually loved being in the cockpit. It was his favorite place in the world.

But right now he'd give a lot to be the one making sure Lennie was handling the flight okay.

And that was an issue.

A few minutes later Abe was back. He didn't say anything as he belted back into his seat.

"So?"

"She's fine." Abe tipped his head to one side. "As fine as she can be considering Elise is talking about food and Lennie looks like she wants to throw up."

"Did you give her a bag?"

"I gave her two." Abe glanced his way. "Just in case Elise can't handle seeing someone else puke."

"Pierce will appreciate that." Rico smiled a little as the sight in front of him eased the tension in his shoulders. "He'd be less than excited to have two women's worth of puke in his plane."

"He'd get over it." Abe went quiet as they both enjoyed the peace of the flight.

There was nothing like it.

Seeing the clouds from the other side. Being far from the world and all the problems that came with it.

Unfortunately his biggest problem was currently on the same side of the clouds as he was.

Their first stop for fuel was in Washington. It was one of the major downsides to the smaller plane. It simply couldn't fly as far as the larger ones without having to stop, which meant they would have to take off and land three times each trip. It was either that or take a bigger, but less comfortable, plane.

He made a judgment call. Hopefully it was the right one.

The landing was as perfect as the takeoff was and it wasn't long before they were in the air again.

Luckily Abe was a quiet partner, and it gave him plenty of time to work through how this trip had to go.

Somehow he was going to have to figure out how to stay away from Lennie. At the very least never end up alone with her.

Because when he had her alone he made bad decisions.

By the time they landed at the small airport just outside of Cincinnati, Rico was prepared. Ready to put down some trenches and dig in.

Because he was not going to fall into the same damn pit everyone around him was.

He'd been there. It wasn't as fun as they all made it seem.

It was agony.

It was pain.

It was disappointment.

Regret.

And as much as he hated to admit it, Lenore Bates was not a woman he'd be able to spend one night with and move on.

Unfortunately.

"Go ahead and get the girls off the plane. I'll be out in a minute." Rico made himself look busy in spite of the fact that Abe knew damn well he wasn't. Luckily his friend didn't call him out on it.

Once he was sure everyone was off the plane, Rico grabbed his bag and made his way to the door. The two unused sick bags caught his eye as he passed the seats where Lennie and Elise sat. At least Pierce would be happy.

Everyone was loaded into the rental SUV when he reached it.

But no one was where they should be.

Rico pulled open the back door. "What in the hell is going on?"

Lennie lifted a brow at him from the driver's seat as Elise turned in her shotgun spot. "You're not from here. Why would you drive?"

"I always drive." Rico looked to Abe for help but Abe was busy on his phone.

Elise grinned at him. "Not today. Today the girls are driving so get in, Miss Daisy."

He dropped his bag on the floorboard and fell into the seat.

Lennie immediately pulled away as Elise hooked her phone up to the navigation system. "This place is going to be so sweet."

"What hotel are we staying at?" Lennie's driving was starkly different this time. She immediately pushed past the speed limit and moved aggressively through the rush-hour traffic.

None of the hesitation he'd seen at the beginning of their first drive together.

"Not a hotel." Elise held her phone Lennie's way. "It's an Airbnb on the river."

"I can't look at that right now. People are driving like assholes." Lennie laid on the horn as a minivan cut her off.

Abe glanced his way, brows lifted.

"That's Cincinnati for you. Everyone acts like they're the only one on the road." Elise thumbed the keyboard on her phone. "Here you go." The map immediately flashed onto the screen in the center of the dash. "Twenty minutes."

"Holy shit." Lennie glanced at the map. "How much did that place cost you?"

"Me? Nothing." She smiled. "Pierce is a different story."

"We could have just stayed in a hotel." Lennie's eyes snapped between her mirrors as she moved through traffic, cutting across two lanes at once to dodge slow movers.

"No way." Elise shook her head. "I told him if we uprooted our whole lives to go to Alaska then the least he could do is rent us someplace nice."

"He paid us to come to Alaska." Lennie's turn signal flicked as she continued driving down the interstate with an easy level of assertiveness that Pierce would most certainly exploit if he knew it existed. "And he gives us a nice place to live while we're there."

"It's a room." Elise relaxed back in her seat, not even a little affected by Lennie's driving. "No living room. No kitchen. Just a bed and a bathroom. I'm taking full advantage while I can."

"You know you don't have to live on campus."

Elise sat straight and turned Abe's way. "I'm not renting a place if I'm not sure I'm staying there."

Lennie frowned. "You're thinking about leaving?"

Elise shrugged. "Maybe." She slumped down in her seat as she faced forward. "It's not really all I thought it would be."

Lennie was quiet for a minute. "Sometimes I think you have to make things happen. Just jump in with both feet and get what you want."

"I'm not sure that's the case for me." Elise sighed. "It just is what it is."

The car fell silent as they closed in on the bridge leading to Newport. The house Elise rented sat just across the river from Cincinnati, and once they were across the bridge it was less than five minutes before Lennie pulled into the driveway of a sleek mid-century modern house surrounded by mature trees.

"It's nice, right?" Elise grinned as she opened her door and climbed out, heading straight for the front entry.

"Is this water-front?" Lennie went to the back of the SUV and opened the hatch. She reached for her bag just as Abe stepped in at her side.

"We'll get your bags."

Lennie gave him a smile. "Thank you."

Rico waited until Lennie was out of earshot before he leaned close to Abe. "You thinking about shooting your shot?"

It was a painful thing to consider, but would be the best for everyone. Abe was a good guy. Grown. Had his shit together.

Abe eyed him. "You want me to go after the girl you want?" He pulled out Elise's bag. "You're taking self-sabotage to a whole new level with that one, man."

"Self-sabotage?" Rico grabbed Lennie's bag. "What the fuck's that mean?"

"Means you do this every time." Abe closed the hatch. "You meet a nice girl and you fuck it all up on purpose."

"There's nothing to fuck-up here." Rico slung his bag over one shoulder and rolled Lennie's toward the house with the other. "So go for it."

"I'm not interested in her." Abe lifted Elise's bag up the steps.

"You want Elise?"

"Hell no. That one's a handful." Abe grinned. "If I ever decide to settle down I want one that won't make me crazy."

"I don't think they make them like that, my friend." Rico scooted Lennie's bag across the travertine tile of the entrance and down a handful of steps, parking it inside the sunken living room. "I'm pretty sure that's just how they are."

He knew. He'd been there.

"Just wait." Rico tipped his head at Abe. "They get you and you don't even see it coming."

And then once you did it was too late.

And everything went to shit.

Elise breezed into the main area, the keys to the SUV dangling from one hand. "I'm going to go get something to eat."

"We've got one car." Abe snagged the keys in a quick move. "That means you can't monopolize it."

Elise scoffed. "Then I'll go rent my own car." She tried to snatch the keys back but Abe held them tight. "Give me the keys."

"How are you going to bring both these cars back?"

Elise smiled at him, her lips curving in a slow slide. "I only care about mine making it back here."

"Sounds right." Abe jerked the keys from her grip. "Come on."

Elise planted her feet. "You don't have to be an ass."

Abe kept walking to the door. "This is me being nice, sweetheart."

"Not your sweetheart, dick."

Abe stopped and slowly turned to face her. "Not your dick, babe."

"Wouldn't want you to be, *babe*." Elise crossed her arms and stared Abe down.

Abe slowly walked her way, keys gripped tight in his hand. He stopped right in front of her. "That makes two of us."

"Good." Elise's smile took on a wild edge. "At least we're on the same page." Her chin lifted and she strode past him. "Come on then. Let's see if you can get me where I want to go."

Abe turned and watched as Elise marched up the three steps to the entry and straight out the door.

Rico smiled. "You're fucked."

"Shut up." Abe grabbed his cell as he walked to the door. "I'll grab us some food while I'm out."

Rico smiled for a good minute, imagining the car ride Abe was definitely struggling through.

Then his smile slipped.

He spun toward the bag he'd brought in.

He was alone with Lennie.

"Shit." Her voice carried from one of the two halls leading from the main room.

"Shit. Shit. Shit. Shit."

She was probably fine.

"Damn it."

Rico edged closer to where he could hear her rustling around in the space. "Lennie?"

She didn't answer him.

He took the three steps all at once to the short hall leading to two bedrooms. Lennie was in the second room off the hall, crouched down beside the bed.

109

Being close to her was not a good idea for him, but if she was hurt…

The thought sent him straight to her side, down to the plush carpet. "What's wrong, Loba?"

She was pressing a towel to the floor. "I knocked my ginger ale on the freaking carpet." One hand came up to push her dark hair from her eyes as she tried to soak up the mess.

"It's okay." Rico grabbed the small nightstand and scooted it away from the spots splashed onto the cream carpet. "It's clear. No one will know."

"But *I* will know." Lennie threw the wet towel over his head into the small bathroom at his back. "You can't just go around messing things up and then walking away like nothing happened."

Rico took the fresh towel from her hands and went to work pressing it into the spill. "That's a good rule to live by."

"I'm pretty sure most people think the same way." She sat back on her heels.

"And I'm pretty sure most people don't." He folded the towel over to a dry spot and put his weight into getting out the last of the liquid.

"Would you have left it?"

He resisted the urge to look at her. "No."

"See?"

"That doesn't mean you and I are the same, Loba." He stood and went to the bathroom to retrieve the wet rag she'd tossed in there. When he turned around she was frowning at him.

Which was good. She should frown at him. It was what he needed.

Lennie shoved up from the floor and came his way, her eyes narrowing.

"What?" He tried to sound put out. Aggravated instead of interested in what she had to say next.

"Why are you being like this?"

"I don't know what you're talking about."

"You do." Lennie stopped in front of him. "One minute you're letting me..." Her eyes dipped for just a second before snapping back to his. "And the next you act like you can't stand to be around me."

She wasn't wrong.

He couldn't stand to be around her. Not without—

"You made me certain offers." Lennie's chin lifted. "Can I assume you're taking them back?"

"I don't think you are ready for what I offered you, Lenore."

One finger came to point right at the center of his face. "Don't you put this on me." The pitch of her voice rose. "I'm not the problem."

The conviction in her tone was strong. Stronger than he expected, and it made everything worse.

Almost intolerable.

Rico dipped his head, aligning his eyes with hers. "Fine, Loba. You want the truth?"

She stood taller. "I think I deserve it."

Rico eased closer, hoping she might back away from him. "I don't want to be around you."

He expected her to be offended.

Upset at his rejection.

Her nostrils barely flared. "Then you should have just said that." She stretched taller, coming toe to toe with him. "Don't pretend I'm the problem when I'm not."

He couldn't look away from her. The way her chin lifted. The way her jaw set. She was fucking stunning. "You are never the problem, Loba."

"You tried to put the blame on me."

"Because I'm a coward, Loba."

Her head bobbed back the smallest bit and her eyes widened. "Oh." Lennie blinked a few times. "Then you should stop being one."

"It's not that easy, Lenore."

"I didn't say it was easy." She sounded a little irritated. "I said you should stop being one."

"Is that what you're doing?"

"Life is too short to spend it being scared." Her shoulders went back. "To spend it believing what other people say you are."

"What do other people say you are?" Rico watched every change of her expression. Every shift of emotion across her eyes.

Lennie didn't hide how she felt. Maybe she couldn't.

The thought made him itch with the need to protect her from people—

Like him.

People who didn't show how they felt.

People who tried not to feel at all.

She scraped her teeth across her lower lip. "That I'm boring."

The admission made him laugh out loud. He couldn't stop his reaction to her.

Yet again.

"Loba," Rico managed to tame the laugh to a smile, "anyone who accuses you of being boring is a liar."

CHAPTER 9

"THAT'S WHY I went to Alaska." Lennie lifted her shoulders. "Because it was the truth. I was boring."

"I'm not sure a change in location is enough to make a boring person into what you are now."

Lennie glanced to the window of the room she chose, looking out over the front lawn. "I was different here. I didn't take risks or put myself out there."

"Why the change?"

"Because I was tired of it." She turned her eyes back to where Rico stood in front of her, his closeness just as confusing as everything else about him was turning out to be. "I didn't want to get old and have regrets."

"Everyone has regrets, Loba." Rico's tone was a little different. A little off.

"Do you have regrets?"

His head dipped in a nod. "Many."

"Do you regret last night?" She'd never in her life been bold.

Never in a million years would she have brought up what she watched last night. Especially considering Rico didn't seem to be having the same reaction to it she did.

But that was the woman she was trying to leave behind. The one who was boring.

Shy.

Backward.

Frigid. That was the one that hurt the most.

"I shouldn't have invited you to my room."

Lennie's eyes drifted down at the memory, her mind snagging on the way he looked standing under the water as it eased the slow glide of his hand. "That's not what I asked." She licked her lips, trying to make them feel less dry. "I asked if you regret it."

She should. She'd stared.

Barely blinked.

Because it was impossible to turn away from him. From his body. She'd never openly looked at a naked man before, let alone one doing what he was.

She'd never really found it interesting, certainly not stimulating. But—

"Don't look at me like that, Loba."

She forced her eyes to his and tried to push the images of Rico from her mind. "How am I looking at you?"

"Like you want to bring me to my knees." He reached up to brush one finger across her lips. "Like you could kill me with that sweet mouth of yours."

"I don't think I could do either of those things." The truth slipped free, exposing the insecurity she hoped to leave behind.

Rico leaned close, the finger on her lips dropping to press under her chin. "I wish I was man enough to prove you wrong, Loba." His body barely pressed into her as his nose skimmed the side of hers. "But I'm not."

"Because you're a coward?" She was a little breathless and every nerve in her body seemed to be teetering on some unseen ledge. Waiting.

For what she wasn't sure.

"*Si*. Because I'm a coward." His lips nearly touched hers as they moved.

"Then don't be." If she was brave enough she would take what was so close.

The thought was barely there before she knew what she had to do.

Rico might be fine with being a coward, but she was not.

Not anymore.

Lennie wrapped both arms around his neck and pulled his lips to hers in a move that went fast enough she couldn't rethink it.

And the second Rico's warm mouth rested against hers she knew she'd never take it back. Even if it all went to hell.

The scrape of the black hair peppering his chin and cheeks rasped against her skin. The scent of his body teased her with the familiar smell of the soap she'd watched running down his naked frame.

A different woman probably would have gotten in the shower with him.

Stripped her clothes off and offered him a hand.

But she wasn't that woman. Not yet.

"Lenore." Rico's lips moved against hers as he said her name.

A name no one but him called her.

"Yes?" It was impossible to breathe around the panic twisting her lungs as it changed, edging closer to excitement with each passing heartbeat.

Rico gripped her tight, one hand at the back of her head and the other at her hip as he turned, spinning them into the tiny bathroom and pressing her tight to the wall. "Why can't I stay away from you?" His lips left hers, moving along the line of her jaw.

"I don't want you to stay away from me." The admission was easier than she expected.

"That's a problem, Loba." Rico's hard body pushed into hers, the line of his rigid dick making her gasp as it rubbed her belly.

"It's not." Her head dropped to one side as his mouth went down her neck, the nip of his teeth on her skin sending a shiver through her body.

"It will be." Rico's hand left her hip, sliding up. "You are a drug, Loba." His palm curved around her breast, fingers immediately coming to work her nipple through the fabric of her bra and shirt. "The more I have the more I want."

She wasn't ever the desirable one. She was the shy one men ignored. Passed over for the women who stood out. The women who knew how to claim attention as their own.

She was never pursued. Never longed for.

She was the woman men ended up with because of proximity and eventuality.

But right now she felt like one of those other women. She felt desired.

And Rico was right. It was like a drug.

He took a deep breath against her skin. "You smell like sin."

"Sin?"

Rico hummed as he let the breath out. "*Si*, Loba. The kind of sin a man would gladly burn for."

"I don't want you to burn." Her head fell against the wall as his thumb and finger continued to work her nipple.

"It's too late." His face tipped to hers, dark eyes filled with something that nearly buckled her knees.

Lust.

No one ever looked at her with lust. Even in the heat of the moment it was absent.

And it left her thinking she simply wasn't a woman men lusted after, but once again, Rico was making her think she could be something different.

Something new.

His hands moved over her, one tucking under her shirt and the other gripping the waistband of her shorts. "I want to make you burn too, Lenore." The hand in her shorts pulled her closer. "Can I do that?" The hand under her shirt pulled down the cup of her bra. "Can I make you burn?"

"Yes." She managed to cut off the please before it slipped out. A confession of sorts.

Because the men she was with weren't the only ones who never had lust in their eyes. Maybe that's why she accepted it from them.

There was no reason to expect something she couldn't offer in return. Lust. Desire. Need. They were all emotions she technically understood, but never really felt herself. Maybe she pushed them down. Maybe she ignored them.

Or maybe she simply hadn't met anyone worthy of desiring, because right now there didn't seem to be an issue. Every nerve in her body was firing, blocking out the thoughts and fear trying to creep in, leaving only one question rattling around in her scrambled brain.

What did a man like Rico do to set a woman on fire?

Whatever it was, she would suffer because of it. There wasn't a doubt in her mind he was completely capable of ruining her for the rest of her life.

And it would be worth it.

Rico's mouth was on hers again, hot and demanding as his hand worked into the loose fit of her shorts. His touch slid under her panties, pushing down until his fingers slid right against her pussy, gliding over her slick skin.

Rico growled into her mouth as his fingers eased into her. The heel of his hand rubbed against her clit, stealing a gasp from her lungs.

"Lennie?"

Elise's voice made her jump, every muscle in her body stiffening at the intrusion.

But Rico didn't flinch. His wide body held her pinned to the wall as his hand continued on. His lips went to her ear. "Tell her you'll be out in a minute."

"I'll be out in a minute." Lennie clamped her lips together as Rico's fingers pulled free and flattened between her labia, rubbing back and forth over her most sensitive spot.

"You okay?" Elise's voice was a little closer.

It should have terrified her.

Sent her into a panic.

It did not do that.

"Fine." Lennie squeezed her eyes closed as Rico's hand continued working her toward a fast and fierce climax, one that was only gaining momentum at the thought of being caught. "I'm fine."

"Okay." Elise sounded unconvinced. "I got us some food if you want some."

Lennie bit her lip as Rico's thumb dragged over the nipple of the breast he bared. "Thank you." She fought in a breath. "I'll be out in a minute."

"Okay." It was a few seconds more before Elise's steps moved down the hall and away from the open door of the bedroom.

She exhaled sharply in relief. Being caught was one thing.

Being caught in the middle of an orgasm was another.

"Did the thought of being caught excite you, Lenore?"

"Yes." There was no sense denying it. If Rico knew half as much about the female anatomy as it seemed like he did then he already knew the answer.

"Mmmmm." His deep hum snaked through her. "Maybe I will come back tonight. Lick your pussy until you want to scream. Leave the door open while you suffer."

There was something wrong with her.

Because the thought of Rico's head between her thighs where anyone could see sent her pussy clenching around his fingers as she came, every ounce of available energy going to keeping her mouth shut. She might find the idea of being caught exciting, but that didn't mean she actually wanted it to happen.

Lennie opened her eyes.

Rico's dark gaze was on her face.

The urge to be embarrassed was strong. Almost unavoidable.

Heat pricked across her cheeks and tried to drag her eyes to the floor.

"No shame, Loba." Rico's finger went to press the tip of her chin, keeping her eyes on his. "Not between us."

"I'm not ashamed. I'm embarrassed."

"Why?" He held her chin firm, refusing to give her the escape she wanted.

"I didn't know you were watching me."

"You thought I wouldn't want to see what I do to you?"

She nearly choked. "No."

In her experience most men were primarily focused on what was done to them. Anything they had to do to get to that point was simply out of obligation.

A requirement to board.

Rico's lips pulled into a slow smile that made her stomach drop. "Then I should tell you now, I will be watching every second of what I do to you, Lenore." He leaned down, his eyes holding hers. "I don't plan to miss a fucking breath you take." He stepped back, dragging her from the wall as he went. "Go eat."

"But—" She wasn't necessarily hungry.

She was more interested in this.

In him.

"No buts, Loba." He tipped his head to the door. "Go. Before your friend figures out what she almost witnessed."

Her brain was racing, tripping over everything that just happened.

And might happen later.

"Okay." Lennie backed to the door. "What about you?" The house was split into two sets of bedrooms. She and Elise on one side, Rico and Abe on the other. There was no way for Rico to sneak from her room without being seen by anyone in the main area of the house.

He smiled. "Don't worry about me, Loba. I'm good at getting out of places I shouldn't be."

The comment could easily be referring to his career choice.

But it didn't seem like it.

Lennie eyed him for a second longer before turning and walking into the short hall, smoothing down her hair before going down the trio of stairs leading to the living room.

Elise glanced her way from where she was sitting on the couch eating from a foam container and watching television. "Your stomach okay?"

"Um." Lennie pressed one hand to her still fluttering belly. "Yeah. It's just feeling a little touchy."

"Probably the flight." Elise pointed to a container on the coffee table. "I bet food will make it better."

"Maybe." Lennie picked the box up and settled onto the sofa beside Elise as she scanned the room. "Where's Abe?"

Elise shoved a bite of corn pudding into her mouth. "Don't care." She tipped her eyes Lennie's way. "Aren't you going to ask me where Rico is?"

Lennie kept her eyes on the food in front of her as she wore her best poker face. "Where's Rico?"

"I dunno."

"Then why did you make me ask?" Lennie scooped up a pile of green beans and brisket and put it in her mouth, trying to look confused.

It shouldn't be that hard considering she was a little confused.

Rico wasn't turning out to be the most consistent man she'd ever met.

Elise lifted a brow. "Don't pretend like you're not interested in him."

Lennie stabbed a chunk of smoked chicken. "Define interested."

She needed someone to, because the original reasons she was intrigued by Rico were shifting. Changing faster than she could keep up with.

"You want to sex him." Elise sipped at the straw sticking out of a foam cup. "That enough of a definition?" She set the cup on the table. "Not that I can blame you. He seems like he'd be really good at it."

"What makes you say that?"

Elise laughed. It was tight and high-pitched. "I don't know. He just does."

"I'll take your word for it." Lennie chewed through a bite of chicken as she tried not to read any more into Rico than she had to.

It would only confuse her more.

She turned toward Elise. "What about Abe?"

Elise's lip curled, lifting one nostril. "What about Abe?"

"You think he's good at it?"

Elise scrunched her nose up. "Who cares?"

"Not you, apparently." Lennie reached out to steal a pickle from Elise's tray.

"Definitely not me." Elise's mouth pushed out in a pout. She looked toward the front door as it opened, eyes narrowing as Abe walked in carrying an armload of bags with Rico following right behind him.

Neither man looked their way as they went to the open kitchen and started putting away the groceries.

"Looks like they're both planning to be assholes." Elise turned back to face the television.

Lennie watched the men a little longer, her eyes lingering on Rico as he lined items down the counter.

Would he really sneak into her room tonight?

Do what he said he would?

Maybe do more?

The thought made her face hot just in time for Rico's eyes to finally lift to hers, catching her thinking of him in a scandalous way yet again.

His lips barely twitched, making it pretty clear he knew exactly what she was thinking.

Or at least close enough.

"What do you want to watch?" Elise snagged her attention. "Movie or sitcom?"

"Movie." She needed some time to work up some bravery.

Just in case Rico decided to show up.

Elise flipped through the menu showing their options, and they settled on watching Thor. The time change put them three hours off, and even after two movies Lennie wasn't feeling even a little tired.

Or maybe that had to do with the panic revving up her insides.

Was it panic?

The line between fear and excitement was blurring more and more, making it difficult to tell the difference.

Elise yawned loud and long. "I'm going to bed." She stood up from the sofa they'd been parked on. "I think the flight wore me out."

"Okay." Lennie stood too, her eyes immediately going to the doorway leading to their rooms. "I'll see you in the morning." She wandered to the kitchen as Elise disappeared into her room, closing the door behind her.

After killing ten minutes getting water and perusing the food Abe brought back, Lennie finally didn't have anything else to keep her from going to her own room.

Abe and Rico had gone to their own rooms when they started the movies, so she was the last one out of the main space. It took a few minutes to find all the switches and shut down all the lights. Then it took a few more minutes to make her way through the dark space without breaking a toe. Finally Lennie made it to her room.

She'd managed to watch two movies filled with gorgeous men and didn't notice a single one of them, which wasn't unusual. What was unusual, was the fact that she spent all four hours thinking about Rico and his hot and coldness. Most of the time going to the hotness part.

Which meant she was no closer to figuring anything out.

Maybe this was just how men like Rico operated.

And if that was the case, maybe he wasn't what she wanted.

She'd known enough men who were wishy-washy when it came to how they felt about her. Men who always ended up moving on to someone they didn't feel so undecided about.

She wasn't necessarily trying to be *with* Rico, but she'd changed her whole life hoping it would make it easier to change herself, and tolerating a wishy-washy man wasn't something she wanted to do ever again.

As much as it sucked, she was going to have to shut Rico down. Tell him to take his sexy, but indecisive, ass somewhere else.

CHAPTER 10

HER DOOR WAS closed.

Rico stood at the barrier she put between them, staring it down, disappointment strong in his gut.

He'd waited for Elise to finally go to bed, thinking Lennie was doing the same.

But now this.

The rejection hit him harder than he expected. Usually being shut down was no big deal.

He simply moved on to someone more interested in his company.

No harm no foul.

But Lennie seemed interested. He would have bet all he had that she was here waiting for him, her cheeks flushed in that way that made him lose his damn mind. Like they were earlier.

When she was watching him in the kitchen.

So why the fuck was her door closed now?

He lifted his hand, intending to knock. Find out what in the hell the problem was.

The door snapped open before he could touch it and Lennie jumped back, her dark eyes wide as she gasped.

"What's wrong, Loba?" It came out accusatory. Maybe it was.

She huffed out a breath. "You scared me."

"No." Rico shook his head. "Why was your door closed?" He eased toward her. "Why did you shut me out?"

Her dark hair was damp, falling in messy waves and bends around her scrubbed face. Seeing her like this felt intimate. Something he tried to never feel toward a woman.

But damned if he could stop it with her.

Lennie's shoulders moved, straightening a little. "I was just coming to talk to you about that."

"Then talk."

Her eyes moved down the short hall toward Elise's closed door. She huffed out a breath then reached to grab the center of his shirt, yanking him into her room and closing the door behind him. She let him go almost immediately and leaned her back against the closed door.

"I'm waiting, Lenore."

She pointed at him. "Don't start with that."

He lifted a brow.

"Don't act like you don't know what you do." She waved the finger around. "The things you say. You know you can pull me right back in and it's not fair."

"Not fair?"

"Not at all." She crossed her arms. "One minute you're all *tell me your secrets, Loba*, and the next you," she lifted her hands, making finger quotes as she continued, "don't want to be around me." Lennie's hands dropped and her chin lifted. "I'm done dealing with men who can take me or leave me."

This was not what he was expecting when he crept through the house, each step coming faster than the last.

"So where does that leave us, Lennie?" He didn't like calling her what everyone else did. Didn't like being relegated to the same place in her life the rest of the world occupied.

"Nowhere." Lennie crossed her arms. "I want excitement, but being yanked around by a man who likes me one minute and doesn't the next isn't what I'm looking for."

"Is that what you think?" The pressure building in his chest eased a little. "That I don't like you?"

"Sometimes you do." Lennie held his eyes as he worked his way closer.

Rico shook his head. "That's not true."

"Then that's worse." She huffed out a breath. "You might be fine messing around with people who don't like you but I'm not."

"Messing around. Is that what you call what we're doing?" He didn't like it. Didn't like the casualness it insinuated.

Even though that's what he pretended this was.

"I don't call it anything now." Lennie's tone was so calm. So even.

Like she'd thought it all out. Maybe been through it before.

"So that's it? You're done with me then?" Rico eased in a little more. "I get you off once and you don't have any more use for me?"

"That's not what I said." She held firm. "I said I'm no longer tolerating men who don't want me."

Hurt edged her words, cutting into the hide he wore like armor, keeping a separation between him and any woman who wanted to get close.

"Wanting you isn't my problem, Loba."

Her eyes dipped a little as they moved over him with suspicion. "Then what is your problem?"

"My problems are too many to count." He rarely offered certain truths. This was one of them.

But he couldn't handle her thinking he didn't desire her.

That she was somehow at fault for his issues.

"Give me one then."

He should keep it simple.

Give her the same bullshit excuse he gave any other woman who tried to get close to him.

But this wasn't some other woman.

This was Lennie.

Lenore.

Loba.

"I want you too much." Rico moved closer. "I want to own every inch of your body." He grabbed the front of the soft shirt she wore and used the hold to pull her close enough he could breathe her in. "I want to fill you, Loba. I want to ruin you. Show you no one can give you what I can."

The words could be misunderstood. Taken to mean only part of his desires where Lenore was concerned.

And he hoped they would.

It was all that could save him.

Her dark eyes were wary. "You mean sexually."

He should have known better. Known she would see through the bluff straight to the core. "I mean what I mean, Loba."

"That's not good enough." Her voice was small. Like these were words she'd never said out loud before.

But always thought.

Rico rocked from one foot to the other as she held firm.

Leaving him two options.

Give her what she wanted.

Or leave.

Leaving was the better idea. The one that would preserve his sanity.

His way of life.

But the thought of leaving her thinking she wasn't enough for him was almost painful. "I wish I just wanted you like that, Loba. It would be easier for me."

Lennie's chin slowly lowered, taking her eyes with it. "Then why are you here?"

"I told you." He leaned close, letting his lips run over the skin just below her ear. "You are my drug." He caught the lobe of her ear between his teeth, teasing it with his tongue before releasing it. "The more of you I have, the more of you I want."

He hadn't offered this much honesty to a woman in years.

This much of himself.

He'd successfully managed to chase the physical connection he craved without falling into anything more.

Maybe it was because he sought women who looked at him as nothing more than what he could offer physically.

And maybe that's all this woman wanted too.

"What do you want from me, Rico?" The question stopped him in his tracks.

"I wish I knew, Loba." He lifted his head, meeting her gaze. "What do you want from me?"

Lennie's head barely shook. "I don't know."

Her answer should unsettle him. The risk that she could want more than he had to offer should send him on his way.

Normally it would.

But nothing with Lennie was normal.

Rico skimmed one hand down her arm, over the smooth skin there. "Do you want what I promised you, Lenore?"

"You didn't promise me anything." She paused as his touch moved to her side. "You said you might."

"How about I make it a promise then?" Rico fingered the hem of her shirt. He'd spent hours thinking of tonight.

Of her.

Her bravery was intoxicating. Her determination to take what she was and make it what she wanted.

He envied her.

"I feel like you're trying to distract me with sex."

"Not you, Loba." He traced along her belly with the tips of his fingers.

"It's not healthy to use sex as a distraction."

"It's fun, though."

"Isn't it more fun when you're doing it because you want to," her eyes met his, "instead of because you have to?"

Once again she cut straight to the quick, slicing through the layers he built up, leaving him with two choices.

Honesty or leaving her behind.

"Sometimes we do the things we have to in order to get through. Does that make sense?"

She tipped her head in a little nod. "Is that how you want to live?" There was no accusation in her tone. Nothing but curiosity.

Still he knew his answer mattered.

"It's where I am, Loba." He had every intention of continuing on like he was. No ties to tangle.

No lives to be left full of regret and pain.

Lennie studied him for a minute. "Do you want to watch a movie with me?" Her eyes moved to the television on the dresser across from the king-sized bed in her room.

He hesitated.

Asking him to fuck her would have been an easier answer. A less dangerous act.

"What movie would we watch?" It didn't matter. In truth he already knew what his answer would be.

She was his weakness. One he never expected to have.

Lennie didn't make a move. "Does it matter?"

Rico shook his head. "No."

Lennie's face fell. "I understand." She turned and went to the bed, pulling back the covers.

"I don't think you do." Rico struggled not to immediately follow her. To find his way into her bed under completely different circumstances than he expected.

"It's fine." She wiggled under the blankets, switching on the television. "Close the door on your way out."

She was drawing a hard line. One that he'd forced on her by fighting the attraction he had for her.

Pretending it wasn't there.

Now she didn't believe the truth when he gave it to her.

She needed to see proof.

Proof he wanted her the way she deserved to be wanted.

Rico turned to the door. He'd walked out of plenty of bedrooms. Left more than a few women behind.

Never once did he second-guess it. If they thought there would be more that was on them. He made his stance clear from the beginning.

He switched off the light, blanketing the room in near darkness. He reached for the door, but instead of opening it and walking out like he had so many times, he twisted the lock. Not because he was worried about being discovered.

Part of him wanted it to happen.

But he was worried about how Lennie might react to being discovered.

Rico turned to where she was tucked into the bed. Her eyes weren't on the television bathing the room in a soft glow.

They were on him.

He peeled his shirt over his head and let it drop to the ground at his feet.

Lennie's eyes barely widened. "What are you doing?"

"I don't sleep in clothes, Loba." He tucked his thumbs into the shorts he pulled on after his shower. "Do you still want me in your bed?"

"You're going to sleep here?"

"*Si*." After too many mixed signals she needed proof he wanted her. Spending the night was something he offered no one.

But he would offer it to her.

Lennie's lower lip tucked between her teeth as she thought it over.

"Did you think watching a movie with me would be like watching a movie with your friend, Loba?" He moved closer. "Because I can promise you it won't." He eased the waistband of his shorts lower. "I'm not interested in being your friend."

"What do you want to be?" Her eyes moved down his bare chest to where his shorts moved lower and lower.

"I want to be your lover, Lenore." Rico pushed the elastic until it caught on the snag of his dick. "No more back and forth. No more hot and cold." He shoved the shorts past his hips and let them drop to the floor. He moved toward the bed, toward the woman still watching him with an unwavering gaze. "You said you want a man who wants you." He crawled over her. "You should probably be careful what you wish for."

"You're naked." The words were breathy. Sounded a little shocked.

"I'm naked a lot, Loba." He eased lower, giving her some of his weight. "You will have to learn to suffer through it."

"I'm not sure I would call it suffering." Her eyes were all over him, raking across his skin without shame.

But her hands stayed where they were, tightly clutching the blankets between them.

"What about you, Loba? Do you like being naked?"

"What?" Her eyes slowly came to his.

"Do you like being naked?"

"Oh." She licked her lips, and the sight of her tongue flicking across her skin shot straight to his dick, making it flex where it rested against her belly. Her eyes locked on it, staring. She didn't even blink.

"Lenore."

"Mm-hmm?"

"I want to know if you like being naked. Tell me."

"No." Her fingers loosened a little.

"Why not?"

"It makes me feel..." One of her fingers came to trace the skin of his chest.

"It makes you feel what, Loba?"

"Exposed." Lennie's finger moved over the line of his pec before dipping to skim across his nipple.

Rico sucked in a breath.

Her eyes jumped to his. "Sorry."

"Did you just apologize for touching me?"

Her finger curled back with the others as her lips rolled inward. "Maybe."

"No, Loba." He shook his head at her. "That's not something we do."

"I thought you didn't like it."

"If I don't like something I will tell you." Rico leaned closer to her. "And I expect the same from you."

She didn't move. Didn't offer the touch she'd rescinded.

"What's wrong, Loba?"

"Nothing." Her eyes moved between them, skimming over his body the way they did the night before. "I just wasn't expecting you to watch movies naked."

"I do everything naked." He teased himself with a drag of his dick across the blanket between them. "If this is what you want then you will have to get used to it."

"Oh." She chewed her lip.

"What are you thinking?" Most women he could read. Know what was moving through their mind when they looked at him.

He couldn't always do that with this one.

"I was just wondering if they wash that blanket between each renter."

Rico looked down. "And now I'm wondering the same thing."

Her eyes slowly came to his. "I guess that means you should get under the covers."

"Are you trying to lure me into the bed with you, Lenore?" Rico flipped the covers back. "Because I thought I made it very clear I intended to be in your bed."

"You are in my bed." She was very still as he moved in beside her.

"Then maybe we have different ideas about what it means to share a bed." He wasn't fucking her tonight.

No matter what.

It felt rushed, which was usually his favorite part of the whole thing. The excitement. The wild abandon.

But not a single cell in his body was in a hurry right now.

Rico lined his body down the side of hers, resting his lips against her ear. "Can I touch you, Lenore?"

"You've already touched me."

"That doesn't mean I have the right to do it whenever I want."

Her eyes came his way, moving over his face for a second before she laid out yet one more thing he didn't see coming.

"Can I touch you?"

"You can touch me any time you want, Loba. I am yours for the taking."

Lennie rolled his way, her soft body brushing his skin as she wiggled into place, every squirm of her hips teasing him in the most perfect way.

Her hands came to his chest, palms resting flat, fingers spread wide. "You are so warm."

"That means I can keep you warm in the winter."

Her eyes lifted to his. "Alaska is so damn cold."

He laughed a little. "*Sí*. Alaska is cold." Rico paused as her hands moved, soft skin sliding over him. "But there are some beautiful things there."

"Is that why you're there? Because it's beautiful?" Her eyes went to where her hands stroked over his shoulders with a slow touch.

"No." He never discussed his life with the women he was with.

They were never meant to be a part of it.

"I came to Alaska because I needed a change." Pierce's offer came at the perfect time. He had no reason to stay in Colombia and every reason to leave.

Start over.

"Me too." Lennie's hand slid down his arm.

"Have you found the change you were looking for?" Rico forced himself not to react when her fingers brushed his stomach, knowing she would stop again.

And he didn't want her to stop.

"Some of it." Lennie's touch teased the spot just below his navel, stalling out before she reached the part of him straining for her attention. "Not everything, though."

"You will find it, Loba. You are brave, remember?"

Her eyes came to his. "You're right."

A second later her hand closed around his aching dick. This time he couldn't control the groan that her touch dragged free.

Lennie inhaled softly. Not a gasp, but close.

She wasn't innocent. He knew that, but she definitely wasn't experienced.

Wasn't confident in the debilitating effect she had on him.

Thank God, or he'd probably be laying on the floor right now wondering what in the fucking world happened to him.

"What about the movie?" Rico speared his fingers into her still-damp hair as he warred with himself.

The drag of her hand over him wasn't anything he wanted to give up, but her need to know he wanted her won out above all else.

Lennie's whole body stilled. "Oh." She pulled her hand from him and started to scoot away. "I thought—"

Shit. Rico grabbed the hand she stole, lifting it to his lips. "That's not what I meant." He brushed a kiss across the inside of her wrist. "I'm trying to give you what you want."

Her eyes leveled on his. "I just want to be wanted."

CHAPTER 11

SHE'D NEVER TOLD a man exactly what she wanted.

Never felt like they'd actually listen if she did.

"I'm here in your bed." Rico's dark eyes stayed right on hers. "Aching." One hand came to rest on the swell of her hip. "I don't know how else to prove I want you."

"Then why did you ask me to turn on the movie?"

"Because I respect you, Loba. I want to give you what you want." His fingers pressed into the fabric of her pajama bottoms. "But I also want to give you what you need."

Lennie closed her eyes. "I don't know what I need."

"Respect, Lenore. That's what you need."

She lifted her lids.

He was still watching her. "That's why I reminded you about the movie. That's what you invited me into your bed for. To watch a movie."

"Is that what you want to do?"

"This isn't about me, Loba." Rico's hand slid to her back, holding tight as he pulled her closer, rolling her to her back as he stayed at her side. "This is about you."

She didn't really know what to do with that. Usually a naked man in her bed meant one thing and one thing only.

Rico curled against her, his face tucking against the side of hers. "Pick your movie, Loba. I'm ready to relax."

How in the hell was she supposed to relax with a completely naked man beside her?

And not just any man.

The single most sexually attractive man she'd ever had her hands on.

"None of that, Loba." He tucked closer. "Not tonight. Tonight you watch your movie."

"I didn't say anything." She fumbled the remote.

"For once I knew what you were thinking." He leaned up to peek at her. "And while I'm proud, I'm not willing to fulfill your wicked fantasies tonight."

"My fantasies aren't wicked." She acted put out that he would think something like that about her.

Because that was how she should act.

How a lifetime of living in a world where women should be sexy, but not too sexy, made her believe she should be.

Experienced but also virginal.

Aggressive but submissive.

Sexually active but only under the right circumstances.

Wearing the right clothes.

Saying the right things.

Get it wrong and you're labeled a slut.

A whore.

Easy.

Unless the pressure gets to you and you're called other things.

The things she was called.

Frigid.

A tease.

Unwantable.

"Your fantasies are definitely wicked, Loba." Rico's voice was low in her ear. "You might not want to admit them yet, but they're there." His nose dragged across her skin as she tried to find a movie to pretend to watch. "And I plan to fulfill every single one of them."

****

"HOW DID YOU sleep?" Elise stood at the counter in the kitchen of their rented house, sipping at a steaming cup of coffee.

"Fine." Lennie grabbed a cup from the hooks screwed into the underside of the cabinets.

"The beds here are pretty decent." Elise set her coffee on the counter as two pieces of toast popped up in the toaster. "And it's so nice to have a kitchen." She stuck a knife into the small jar of peanut butter Abe brought home the night before. "It is a little strange not to have ten people fighting over the first pot of coffee."

"It is." Lennie peeked into the fridge to see if Abe happened to pick up anything that might make the coffee more palatable. As hard as she tried, there was nothing in her that could ever tolerate the stuff straight up.

A small container of her favorite creamer stared out at her from one of the shelves.

Lennie pulled it out and added some to her cup. "Did you give Abe a shopping list?"

Elise took over the grocery orders for headquarters almost immediately, keeping the fridges in the rooming house and the break room stocked with everyone's favorite things.

Elise snorted. "I'm not giving him anything."

Lennie twisted the cap back onto the creamer. She was almost positive Elise ordered it just for her. It never seemed to run out faster than she expected, so if Abe liked it he didn't use much.

Elise picked up a pen from the counter and started writing across the pad directly next to it. "I think I have the best plan of attack figured out to make this go as smoothly as possible."

Lennie leaned in to scan the paper Elise was writing on. It was a neat and extremely thorough list of what needed to be done. "Holy crap. Were you up all night working on that?"

"I didn't have anything else to do." Elise finished the line she was working on. "Figured I might as well make sure we were ready." She wiggled her brows at Lennie. "Besides, the faster we get done the more time we have to go out and have fun while we're here."

"That sounds nice." Going out wasn't really at the top of her list of fun things to do right now.

Not when she might end up with a naked Rico in her bed if she stayed in.

Elise polished off the last bite of her toast before swallowing down the remainder of her coffee. "I gotta pee. I'll be back."

Lennie stood at the counter sipping her coffee as Elise disappeared into her room.

"Good morning." The heat of Rico's body blanketed her back a second after the heat of his voice warmed her ear.

"You already told me that." Lennie peeked at him over one shoulder.

"I wanted to tell you again." He pressed against her. "How did you sleep, Loba?"

"Fine." She took another drink of coffee to fight the urge to say more.

"Just fine?" Rico's hands came to rest on her hips. "That's disappointing."

"I slept well." Admitting she slept amazingly, cuddled up to a Colombian who could stand in as a whole-house furnace, would land her directly in clingy-girl territory.

It was one more pitfall women had to watch out for. Enjoy being with a man too much and you're being crazy. Don't like being with him enough?

Frigid.

"What's wrong, Loba?" Rico swept her hair to one side and tucked his chin against her shoulder.

"You ask me that all the time."

"It's because something bothers you all the time." The hands on her hips moved over her belly as his arms wrapped around her middle. "It holds you back." His palms flattened, one moving up while the other moved down. "I want to see you when nothing holds you back."

"I'm not sure that will ever happen." It was the cycle she always ended caught up in.

What she should be.

What she shouldn't.

If any of it mattered anyway.

"It will happen." Rico's lips moved against her ear in a way she was starting to crave. Like he was telling her a secret. Something he only wanted her to know. "I promise."

Then his heat was gone.

"I think the first thing we need to do is a basic inventory. Make sure everything's there." Elise came down the steps leading from their rooms. "Then we can start packing up what we're taking and get it into the moving units." She frowned at the sight of Rico at the coffee maker.

Rico turned toward Elise, cup right under his lips. "Good morning."

Elise straightened. "Morning." Her eyes slid toward Rico and Abe's rooms. "Where's your buddy?"

Rico's lips twitched. "He'll be back any minute."

Elise scoffed. "We don't have time for him to go—"

The front door to the house opened and Elise spun toward it, hands already hitting her hips.

But instead of laying into Abe for not being ready to go her mouth dropped open.

Abe stopped in the entry, reaching up to tug one earbud free as he lifted a brow. "What?"

Lennie struggled to keep her own jaw from going slack at the sight in front of her.

All the men at Alaskan Security were in good shape. They had to be. Their lives could depend on it.

But this.

This that she was witnessing right now.

It was just stupid.

"Something wrong?" Abe checked the watch strapped to his wrist as he waited for one of them to answer him.

It wasn't going to be her. She was too busy trying not to stare at what his grey shorts did nothing to hide. She blinked a few times, trying to work up the will to look away.

"It's okay to look, Loba." Rico's voice was barely audible in her ear. "There's no shame in it."

Looking was all she was actually doing. She could recognize an attractive man. Acknowledge he was well-assembled, but that was as far as it went. None of her parts ever really became involved in the process.

With one exception.

Elise seemed to suddenly pull from her stupor, and she came out of it ready to fight. "Where have you been?" She marched toward Abe, her eyes somehow managing to stay above his bare chest. "We are supposed to leave in ten minutes."

"That's not a problem." Abe went straight past her.

"How is that not a problem?" Elise followed behind him, chasing Abe as he went toward his room. "You are nowhere near ready."

Abe suddenly turned, causing Elise to run right into him. His blue eyes stayed on her as she jumped back, wiping the hands that landed in the center of his chest down the front of her pants. "You're all sweaty."

He smirked. "I just ran ten miles, Babe. It gets sweaty."

"Why would you do that to yourself?" Elise's nose scrunched up.

Abe leaned down. "Stamina."

Elise blinked a few times at him as he turned and strutted to his room. As he rounded the corner she took a few steps in his direction. "You better hurry, Abraham. We have shit to do."

Lennie almost laughed, managing to smother it out at the last possible second. "Did you just call him Abraham?"

Elise turned toward her. "That's his name." She went to where her purse was on the coffee table, snatching it off before stomping to the front door. "Tell *Abraham* I'm timing him." She opened the door and paused. "I'm going to make some calls while I wait." Then she went out the door, slamming it shut behind her.

"I thought she was excited to come here." Rico passed Lennie a strawberry breakfast bar.

"I'm not sure it's going the way she wanted it to." Lennie opened the wrapper and took a bite. "Any of it."

Rico shook his head a little. "It never does." He bit his own bar.

"That was nice of Abe to get us groceries." Lennie hadn't really looked through what all he got, but it appeared they were covered for the majority of the trip.

"Abe's a nice guy." Rico shot her a wink. "Not that you should get any ideas about him."

"I thought I shouldn't be ashamed of looking."

"Looking is one thing, Loba." Rico moved in close to her, crowding her until she backed into the counter. "But the only ideas I want in your head involve me."

"I don't have ideas."

He clicked his tongue at her. "We talked about this, Loba. No shame." Rico reached out to slide one finger along her jaw. "Not with me."

"It's not as easy as you make it sound." Rico might be used to vocalizing anything his brain could conjure up.

She was not.

"It's not as hard as you want it to be."

"I don't want it to be hard. That's just how it is." She wiggled her way out from the counter. "It's not okay for women to be like men and it fucks us up." She grabbed her cup off the counter, embarrassment and the shame he was so sure she shouldn't have making her cheeks hot.

If it was easy to be a sexy seductress she wouldn't have had to move to Alaska.

She would have still been with—

"I'm going out with Elise." Lennie grabbed her purse, hooking it over her shoulder while she held her breakfast with her teeth and her coffee in her free hand.

She needed some air.

Some space.

Elise was sitting on the steps outside, staring at the yard.

"I thought you had calls to make." Lennie dropped down beside her, taking out some frustration on the remainder of her breakfast.

"I just couldn't deal with them anymore." Elise eyed Lennie's coffee. "I should have grabbed another cup before I threw a fit."

"I'd offer to go get you a cup but I might have just done the same thing." Lennie held out her drink. "You can have some of mine."

Elise wrinkled her nose. "Not with that shit you put in it."

"I like it." Lennie took a drink. "Makes it taste like it's not coffee." She peeked into the cup to gauge how much she had left. "Thanks for telling Abe to get it for me."

"I told you already. I didn't tell Abe anything." Elise leaned back, resting her elbows on the step behind them. "He makes me ragey."

"Even now that you know what he looks like without his shirt on?"

Elise pursed her lips. "That's an unfortunate waste."

"Not into older guys?" Lennie popped in the last of her breakfast and washed it down with a drink of her sweetened coffee.

"Not into him." Elise sighed. "And I'm sure older guys wouldn't be into me."

"Not true." Lennie waved one hand Elise's direction. "You're exactly what every man wants." Elise was tall and slender. She was smart and funny and bitchy in a good way.

"I have a certain amount of baggage most men won't touch with a six-inch pole."

"A six-inch po—"

"Nine minutes and forty-six seconds." Abe walked out the door behind them.

"Congratulations." Elise peered up at him. "You managed to meet the minimum requirement."

Abe's eyes narrowed. "You're a hard woman to please, aren't you, Babe?"

"You'll never know." Elise stood up. "Babe." She spun on one heel and stalked toward the SUV they drove home from the airport, opening the driver's door and climbing in.

Abe marched right after her, opening the passenger's door and climbing in beside her. Elise's mouth dropped open as she stared across the console at him.

"Should be an interesting day." Rico stopped at Lennie's side, passing over a lidded cardboard cup.

"What's this?"

"Fresh coffee." He took her mostly empty cup and tossed the rest into the bushes before tucking the mug into a hidden spot on the porch. "There was a little left and I thought you might want it."

Lennie eyed him as she lifted the cup to her lips, uncertain what she was about to have in her mouth.

Hopefully it wasn't straight black coffee. She'd hate to have to spit it out at him.

Rico watched as she took a cautious drink. "How is it?"

She followed the first swallow with another. "It's perfect. Thank you." Lennie started to walk toward the SUV where Abe and Elise were in a heated-looking discussion. She paused and turned to Rico. "Did you tell Abe what I drink in my coffee?"

His lips barely lifted. "I pay attention to what matters to me, Loba." He reached one hand her way, resting it on the small of her back. "We should go before one of them kills the other." He eased her toward the SUV. The second Rico opened the door Elise's shouts carried out into the morning air.

"You just think you're so freaking hot."

"I am hot, Babe."

"Oh, shut up. A set of abs doesn't make you hot."

"Based on the way your jaw dropped when you saw them I'd say they do."

Lennie looked at Rico, widening her eyes.

He leaned into the SUV. "If you two don't quit I'll leave your asses here and we'll fly home."

Elise's head snapped Rico's way. "You better not."

Lennie dropped into the seat, holding her breath until Rico was in the seat beside her.

Elise pulled out onto the road, her lips pressing together more with each passing second.

The tension was palpable. High enough that the second they were parked outside of their old building Lennie jumped out of the SUV and made a beeline for the front door. Hopefully a day of work would calm everyone the heck down because she didn't want to deal with Elise and Abe if they were going to be at each other's throats for the whole trip.

Investigative Resources took up half the top floor of a large building just outside downtown Cincinnati. It was strange to be back. Walking through the same halls. Riding in the same elevator.

It was so familiar but still seemed so foreign.

Like it was part of a different life.

And in some ways it was.

No one said a word as the elevator made its climb, each floor passing with a flash of light on the numbers above the doors. They reached the top and Lennie was the first to step out. In her haste to get out of the uncomfortable space she didn't check to make sure the path was clear, and ended up running right into the person waiting to take the elevator down.

But it wasn't just any person.

"Lennie."

She took a step back, choosing one discomfort over another, but instead of bumping into Elise or Abe, she backed straight into a hard wall of chest. Rico didn't move as she stared down the man in front of her.

She knew this was a possibility.

Probability.

It was just so soon.

Lennie resisted the urge to offer a polite smile.

This man didn't deserve one.

Instead she lifted her chin, took a deep breath, and met his eyes.

"Kyle."

CHAPTER 12

RICO EYED THE man standing in front of Lennie.

The guy was decent enough looking, but there was something about him he didn't like.

And it had nothing to do with the fact that he and Lennie clearly had a past.

"What are you doing here? I thought you moved?" The man's eyes hadn't come Rico's way once.

Not so much as a glance.

They were only on Lennie.

"I did move." Lennie shifted from one foot to the other.

"But you're back now?" He sounded a little too interested in the possibility.

"No." Lennie stepped around the man still focused completely on her.

He turned to follow as she walked toward a glass door emblazoned with the logo for Investigative Resources. "What's going on?" Kyle's gaze finally came Rico's way, eyes sharpening. "Are you in some kind of trouble?"

Lennie stopped, her head slowly turning to the man chasing her. "Why would you ask me that?"

Kyle let out an awkward chuckle. "I mean, come on. You're not the kind of person to just up and disappear."

Lennie turned to face Kyle fully. "I didn't disappear, Kyle." Her eyes narrowed. "I moved."

"To Alaska." Kyle tucked his hands onto his hips, flapping out the sides of his suit jacket. "You're not the kind of person who just up and moves to Alaska."

"I am now." Lennie turned from him for a second time.

For a second time he chased her.

Abe leaned close, his eyes locked on where Lennie was once again facing Kyle down. "You think she's going to clock him?"

"We can only hope." Elise shouldered her way past Abe, glaring at him as she passed. "Thanks for just standing there instead of going to help her." The heels of her shoes clicked against the tile floor as she went straight for her friend, shoving one finger toward the other end of the building. "Go back to your cave, Kyle."

Kyle sized Elise up, his lips twisting into a smirk. "Hello, Elise."

She ignored him, grabbing Lennie as she went and leading her straight to the glass door. The second Elise had it unlocked they were inside, leaving Kyle standing alone in the hall.

He turned to Rico and Abe and looked each one of them up and down.

It was the act of a man who didn't realize how far he was in over his head.

Kyle shot his smirk their way as he went down the hall and disappeared through a door into a posh-looking office.

"I feel like one of us is going to end up kicking his ass."

Rico shook his head. "I feel like one of us is going to have to stop one of the girls from kicking his ass."

"Hell." Abe huffed out a breath. "I think I might just let it happen."

"I'm not interested in having to bail them out and fly them back for court dates." Rico walked toward the door to Investigative Resources, taking a long glance into the office where Kyle must work. "No matter how much he probably deserves it."

"Seemed like Lennie knew him." Abe opened the door to the office where most of Team Intel used to work.

"Seemed like." Rico stepped inside and scanned the space. It was bigger than he expected. A few offices lined one side of the space and the rest was filled with grey-walled cubicles.

"How do you feel about that?" Abe frequently toed the line between conversation and therapy session.

"Not interested in discussing it with you." Rico walked to the rows of cubicles, looking for any sign of Lennie's dark head. "Where did they go?"

He stood still for a second, listening.

Hushed voices came from the other end of the large office.

Abe's head barely tilted. "Sounds like someone's willing to talk about how Kyle makes them feel."

"Shut up." Rico walked in the direction of the soft conversation. The smell of brewing coffee hit right as he stepped into what was definitely a break room.

Lennie was going through the cabinets, pulling out everything inside and lining it down the counters as Elise stared at her, arms crossed.

"Let Abe kick his ass then. It's the least he can do."

"No one's kicking Kyle's ass." Lennie squinted at a container of coffee. "It's not worth the effort." She slid the unopened can to one end of the counter. "That can go in the donate box."

"It's worth the effort for me." Elise grabbed the coffee and set it on the small table in the center of the room. "If for no other reason than because of what he said to you."

"What did he say?"

Elise's eyes lifted to Rico and widened just a hair.

Lennie pulled a container of peanut butter from the cabinet and set it beside the coffee. "Nothing that matters." She went back to the cabinet, turning her back on him.

Elise straightened, turning to where Rico and Abe stood. "We need boxes. There should be a whole stack of them in the supply closet." She held out a key and pointed to a closed door at the opposite end of the office. "There's packing tape in there too."

Abe snagged the keys, glancing Rico's way before turning to head to the closet.

Rico held back, watching Lennie a second longer.

She might say that prick Kyle's words didn't matter, but right now it sure seemed like they did.

He pulled himself away, forcing his feet to the closet where Abe was sifting through the collapsed boxes, pulling out the shallow ones and opening them up. Rico found a roll of clear packing tape and went to work sticking them in place, adding a couple extra layers to be sure they could support the weight of the food Lennie and Elise were clearing out.

It took an hour to pack the break room up and carry it all down. Unopened items went into the back of the SUV to be delivered to a local food bank, and opened items went to the dumpster at the back of the building.

"What next?" Abe was rocking on his feet, ready to move on. It was his one downfall. The man never fucking stopped. Never relaxed.

"Next we need to shred any hard files left." Elise's eyes moved down the list. "Then we collect all the office supplies and pack them up to be shipped to Alaska."

"You guys used hard files?" Rico rested his arms on the top edge of one of the cubicles and peered into it. The desk was cluttered with papers and crumbs. A half-consumed cup of coffee sat at one corner and a stack of wadded-up tissues took over another.

"Sometimes." Lennie pushed up on her toes to peek into the space. She wrinkled her nose. "Who worked here?"

Elise glanced up. "Rob."

Lennie rounded the side of the workspace. "He didn't bother cleaning up his mess when he left." Her eyes snagged on the papers, narrowing a little as she pressed her finger to one and pulled it closer. "Do you know what he was working on before we closed?"

"I'm not sure. You'd have to ask Eva." Elise walked around to join Lennie in the cubicle. "What in the hell?" She picked up a half-printed sheet of paper. "This is a roster."

"The people who worked here?" Rico scanned the space as Abe stood straighter beside him.

Lennie shook her head. "Clients." She turned the paper his way, showing the faded ink. "It looks like he had an issue with the printer."

Rico took the paper. "Anyone important on here?"

Lennie took the paper back. "When we found out we were closing, Mona and Eva had us finish any projects we were working on. Anyone new was refunded their money and their contract was nullified." She twisted her lips to one side as she read through the names. "These sound familiar, but I'd have to get into the system to know for sure where they fell in the process. Maybe he was trying to start up a business of his own."

Abe turned in place. "There's still plenty of computers here. You want us to set you up a spot to work?"

"These computers won't help anymore." Lennie collected the papers into a stack and tapped them against the desk to straighten them. "Heidi cleared the whole system and moved it to a secure server before we left to come here." Her dark eyes drifted down to the paper in front of her. "Rob must have done this before that happened."

"And ran out of printer ink early in the process." Elise wrinkled her nose at the mess covering the desk. "Then made a fucking mess."

Lennie eyed the papers in her hand as she slowly backed out of the cubicle. "The supply closet was locked." Her gaze drifted to the heavy steel door they'd opened to get the boxes. "So he couldn't have gotten the printer ink."

"He could have gone and bought some." Elise followed behind Lennie as she went to the next cubicle over. "Then come back and printed off what he wanted."

Lennie pointed to the computer on the desk in the cubicle next to Rob's. Her eyes locked onto Elise's as she went to the next workspace in line. "There's a computer here too."

Elise turned and checked the cubicle at her back. "His desk is the only one missing a computer."

"So he took it." Lennie huffed out a breath. "Mona's going to be pissed as hell."

"Mona's probably not the only one." Abe glanced Rico's way.

Rico backed toward the hall leading from the room they were in, scanning each cubicle as he passed.

Abe casually wandered to the cubicle they'd been inspecting and picked up the coffee cup. He tipped his head in a barely-perceptible nod.

Rico slowly turned his head from side to side, listening for any sign of the man who could fuck this whole day up.

They weren't in Alaska anymore. The police here didn't know them. That meant this had to be handled differently.

Lucky for Rob.

Abe eased a little closer to where the women were still chatting, discussing their thoughts on Rob and what he might be up to.

As Rico reached the first door, Lennie's eyes lifted to his, holding a second before snapping to where Abe was creeping in.

She suddenly straightened, her big brown eyes darting around the space.

Rico shook his head as her panicked gaze came back to his. Her lips immediately flattened into a thin line as the color drained from her face.

She didn't need to be scared. He would do whatever it took to make sure she was safe. Even if it meant his life got a little stickier until Pierce could straighten things out.

The first room was a windowless space. The darkness inside was smothering, making it impossible to see anything that might be lurking there. Rico slowly moved to the doorway. Chances were good this guy didn't come here expecting to be caught, which meant the threat was relatively low. He was probably hiding, hoping to wait them out so he could escape undetected.

Unfortunately, Rob decided to fuck with something that was important to women he cared about.

Rico slowly reached out to flip on the light.

The second the bulb flashed to life his body lurched back, slamming into the wall of the hallway as a surprisingly large man knocked him out of the way.

Rob managed to clear the door, but he didn't make it much farther. Rico had him in two strides, pinning Rob's arms at his sides as he took him to the ground, their bodies hitting hard as they landed on the industrial carpet.

Rob grunted as he struggled to get free. "Get off me."

"Not gonna happen." Rico pressed one hand to Rob's back as he straddled his torso, keeping him pinned in place as he pulled a zip tie from one pocket of his tactical pants. He managed to pin one hand behind Rob's back before the man figured out the full scope of the position he was in.

"You can't fucking cuff me. I work here." Rob was decently strong, but his lack of skill proved his downfall. It took less than five seconds for him to land his other hand in a spot that made it easy to snatch.

"No one works here, *hombre*." Rico held tight to Rob's wrists, waiting as the other man fought against his hold. "You're making this harder than it has to be."

"I'm calling the cops." Rob started kicking his feet like he'd be able to do some sort of damage.

"I already did." Elise shoved past Abe and came straight to where Rico was still wrestling Rob, her phone pressed to her ear. "You can't just break into buildings and steal shit that's not yours, Rob."

Rob craned his neck to glare up at Elise. "Fuck you, Elise. You're such a bitch. That's why no one wants to fuck you."

"That's it." Rico hefted Rob's torso off the ground before slamming it back down, knocking the wind out of him. "Shut your mouth before you piss me off."

Rob wheezed a second before smirking up at Elise. "Looks like you found someone to fuck you after all."

"I don't have to sleep with a woman to make sure she gets the respect she deserves." Rico slammed him a second time just for fun. "Stop moving."

This time the hit stunned Rob long enough that Rico managed to get the zip tie around his wrists. He pulled it tight before climbing off his back and leaving him to roll around on the floor. He glanced at Elise who was suddenly quiet. "How long till the cops are here?"

She blinked a few times. "Uh." She took a step back as Rob wormed across the carpet. "They said they were on their way."

Rico looked to Lennie. "Call Pierce. Let him know what's going on in case we need him." He pointed toward the door. "Go out in the hall and wait for the cops."

He didn't want Rob spewing anything else that might upset one of them.

He also didn't want any witnesses in case Rob decided to be a pain in the ass.

Lennie grabbed Elise, who was still staring at Rob, and pulled her toward the door, leaving him and Abe alone with Rob.

Abe crouched down near Rob's head. They had a limited amount of time to get any information they could out of this guy before the cops took him. "Anthony's dead you know."

Rico waited, holding his breath as he watched Rob's reaction to the name of the man who tried to take Alaskan Security down.

Rob grunted as he continued to struggle, finally managing to roll to his side. He squinted at Abe. "Who the fuck is Anthony?"

Abe studied Rob for a second before his eyes lifted to Rico.

Rob's confusion was genuine. He didn't know who Anthony was.

Which meant he was here for completely different reasons.

Abe stood up. "Guess you're not as popular as I thought you were."

"Fuck you." Rob glared at them as he puffed out labored breaths.

Rico rested one arm across the top of a cubicle. "You get all those names you came for?"

Rob's mouth clamped shut.

Abe walked back to the room where Rob had hidden. He came out with a laptop in his hand. "Looks like we got here just in time." He grinned.

"Rob-o almost got what he thought he needed." He tucked the computer under one arm. "Bet you were pissed when you came back and realized the whole system was wiped."

Rob stayed silent.

Abe shrugged. "Be that way then." He opened the laptop and switched it on.

Suddenly one of Rob's legs shot out, catching Abe in the ankle hard enough to make him look down. He lifted a brow. "That was un-fucking-called for."

"You've got me hog-tied." Spittle flew out of Rob's mouth. "Like an animal."

"First of all," Abe didn't look away from the computer screen, "you're not hog-tied, but you will be if you don't start acting right." He tapped a few keys. "Second, you insulted a woman. That makes you worse than an animal."

"You'd insult her too if you knew her." Rob balanced on his side. "She's a fucking bitch."

Rico's kick to Rob's gut was swift and strong.

Abe closed the laptop and turned away, moving out of Rob's view before sliding it onto a chair and shoving it under a desk. He snagged a second computer from the next cubicle over, grabbing it just as the police came rushing into the office.

It was a drill he and Abe were familiar with. They each immediately held their hands out at their sides. Nothing made cops jumpier than coming into a place with semi-armed men who clearly knew how to handle themselves.

They caught a few cautious stares as the police went to work collecting Rob. As soon as Rob was secured they hefted him up and hauled him out.

Lennie and Elise edged their way into the space, watching as Rob passed with an officer on each arm.

Rico stood with Abe while another officer asked them questions. His gaze kept trailing to where Lennie stood.

She looked okay. Maybe a little shaken up.

Rico turned to the officer. "I'll be right back. I need to check on something." He didn't wait for permission.

Lennie's eyes stayed on him as he came her way. The second he reached her his hand went to her face. "Are you okay, Loba?"

Her lips twisted around a little and she barely leaned into his touch, eyes dipping. "I thought he was going to hurt you."

CHAPTER 13

SHE WANTED EXCITEMENT.

Adventure.

But this…

"I'm fine." Rico stepped closer, the hand on her face sliding to rest on the back of her neck as he pulled her closer. "If someone like that can hurt me then I'm in the wrong profession."

She snorted out a horrible-sounding laugh against his chest. "I guess that's true."

"Things like this happen, Loba. We handled it, and now it's over."

The cop interviewing her and Elise continued on in the background. "Where did you say the computer he was trying to take is?"

Elise glanced around. "Um—"

Rico turned to where Abe stood. "It's on the desk over there."

Lennie tipped her head to look up at him. "You found it?"

"It was in the room where he was hiding." Rico's hold on her eased. "We must have caught him when he came back to refill the ink and realized everything was wiped."

Lennie rested one hand on her head, trying to ground the spinning. "I can't believe he was here the whole time."

The rest of the morning passed in a blur of questions and statements. Pierce called every fifteen minutes to make sure everything was okay until finally Lennie had to tell him they would call him if there was a problem.

Luckily there wasn't. The police seemed a little odd when they spoke with Abe and Rico, but other than that things seemed normal.

As normal as a breaking and entering could be.

By the time the cops were gone it was after one, and somehow Lennie's stomach was growling.

"Let's go get some lunch and come back to regroup." Elise smoothed down the fabric of her skirt. "Maybe have a drink while we're out."

"I'll buy." Abe walked to Elise's side. "Don't let what that prick said bother you. He was just pissed we ruined his morning."

Elise gave him a tight smile. "Thanks."

Abe opened the door and held one arm out, motioning for Elise to go first. Lennie followed behind her. Almost immediately Kyle came through the door of the office where he worked and sprinted their way.

"What in the heck just happened?"

"Misunderstanding." Rico stepped in at her back, standing tall and broad as he faced Kyle down. "That's all."

Kyle kept his eyes on Lennie. "Was that Rob I saw them taking out in cuffs?"

Rico's hand came to rest on the small of her back. Somewhere Kyle couldn't see, but she felt like it was the only thing in the universe.

Lennie managed to put on a small smile. "It was just a misunderstanding."

Elise reached out to take her hand. "Come on. I'm hungry." She pulled Lennie away and toward the elevator.

Lennie pushed in close to Elise's side. "Thank you."

"No problem." Elise pushed the button to call the elevator. "I don't know why he thinks you'd have shit to say to him."

"I was cordial to him after we broke up." She'd wanted to keep the peace since she had to see his face in the halls almost every day.

"Well you should stop." Elise stepped into the elevator the second the doors opened. "He doesn't deserve for you to be anything but a bitch to him."

She wasn't wrong.

"I wasn't nice to him back there." Lennie didn't tell Kyle what he so clearly wanted to know.

"You didn't kick him in the balls though, which is what he deserves."

Lennie stood at Elise's side, trying not to squirm under Rico's gaze. She could feel it resting on her as Elise went on about Kyle.

"I'll kick him in the balls next time." Elise lifted one foot, hooking the narrow heel of her pump forward. "And I'll dig in there."

"It's not worth messing up your pretty shoes." Lennie tried to diffuse her friend's anger. It's probably a good thing she and Elise weren't closer when she and Kyle actually broke up.

Elise might have actually followed through on her threats.

"If Kyle needs a perspective adjustment Rico and I will be the ones to handle it." Abe pressed the button for the ground floor. "This isn't like Alaska where you can go around doing what you want without getting in trouble."

Elise's eyes widened. "We can do that in Alaska?"

Abe stopped short.

Elise rolled her eyes. "I'm kidding."

Lennie started laughing. She'd been stressed out all morning, worried about Rico and Abe and what in the hell was going on with Rob. Speaking of. "Did they figure out what Rob was up to?"

Rico looked toward Abe. "Seems like he was just trying to steal contacts from Investigative Resources."

Abe tipped his head in a nod. "Seems like."

The elevator stopped and the doors opened. Elise strode out. "I'm picking where we eat."

Abe scoffed.

Lennie paused at his side as she walked out of the elevator. "You should probably let her pick. She knows all the little places around here that serve the best food."

Elise unlocked the SUV and climbed into the driver's seat. She immediately turned on the air, kicking it up as high as it would go. "Does it seem hot as hell?"

"You're getting used to Alaska." Abe snagged the front passenger's seat.

"I'll never get used to Alaska." Elise closed her door as Lennie reached for the handle to open her own door.

"How you holding up, Loba?" Rico's hand rested on her back as he beat her to the handle with the other. "You doing okay?"

"I don't like that he was there and we didn't know it." She rubbed a hand down her arm as the hairs there lifted. "It bothers me."

"It won't happen again." Rico leaned close as he opened the door. "I promise."

He literally couldn't promise that, but somehow it made her feel a little better.

Rico closed her door as soon as she was seated and jogged to the other door before climbing in next to her.

"I hope you boys like noodles." Elise pulled out of the lot and headed into downtown, navigating the roads easily during the busy lunchtime traffic. She parallel parked along the road in front of a tiny ramen shop near the museum center.

Elise got out as Abe went to pay for their parking. She watched as he reached the kiosk.

Lennie gently worked her elbow into Elise's ribs. "You hate him a little less than you did this morning?"

Elise's eyes snapped away from Abe as he started back their way. "Paying for parking doesn't make him less of an asshole."

"No, but sticking up for you when Rob called you a bitch does."

It sucked that women were so easily boxed in. Act too organized and on task and you were cut-throat.

Don't take shit? You're a bitch.

Like having sex? Someone's gonna call you a slut.

Elise spent her time at Investigative Resources running the office and she did a hell of a job.

But she didn't take any shit, and if someone was being a problem she called them out on it.

Which led to many of the men on staff calling her a bitch behind her back. All because they didn't like being told to clean up their own messes and reload the printer paper.

It was freaking stupid.

"Hurry up. I'm hungry." Elise scowled at Abe as he slowly ambled down the sidewalk.

"Patience, Babe."

Elise huffed out a loud breath as she turned to the door and yanked it open, walking straight to the hostess station.

Rico snagged Lennie, pulling her to one side as Abe seemed to come out of nowhere, his tall body dominating the space as he stepped in at Elise's side and stole every bit of attention the poor hostess had. He held up four fingers. "Four."

The hostess practically passed out. Her cheeks flushed as she tried to collect the stack of menus and fumbled with the napkin-wrapped flatware, smiling at Abe the whole time. "Right this way." She nearly tripped, trying to keep her eyes on Abe as she walked. "How has your day been?"

"Eventful." Abe's gravelly voice snagged the attention of a few women sitting at the counter as they passed. Each one looked him up and down before they leaned together and spoke in hushed whispers.

Lennie rolled her eyes Rico's way.

His voice was low in her ear as he leaned close. "It's the grey hair." He rested one hand on her back as the women's eyes landed on him. He tipped his head at them as they passed, his hand slowly creeping around to curve against her hip.

When they got to the table Abe was still on his feet as Elise slid into the booth side of the four-top. Rico's hand moved to Lennie's back, easing her toward the other booth seat. Once she was sitting, he and Abe sat in the chairs across from them.

Elise leaned across the table. "I thought men like you didn't leave their backs to the door."

Abe leaned toward her. "You ever tried to fight your way out of a booth and around a bunch of chairs?" One corner of his mouth lifted. "It's not as easy as it sounds."

Elise's eyes dropped to the menu in her hands. "It doesn't sound very easy."

Abe studied her for a second longer before scanning his own menu for a half second. He set it down on the table in front of him.

Elise's eyes jumped to the menu then to him. "You already decided what you wanted to eat?"

"I'm gonna let you decide."

Her brows shot up. "You want me to decide what you eat?"

"Why not?" Abe slid his menu across the table. "You eat here. Might as well let you pick."

Elise stared at him. "But—"

"Listen, Babe." Abe folded his hands on the table and leaned in. "Some things I care about and some things I don't. Food is one of the things I don't care about."

Elise wrinkled her nose. "Are you one of those 'food is fuel' monsters?"

Abe started laughing, his deep voice carrying around the small space and drawing the eyes of every woman inside it his way once again. "I wouldn't say I'm a monster."

One side of Elise's nose lifted. "You and Shawn." She shook her head. "Missing out on so much joy because you won't admit food is amazing."

The waitress came to the side of the table with a wide smile. "You guys ready to order?"

Lennie ordered a bowl of her favorite shoyu ramen. Rico ordered a bowl of miso ramen, which was actually her second favorite option.

Elise lifted her brows at Abe, giving him one more chance to determine his own fate.

He held his hands out, palms up, passing it off to her.

Elise pursed her lips for a second. "Can we have the spicy ramen and the loco moco?" She passed the stack of menus off and leaned back in her chair, eyeing Abe across the table. "Are you going to ask which one is for you?"

He shook his head. "Nope."

Elise lifted her shoulders. "Fine. Then I'll just pick the one that looks the best when it gets here."

Abe's lips twitched a little as he watched her across the table. "That seems fair."

Lennie shifted in her seat. She'd hoped lunch would take her mind off the events of the morning, but they still lingered. "What's going to happen to Rob?"

"Right now?" Rico sipped at his water. "They'll probably charge him with breaking and entering. Possibly theft, but he didn't make it off the premises with anything, so he can fight that pretty easily."

"Will they keep him in jail?" She played with the wrapper of her straw as she thought of all the reasons Rob might have come back to the office.

What he might be up to.

"No." Rico reached across to slide his fingers over hers. "He'll probably be out by the end of the day."

Lennie sighed. "I guess that's fair. He didn't actually take anything"

"He tried to take confidential information." Elise unrolled her napkin and spread it across her lap. "I'm not sure I'd call him getting out in a few hours fair."

"They can't hold him for being an asshole, Babe." Abe glanced up as their waitress came back to check drinks. No one spoke until she was gone again.

"What do you think he was going to do with those names he was trying to get?" It was what bothered Lennie more than anything. "Do you think he's connected with—"

She hadn't realized going to Alaska was going to be walking into a full-on shit storm, and the chance that it might not really be over sat like lead in her belly.

"No." Rico sounded sure. "I'm almost positive he's not connected in any way to the people who tried to take the company down."

She let out a breath. "That's good."

"Is it?" Elise drank a few gulps of her soda. "Because if he's not, then there's some other reason he was trying to steal information."

Rico shifted in his seat.

It was subtle.

Barely noticeable.

A move Lennie might not have noticed a few days ago.

But today she couldn't miss it. Rico was always so calm. Intense and focused, but always relaxed.

This little move was different.

Before she could think any more about it, their waitress was back, balancing a tray of bowls on one hand. She set Lennie's and Rico's down first, then delivered the two dishes Elise ordered before leaving them to eat.

"Take your pick, Babe." Abe scooted both bowls Elise's way. "Unless you want to taste them both before you decide."

Elise pressed her lips together as her eyes dropped to the food.

"Do it." Abe tipped his head toward the lunches. "See which one you like better."

"That doesn't seem fair." Elise's fingers wiggled on her chopsticks.

"Wouldn't be fair for the one who loves food to end up with something she didn't like." Abe bumped both bowls again. "Hurry up before they get cold."

"Well, this one's spicy so..." Elise caught a mouthful of noodles with her chopsticks and managed to eat them without sending any of the broth flying. She eyed the loco moco as she chewed.

Abe lifted his brows. "Get on with it. I don't want to be here all day."

Elise worked her chopsticks into the fried egg and beef patty sitting on a bed of rice. She swiped her bite through the gravy and shoved it in her mouth. Her eyes narrowed as she chewed. After a few seconds she hooked her finger at the edge of the spicy noodle bowl and pulled it closer.

Abe grinned. "I was hoping you'd pick that one." He snagged the bowl of loco moco and dug into it.

As they ate Elise laid out the plans for the afternoon which were actually the plans for the morning that went sideways. By the time they were finished Lennie was ready to go back and get it over with. The faster they got the office cleared out the sooner she wouldn't have to worry about running into Kyle every five minutes and the sooner they could go home.

When they got back to the building Rico and Abe went in first, clearing the office before they would let Lennie and Elise inside. The moving units were being delivered tomorrow morning and picked up tomorrow afternoon, so they had to be ready to pack them. That meant the rest of the day was spent doing a quick inventory and organizing what was going to be shipped, which was most of the office furniture and supplies, along with the electronics like computers and printers.

Mona and Eva's offices were to be packed up and sent in a separate shipping unit that was being delivered the day after next, so that meant they could be handled later.

By the time they had everything moderately organized Lennie was exhausted and ready for a shower. She'd managed to avoid the halls, and therefore Kyle, which was nice, and it was late enough by the time they left that Kyle was long gone for the day.

Elise drove back to the rental. Lennie rode in the front seat while Abe and Rico sat in the back chatting about Rogue's plans for the future.

"The other teams have clear objectives." Abe shook his head where he sat behind Elise. "We don't. Not anymore."

"I'm not interested in joining Alpha or Beta." Rico's voice sent a prickle of awareness across her skin. She couldn't see him, but she could picture the expression on his face. The way his dark brows would pull together. The seriousness in his eyes.

"You okay?" Elise reached out to turn up the blower on the air. "You look all flushed."

"Just a little warm." Lennie plastered on a smile as she directed one of the vents right at her heated cheeks.

She was never like this. She liked men well enough. Dated a few.

Her lust level just wasn't usually very high.

Might even have been called low a few times.

But recently she'd been running into the opposite problem.

Elise parked the SUV and they all got out. Abe tipped his head to the car Elise rented. "You gonna keep that?"

"Yup." Elise went straight to the front door. "Lennie and I might want to go out one night, and I don't have any interest in chauffeurs."

Lennie resisted the urge to look back to see where Rico was. The last thing she needed was to look at him and make the reasoning for her pink cheeks obvious.

She followed Elise into the house and went straight to where her bedroom was. "I'm going to take a shower."

"You want me to order us some dinner?" Elise was already on her phone.

"No thanks. I'm not really hungry." Lennie went up the few steps and escaped into her room, closing the door and taking a deep breath. She needed to get her libido under control.

Otherwise she was going to catch on fire.

CHAPTER 14

"SEND IT TO Vincent." Pierce's tone was sharp through the speaker of Abe's cell phone. "We simply don't have the resources available to deal with this issue as quickly as he can."

Abe was packing the computer they'd lifted from Rob into a box. "You're sure you want Vincent to be a part of this?"

"I'm sure I want this handled now and I want it handled quietly, so yes. I'm positive I want Vincent to be a part of this."

Abe's eyes lifted to Rico's and held.

Pierce could make all the claims he wanted, but his reasoning for sending this computer to Vincent had to do with only one thing.

One person.

"Does anyone else know you have the computer?"

Abe pushed newspaper in around the laptop, wedging it in place. "Are you asking if Lennie and Elise know we have it?"

"I'm asking if anyone knows." Pierce dodged the question. "The police. The man attempting to take it. Anyone."

"As far as I know no one else knows we have it." Abe pushed the flaps of the box into place, holding it as Rico lined a length of packing tape across the seam and pressed it down.

"I would prefer to keep it that way."

Of course he would.

"This was her business, Pierce. She deserves to know what's going on."

"She deserves to have peace, and I will do anything in my power to give that to her." His voice carried an unyielding edge.

"What if he finds something? Then what?" Abe picked up his phone and started to pace with it, walking up the side of his bed and back down again.

"If he finds something we will deal with that when it happens."

Rico pulled up the address Pierce sent to his own phone and went to work addressing the label for the package.

"It's on you then." Abe was not happy with how Pierce wanted to handle this situation. Abe wanted their in-house team to deal with the computer and anything that might be on it. Unfortunately, what might be on it would affect at least two members of their in-house team directly. One of them being Pierce's wife.

"Pierce is right." Rico pulled the label from its backing and stuck it to the box. "If there's anything problematic on that computer it will be a huge conflict of interest to have Heidi working on it. It's better to let Vincent's team deal with it."

Abe held his hands out at his sides but didn't say a word.

Heidi was more skilled than anyone Vincent had. No one would deny that. Including Vincent.

But her past employment at Investigative Resources meant she was too connected. If Rob was doing something shady and Mona and Eva wanted to press charges then anything Heidi found would be called into question.

No one would question Vincent.

"Fine." Abe huffed out the air from his lungs. "I'll ship it first thing in the morning."

"Good. I will be in touch."

Abe disconnected the call and tossed his phone onto the bed. "Heidi would find anything he put on that damn computer and she'd do it in half the time Vincent's people will."

"You're not wrong." Rico slid the box Abe's way. "But no one will question Vincent's motives if his team finds something."

Abe lifted a brow.

"Maybe there's something illegal on there." Rico lifted his shoulders. "I'm just saying I think Pierce is doing the right thing."

"You think Pierce is doing the right thing because you want to protect Lennie the same way he wants to protect Mona."

"I think he's doing the right thing because I'm willing to look at Vincent as a tool we use instead of hating his guts for being an asshole."

"He goes around doing whatever the fuck he wants. He doesn't give a shit about anyone but himself and his own agenda." Abe grabbed the box holding the laptop and shoved it into his bag. "And that's exactly what he's going to do with this."

"Without him our jobs are gone." It was the honest truth. Without the liberties their relationship with Vincent and GHOST afforded them, Shadow and Rogue would be limited to the point they would be useless. Relegated to the same boring bodyguard shit Alpha and Beta were assigned to.

"You think Vincent is the only man running a team like GHOST?" Abe shook his head. "I can promise you there's ten more of him doing the same damn thing. Hunting down and cleaning up messes the government pretends not to know about."

"And I can guarantee you each of the men running them is exactly like Vincent is." It took a special kind of man to live that life. Hiding what you are from everyone around you.

No family.

No friends.

No home.

Rico rubbed one hand across a sudden ache in his chest. "I'm going to bed."

"Sure." Abe turned toward the bathroom attached to his room, walking inside and shutting the door. A second later the shower switched on.

Rico went to his own room and took a quick shower before pulling on a t-shirt and a pair of shorts.

The call with Pierce was unavoidable. It had to be done, but it was the last thing he'd wanted to do, and as the minutes dragged out he became more and more restless.

Rico opened his door, listening for any sign that Elise was still up and moving around, but the house was silent and dark. A thin line of dim light marked the bottom of Elise's door as he crept toward their side of the house.

The closer he got, the more a single question burned through him.

It was a question he had no right to ask.

A question he shouldn't care about the answer to.

But it was all he could think about.

There was no sound coming from the other side of Lennie's door when he softly tapped against it.

Nothing.

He tapped again, keeping the sound quiet enough Elise wouldn't hear.

Still nothing.

Rico turned the knob and slowly let the door swing open.

His eyes immediately met hers and the question he shouldn't ask was between them before he realized it.

"Who's Kyle?"

Lennie stood just inside the small bathroom off her bedroom, her hair dripping wet and a towel wrapped around her body. "You keep showing up right after I get out of the shower."

That didn't answer his question. "Because you don't invite me to watch."

Color crept across her cheeks and down her neck. "I didn't know that was something you were interested in."

"You don't think I'd want to watch you?" He took a step toward her. "Naked." Another step. "Wet." One more step. "Slippery and soaked."

The pink on her skin intensified and she visibly swallowed. "No." It was barely a whisper. "Not really."

He was used to women who owned their sexuality. Flaunted it proudly.

He sought them out. They were looking for the same thing he was.

An interaction with limits.

Lennie had no limits, and it should scare the shit out of him.

But he was too busy being bothered by the rest of the situation.

"Why don't you know that, Loba?"

She blinked. "Why?"

"*Si*. Why."

Her eyes went to one side. "I don't know. It's just how it is."

"Is it not clear I desire you, Lenore?" He couldn't help but move closer to her. "You slept next to me." Rico reached to trace down the side of her arm. "How can you still pretend not to know I want you?"

Her attention went to where he touched her. "You kept giving me mixed signals." Her gaze followed as his fingers ran over her shoulder, eyes dropping as his touch slid up her neck to her chin, lifting her face toward his.

"No more of that."

He'd never been jealous in his life. Not a single day.

Not until this one.

Rico tipped Lennie's chin up until their eyes finally met. Then he repeated the question that had been burning through his mind all day.

"Who is Kyle?"

Her lips pressed together and for a second he thought she might not tell him. Might choose to leave him suffering with an emotion that was unfamiliar and unwanted.

"We dated."

"I know that much, Loba." Rico moved closer, the talk of the man she used to know making the urge to prove who she belonged to impossible to control.

Only Lennie belonged to no one.

And that almost bothered him more.

"I want to know who is he to you." He needed to know why this man mattered. Why she reacted to him the way she did.

Lennie barely lifted one shoulder. "He's no one to me. Not anymore."

"Is that the truth?"

She scoffed, the sound surprising him. "Do you think I'm lying to you?"

"No." Rico shook his head. "But I think you might be lying to yourself."

Lennie held his gaze. "He doesn't deserve to be anything to me."

"I agree." He understood the situation more than she realized. "But that doesn't mean he isn't."

The truth was a difficult thing to face. He'd been running from it himself for years.

Too long.

Long enough he was tired. Worn down from trying to escape the inescapable.

"I was married, Loba."

Lennie's dark eyes widened but she didn't say anything.

It made him press onward, spill more of his past at her feet.

"We were very young." No one knew the full truth of the life he had before Alaskan Security.

The man he used to be.

Maybe could be again.

"I loved her with everything I had." Rico submitted to the need to be closer, easing in until Lennie's body rested against his.

That was the most difficult part of the way he chose to live.

The lack of contact. Any he had was short and sharp. There and gone, like a flash in a pan.

"She was supposed to be my only." He tucked his chin until his forehead rested against her damp hair. "And then she left."

"Wait." Lennie's hands lifted from where they'd been at her sides, tucking between them, one fingertip resting between his ribs. "She left you?"

"*Si.*"

"Why?" The incredulity in her voice made him smile.

"Because she wanted to experience the world."

So he'd done the same thing.

Lennie's lips twisted into an odd little smirk.

"What makes you smile, Loba?"

"I'm just thinking about how disappointed she probably is right now."

Rico lifted his head in an unfiltered laugh, one he didn't know was coming until it was there.

One she brought him.

"You might be surprised." Rico ran his hands down the soft skin of her arms. "The man you know is not the same man she knew."

He'd changed so much after Paola.

Because of her. In good ways and in bad.

"I bet you were still better than most of them."

Rico's hands stopped where they curved against her biceps. "Am I better than Kyle?"

Lennie laughed, her head falling back. She reached up to wipe under the corner of one eye. "You're definitely better than Kyle."

"How?"

She sobered, eyes coming to his as she went quiet.

He was sure she would hold back again. Keep the truth she didn't want to face.

"You don't make me feel bad about myself."

It took great restraint to keep his hands relaxed. To keep his expression neutral.

Rico took a slow breath. The kind that got him through the most dangerous situations he'd been in.

Through bad flights and terrible landings.

Through missions that almost went wrong.

Through the kidnapping of his friends. The constant worry he wouldn't be able to keep them all safe.

Lennie's eyes moved over his face. "You look like you're going to kill someone."

"Are you sure?" His face felt fine. Relaxed and calm.

Her head lifted and lowered in a slow nod. "Positive." She lifted one finger and pointed it toward him. "It's in your eyes."

"My eyes?"

"Yes." She rubbed her lips together. "Your eyes always give you away."

No one read him. No one thought he was anything but calm. Relaxed.

No one saw through what he showed them.

Or maybe no one really looked.

"What do my eyes tell you now, Loba?"

Lennie's gaze immediately dropped his. "Nothing."

"Look, Loba. See it. Own it."

She stared at his chest for a heartbeat.

Two.

Three.

Slowly her eyes lifted, finding his.

He didn't hide the need he felt. A need that was more foreign than it should be.

He thought he'd been happy. He thought he'd been content.

Now all that seemed wrong.

Lennie's skin flushed as she stared up at him, lips barely parting.

"You see it, don't you?"

"I—" She tried to look away.

"No." Rico caught her face in his hands. "See it, Loba. See what you really are." He pressed into her, his desire for her obvious and undeniable. "You make me fucking crazy. You are all I can think about. All I can want."

Lennie was always shy. Hesitant. And this moment was no different.

She was still shy. Still hesitant.

But she took a chance anyway. Proving she was what he'd always known.

Dangerous. A woman he should have run from.

Her head tipped his way, pausing before coming closer, her lips lifting to his, slaying him with a tenderness he hadn't experienced in so long.

Too long.

Reminding him there was a time and place for everything.

The sweet and calm.

The needy and rough.

He loved it all. Wanted it all.

From her.

He reached between them and gripped the front of the towel keeping her from him, tugging it free in a quick move.

Lennie's lips pulled from his as a gasp raced free.

His eyes dipped, unwilling to ignore the sight in front of him. "*Estás más sexy que el carajo.*"

Her lips pressed together. "I have a confession to make." Lennie held perfectly still as he continued taking in every dip and curve of her body. "I only took Spanish in high school." Her fingers curled into loose fists at her sides. "So there was only one word of that I understood."

"What word was that, Lenore?" He knew what word she understood, and he wanted to hear it come out of her mouth.

"*Carajo.*"

Rico lifted his eyes from where they'd stalled at the softness of her belly. "In English, Loba." He moved close to her again, bringing one hand to the silky skin of her stomach, imagining how it would feel to rub his dick against the satiny softness until he came. "Say the word." He flattened his hand and pushed it downward, easing between her thighs to cup tightly against her pussy. "Say it."

Her lids dropped as his hand pressed against her.

The line of her teeth pressed against her lower lip, teasing him, sending him to an unseen edge as he waited, eyes locked onto her mouth.

"Fuck."

He'd heard the word said by women more times than he cared to admit. At the time he thought it was sexy.

But those women had nothing on this woman.

"You will kill me, Loba." He wrapped one arm around her waist, holding her against him as he turned to the bed, pulling his hand from between her legs to grab the stack of pillows from the headboard. "But I will take you down with me." He pushed her butt to the bed, dropping the pillows right behind her back. "And I will make you watch me do it."

Lennie's eyes went wide as he hooked his hands behind her knees and lifted her feet off the floor, forcing her body to rock back against the pillows that would keep her how he wanted her.

Sitting in a front row seat.

Rico went to his knees, shoving her thighs wide as he hit the ground.

"What are you do—"

His mouth was on her before the question was fully out of her mouth, cutting it short.

Rico lifted his eyes.

Lennie's gaze immediately darted away.

"No shame, Loba." He couldn't make himself move away from her so the words pressed into her flesh. "Watch what I do to you."

She was slick and sweet. Hot and tempting in a way he would never have been able to resist.

No matter how hard he tried.

Her thighs were full and soft, easy to sink his fingers into. Easy to imagine wrapping around his hips while he—

"Stop." Lennie's hand shoved between her body and his mouth as she scooted away from him and toward the center of the bed, grabbing blankets as she went.

"Loba?" He was a little stunned.

Women didn't normally reject what he was offering.

"We can just," she waved one hand around, "have sex. You don't have to do all that."

"All that?" She'd thrown him off in a way that left him speechless.

"It's fine. I don't really need all that extra stuff." Lennie laid flat on her back, assuming a position he hadn't used in years.

"Are you saying you just want me to fuck you and get it over with?"

She blinked at him. "Well isn't that what you want?"

"I need to make one thing clear to you." Rico grabbed the covers she'd used to hide herself from him, yanking them away and launching them toward the foot of the bed. "There is no limit to what I want from you." He crawled onto the mattress, working his way over her naked body. "Fucking is dessert, Lenore." He shook his head at her. "Not dinner." He leaned close enough their noses almost touched. "And I'm hungry."

CHAPTER 15

SHE WANTED A man who was into her.

A man who desired her.

It sounded good in theory.

But now that she was staring it down, that theory was turning out to be a little terrifying.

A little more than she bargained for.

"You're looking at me like I'm crazy, Loba."

She was lying naked on a bed under a fully-clothed Colombian who basically just said he wanted to eat her for dinner. She couldn't be held responsible for what her face did right now.

Lennie took a breath and dug deep, scrounging up the balls to say what she was thinking.

"I thought you were just doing that because..." Her nerve ran dry.

Rico's eyes narrowed on her. "Because why, Loba?"

"Because that's what you have to do the first time." Men always put their best foot forward at the beginning, trying to look like they were better than they were.

They were usually even bad then, which was fine. Sex wasn't really a big deal, and once a guy stopped pretending like they were actually good at it, things were much faster and easier.

Wham, bam, not even usually a thank you ma'am to slow it down.

One of Rico's dark brows slowly climbed his forehead. "The first time?"

Lennie nodded.

"Do you like when a man licks your pussy, Lenore?"

Her skin went hot and an answer automatically ran through her lips. "No."

"Don't forget I just tasted you." He leaned closer. "Don't think I can't tell when a woman likes what I do to them, Loba."

She wasn't really lying. She didn't like when most men did that.

And maybe that was the problem.

Rico wasn't turning out to be most men.

He also wasn't turning out to be the fast and fun excitement she'd been seeking.

This man was turning out to be something else altogether. Something that made her insides twist in every way possible. Made her feel more things than she knew existed.

But right this minute it was the panic that was winning out.

Rico's dark eyes moved over her face in a slow sweep.

His weight suddenly shifted.

He was leaving.

It made sense. He was finally seeing the real her. The one that made other men call her what they had.

What made them move on every time.

The wring in her belly pulled tighter, bringing on a level of discomfort she wasn't expecting.

Because, in all honesty, she hadn't been that upset when Kyle dumped her.

She hadn't been that upset when anyone dumped her.

What bothered her was why they did it. The faults they found in her and used to explain their exit from her life.

Because most of those reasons were possibly true.

She wasn't particularly interested in sex. Usually.

She wasn't particularly open to different things when sex was involved. Usually.

And she wasn't particularly affectionate. She didn't desire to be held or doted on.

Usually.

Unfortunately she was not feeling like her usual self lately, and it was uncomfortable.

But Rico's body didn't leave hers. It just eased away a little as he reached back to grab the covers and pull them up to cover both their bodies. He settled in so close it was impossible to decide if he was still on top of her or beside her. "Why did you stop me?"

It was an uncomfortable question to consider, let alone answer. "I don't know."

It wasn't a lie.

One of Rico's legs slid along hers, his knee pushing between her thighs. "Were you embarrassed?"

She tried to think about it, but the pressure of his leg as it climbed higher was more of a distraction than it should be. "I don't think so."

"Were you afraid?"

That didn't make sense. "What would I be afraid of?"

"That's an interesting question, Loba." Rico's thigh wedged tight against her, pressing into the part his mouth almost explored. His nose grazed across her jawline as his hand skimmed over her belly. "Are you still afraid of me?"

"Yes."

Damn it. She hadn't even known the answer was coming. Her brain had so many things to juggle it apparently couldn't also filter her mouth.

But Rico didn't seem upset at all by the accidental admission. He laughed, low and deep. "I think that's what we should fix first." The hand on her belly flattened, sliding up to curve against the underside of one breast, finger and thumb coming together on each side of her nipple to roll with a perfect amount of pressure. "I don't want what you feel for me to be fear, Loba." His lips moved over the skin of her shoulder, creeping toward her untouched breast.

"I don't fear you." She sucked in a breath as the heat of his mouth closed around her neglected nipple.

Her lids dropped, closing as the feel of his hands and mouth on her breasts coupled with the press of his leg made it impossible to continue discussing whatever it was they were discussing.

It didn't really matter anyway.

What mattered was how much she liked what was happening.

How much she wanted it to continue.

How much she wanted it to stop.

Lennie's eyes flew open and her whole body went stiff, tensing up as she tried to shut out what she was feeling.

Rico's hand immediately left her body and his head lifted, dark eyes finding hers.

Well.

Shit.

She pressed her lips together.

There wasn't really anything to say.

Any explanation to give.

Because none of this made any sense.

She'd had sex. More than a few times with more than a few men.

She'd never had this issue.

But none of those men ever turned down her offer of just sex either.

Each and every one was happy to go straight to penetration.

"Why can't we just," Lennie huffed out a breath of frustration, "have sex?"

"I thought that was what we were doing, Loba."

"That's not what we're doing." She wiggled a little, trying to work away from where his leg still pressed into the part of her that was beginning to throb with an almost unbearable ache. "This is not that."

"If you don't think this is how you have sex then you're about to be in for a rude awakening." Rico leaned closer to her. "Because I will never just fuck you, Loba."

"Why?" It would be so much easier.

So much simpler.

His lips curved into a slow smile that made the pulse between her legs pick up speed. "Because I'm greedy." His hands were on her again, but they didn't go anywhere useful. They moved over her arms. Over her hips. Across her stomach.

"I love this part of you." Rico stroked the bit of her that gave away her love of carbs and cookies. He sank his fingers into the fullness there. "I want you to get used to the way we're going to be doing things so I can have all I want, Lenore."

She shouldn't ask. It would probably just complicate things further.

"What do you want?"

"Everything." Rico leaned into her, the ridge of his dick pressing into her belly as his thigh pushed against her, sliding along her slit. "I want to rub against your skin until I come." His hands came up to her chest, fingers and thumbs spreading wide, one catching each breast and pulling them together. "I want to fuck your tits." One hand slid over her collarbone and up her neck, two fingers catching her bottom lip and pulling it down. "I want to fuck your mouth."

What in the hell was it about him?

She'd spent her whole life knowing she liked men but struggling to find that sexual attraction so many women spoke of.

The desire.

The lust.

They were not anything she normally had to deal with.

Not until this man came along, bringing a whole slew of new feelings and sensations with him.

It was overwhelming. It was—

Terrifying.

And yet she wanted it.

"Do those things then."

Rico slowly shook his head at her. "No."

"But you said—"

"Not tonight, Loba." He looked so much more serious than normal. "This is not the night for those things."

"What is it the night for?" A tiny thrill cut through her, distracting from the fear still trying to close her off.

"Tonight I take what I want from you." His head dipped, lips catching a nipple and sucking it deep into his mouth before letting it drop free. "As much as I want of it."

Another stab of need cut through her insides and shot straight to where his leg rubbed against her. "Okay."

"You say okay, Loba, but you don't know what I want."

"What do you want?"

"I want to feel your pussy clench around my fingers while I suck your clit." He pinched her nipple as his words registered, the image they conjured up coupling with the sensation to make her thighs clench.

"Then, maybe I will fuck you." Rico's leg worked against her, the pressure no longer being enough. Her hips worked into him, trying to get more.

"Are you ready for me now, Lenore? Are you ready for my mouth on your pussy?"

"Yes." The breathy word sounded like it came from a different woman.

A woman who was sexual and filled with the desire she'd only just begun to know.

Rico's hand replaced his thigh and the sudden shift in sensation made her cry out.

He leaned into her ear. "You are wet for me, Loba. Ready for all I want to give you."

She whimpered as his fingers pressed right against her clit, working it in small circles that had her thighs shaking in seconds.

"My fingers scare you less than my mouth does, don't they?"

She wanted to tell him he was wrong, but all her attention was focused on where he touched her.

What he was doing.

And the anticipation of what he would do next.

Excitement pushed at the fear, shoving it back, tamping it down.

Rico caught one of her hands, placing a kiss on the center of the inside of her palm before lifting it to his head, pressing her fingers into his black hair as his body moved. He put pressure on the back of her hand, as if she was the one pushing him down.

Down.

Down.

"One day you will do this, Loba. You will put me where you want." His breath was warm against the inside of her thigh. "You will take what you want from me." The rasp of his jaw teased her skin. "And I will beg to give you more." His mouth locked onto her, lips pressing into her flesh as they wrapped around the most sensitive part of her.

Rico's face, the part of him the whole world saw was there, wedged between her thighs, doing horrible, wonderful things with his tongue and teeth as his fingers—

"That's it." He growled so low she almost couldn't hear his muffled words.

No. That wasn't why she couldn't hear him.

Both her hands were at the back of his head, holding him there, keeping him from stopping as she started to shake.

Started to trip toward something she thought she was incapable of.

Not an orgasm. She'd had those. They were fine.

This was not fine. This was consuming. The heat, the need, the urge to have all he would give her.

This was new, and only minutes ago it was also terrifying.

Scary enough to make her run away.

But somewhere between here and there she'd crossed a line.

A point of no return. The same one she'd crossed in the bathroom when he offered a taste of what he could do to her.

Bring out in her.

She'd been warned.

Lennie's fingers dug in. The thought of him stopping was unbearable.

Losing this feeling.

This want.

It was a high she'd never really known.

Rico's arms looped around her thighs and hefted her closer, smashing his face against her as his mouth pulled at her clit, the pulse of it relentless as it sent her back bowing and her lungs seizing as she came.

She lost control of her limbs. Of her voice.

Of her mind.

And Rico wasn't done.

He hefted her up off the bed, ears still ringing, legs still shaking, unable to support her weight as he pulled her back against his front, pinning her to him with one arm around her waist. "Tell me you want more from me, Lenore."

More?

There was *more*?

The slide of his dick along the crack of her ass made her instinctively press back against him.

"You have to say it, Loba." His cock pressed between her thighs rubbing against her still-throbbing pussy. "If you want it you have to tell me."

She'd never wanted more from a man. Not sexually.

Quite the opposite, actually.

For a long time she assumed there was something wrong with her.

And the men in her life definitely reinforced that belief.

"I want it."

Rico pulled back before thrusting, driving his length between the press of her upper thighs, dragging it along her clit as he did.

Lennie started to tip forward as her legs lost any ability they'd worked up to support her.

Rico pulled her tighter to him, grabbing one of her arms and lifting it over her head to loop around his neck. "Hold on to me, Loba."

She flailed her other arm to join the first, locking her hands on her forearms just as the angle of Rico's thrust changed.

In one long, strong stroke he filled her from behind, his hips meeting her ass.

His arms banded around her, holding tight as her body rocked. One hand pressed between her thighs, a single finger pushing deeper to rest right against her clit, the thrust of his body into hers forcing her to slide against it.

It was unbelievable. All of it.

How good it felt.

How much she wanted it.

But only from him.

Rico was the only one she wanted like this.

The only one who made her feel like this.

His lips locked onto the spot where her neck and shoulder met, teeth sinking into the tense line of muscle there.

It sent goosebumps running over her skin and a bolt of pleasure straight to where his body shoved into hers. It was too much. More than she could sustain.

As she started to come Rico's body took her down to the mattress, his weight heavy on her back as he fucked her. Fast.

Hard.

Wild.

And thank God her face was flat against the sheets. It was all that smothered the sounds that came from her as she twisted and writhed.

Like an animal.

Feral.

Rico pushed deep, holding still as a low growl rumbled where his chest met her back, dick swelling as he came.

Holy.

Hell.

"What just happened?" She had to take a word between each breath, a clump of hair tickling her nose and mouth with each inhale.

Rico's lips ran along her shoulder, the dark hairs peeking out the skin of his jaw scraping her skin. "That was just the beginning, Loba."

****

"WHAT ARE YOU doing?" Lennie whisper-yelled as Rico yanked open the door to her room.

"Going to get us some coffee." He stood in the doorway wearing nothing but a towel tucked precariously around his waist.

The man hadn't been lying about his love of being naked. Once the clothes were off they didn't seem to go back on until the last possible second.

"What if someone sees you?" She craned her neck to look around him and out into the tiny hall connecting her room and Elise's.

Rico's hand dropped off the knob and he slowly came her way. "Are you ashamed of me, Loba?"

"No." The answer came out loud and fast. She took a breath and lowered her voice. "I just thought you wouldn't want anyone to know—"

"You think I don't want everyone to know I'm the man you chose for your bed last night?" He crawled onto the mattress, the towel at his waist losing more ground with each move. "And the night before that?"

"Kinda?" Lennie pulled the covers between them higher. "I just assumed you wouldn't want the pressure of them knowing you were here."

"The pressure?" His expression suddenly darkened. "What kind of men have you been allowing in your bed, Lenore?"

"The normal kind." Men were supposed to be less attached. Skittish about commitment and any other sort of tying down that might make them feel boxed into one woman.

"You call men like Kyle normal?" He came to a stop directly over her and leaned close, running his

208

nose along hers. "Because all the men I know would kill to be able to claim you as theirs."

She didn't really have any sort of response to that, and any attempt to think of one was cut short by an awful howling noise in the hall.

Elise screeched from just outside the door. "Ew. God. What the fuck, Rico?"

Lennie's hand came to cover her mouth as Rico rolled to his side, propping one arm under his head, like this was a completely normal situation.

She sat up to find Elise with her back to the open doorway.

"I saw his butthole." Elise bent at the waist. "It was just staring at me when I came to see if you wanted some coffee."

"We would love some coffee." Rico grinned at Elise's back. "Thank you."

"No coffee." Elise held a hand over her eyes as she turned to the side and stomped toward the stairs. "You get no coffee from me ever again."

Rico turned to Lennie. "Was that so terrible?"

"I think Elise would say yes."

"It's just an ass." Rico stood up and retucked the towel he clearly thought worked better than it actually did. "Everyone has one."

"How would you feel if Abe saw mine?"

His expression hardened. "Jealousy is a new emotion to me, Loba. One I'm not used to having to control."

"You would be jealous if Abe saw my—"

"Stop." Rico's tone was short and sharp. His eyes held hers for a few long seconds. "I will learn to handle it, but for now just know I am jealous when another man breathes your air."

Well.

That was something new.

The darkness in his eyes and the set of his jaw eased. "What are you hungry for, Loba? Toast? Eggs?"

Was he offering to bring her breakfast? "I can get it." Lennie started to get out of bed.

"No." Rico shook his head. "I will bring it to you."

"Um." She smoothed down one side of her hair. "Whatever is fine."

Rico's brown eyes skimmed over her face. "I will accept this now, but not forever."

"I don't know what that means."

"It means I want to know your needs, Loba." His voice dropped. "Your desires. I want you to give them to me."

Nothing in her life had prepared her for a man like this.

One that demanded so much but also so little.

"I'm not sure that will be easy for me."

"I don't expect it to be easy, Loba." His lips curved in a slow smile. "But I promise you I can make it worth it."

Her stomach dropped and her whole body went hot.

It was difficult enough to tell someone what she wanted to eat, let alone what Rico was clearly asking for.

"We will start small." He checked his towel. "What do you want to eat?"

Did she really want to open this can of worms?

Her eyes dipped to where Rico's hand rested in the bound waist of the towel, just above his—

"Lenore."

She jumped. "What?"

"If you look at me like that you will have to wait for your breakfast." He lifted a brow. "And considering your friend is already awake, she will know why."

Lennie rested one hand to her head. "Elise is going to kill me."

Rico chuckled low. "I never thought a woman could be sexy and cute, Loba. Somehow you've managed to do it."

"I think I feel sick." She couldn't face Elise. Not after Rico being caught naked in her room, and definitely not after the butthole sighting.

"You are fine." He stood tall. "I will take all the blame for seducing my way into your bed." He winked. "But I will also make it clear I plan to be there again tonight."

Lennie slouched down in the bed as Rico disappeared from the doorway. She pulled the covers over her head.

"Don't even think about hiding."

Lennie lowered the sheet so she could peek at Elise with one eye. "Go away."

Elise crossed her arms. "I'd come sit with you but my guess is Rico's dragged his balls all over that bed."

Lennie tucked the covers under her chin. "What kind of weirdo sex are you having?"

Elise straightened.

"You know what? Never mind. I don't want to know." Lennie flipped the covers back.

Elise yelped as her hands went to her eyes.

"I'm not naked." Lennie stood and headed for the bathroom.

Elise peeked through her fingers. "Why was he naked then?"

"He's always naked." Lennie went in and grabbed her toothbrush. "I wish I was that comfortable naked."

"I don't. Seeing his butthole was more than enough. Seeing yours would give me a heart attack." Elise edged into the room, staying far from the bed. She stopped in the doorway of the bathroom, peeking out over her shoulder once before leaning in. "When were you going to tell me you were boning Rico?"

"Honestly?" Lennie spit out the toothpaste in her mouth. "Never."

CHAPTER 16

ABE EYED THE towel wrapped at Rico's waist. "Fun night?"

"I'm not sure I'd call it fun." Last night wasn't about fun.

It was about something very different.

Something he wasn't expecting to find.

Or want.

"Really?" Abe let out a low whistle. "You guys are killing me."

"Watch your back, man." Rico poured some freshly-brewed coffee into a mug and added the creamer he'd made sure Abe bought from the store. "They're like ninjas. They come at you out of nowhere and there's nothing you can do about it."

"I'm sure there's plenty you can do about it." Abe pulled out one of the chilled, pre-mixed protein shakes he started each day with and twisted off the cap. "You just don't want to."

Rico shook his head. "You don't even know it happens. One minute you think they're going to get you killed on the interstate, and the next you're getting them coffee and making them breakfast."

Abe tipped back his shake and drank it all in one go. When it was gone he crushed the cardboard container with one hand and replaced the cap. "That sounds an awful lot like you happily falling right into it."

Rico picked up the coffee and the plate of eggs and toast he'd made, shrugging as he walked toward Lennie's room. "It is what it is, my friend."

Lennie was dressed and working a brush through her long hair when he walked in. She peeked at him from the open bathroom door and her cheeks immediately pinked before she disappeared deeper into the space.

He smiled. "Are you thinking about what I did to you last night, Loba?"

Her head snapped out the opening, eyes bouncing around the space. "Be quiet."

Rico set the food and drink on the top of the dresser and went to lean against the jam. "I thought you wanted excitement, Loba?"

"I do." Her eyes went over his shoulder. "But I want excitement with limits."

"What are the limits?" He thought it would take her longer to open up to him. Expected he would have to gently coax Lennie from her shell.

"No traumatizing my friends." She wiggled one finger toward the spot where Elise almost caught them the day of their arrival. "No more doing things when someone could walk in." Her finger went to his towel. "And no more nakedness when the door's open."

"So you want my body to be for your eyes only."

Lennie's chin dipped. "That's not what I said."

"But it's something we have to talk about, Lenore."

She eyed him. "What is?"

"I am with no other women now. Only you." He eased closer. "I want you to be only with me."

"Already?"

"*Si*, Loba. Already." He'd spent years seeking out the temporary.

Being it.

Never expecting something would make him reconsider.

Not just reconsider.

Straight out reject the thought. Lennie was not filling a temporary place in his life.

She was reminding him of a spot he thought no longer existed.

"I mean. I'm not—" She huffed out a breath, running one hand through her hair. "There's no one else who wants—"

"Stop there." He grabbed her and pulled her close. "Not all men make their interest clear, Lenore. A man can find you desirable without acting on it. Without voicing it."

"Are you trying to make me feel better about never being the girl men picked?" Hurt edged her soft voice. It surprised him almost as much as the confession.

"Boys look for the path of least resistance, Loba." He ran one finger along her jaw. "You are more cautious. More careful. You take effort and commitment. The boys you refer to as men aren't capable of things like that. They are just looking for a good time."

"Isn't that what you were looking for?"

"*Si*." He couldn't stop the smile at her ability to slice the conversation straight to the core. "But I was honest. I made my intentions clear. I found women who were looking for the same thing I was."

"But that's not what you're doing now?"

"It is what I'm doing now, Loba." He leaned into her. "I told you what I want. I asked you for the same in return."

"Why do you want something different now?"

"I don't want something different *now*." He hadn't planned it. Wasn't necessarily even interested in it. Not until she showed up. "I want something different *with you*."

"It just seems like an abrupt change."

"It's not a change." This was a man he'd been before. A man he'd expected to be forever. "It's a reversion." Rico backed away from her. Lennie was cautious. It made sense she would show that now. "Your breakfast is on the dresser. I will give you time to think about what I want from you. Time to decide if you want the same from me." He gave himself one final look at her before turning away and going to the room he had yet to sleep in.

Rico took a quick shower before dressing and going to find Abe. His partner for this job was back in the kitchen, eating his second breakfast. "Did you get that computer shipped out?"

"Yup." Abe shoved in a spoonful of plain oatmeal. "Did it as soon as they opened."

"Good." Rico eyed the hall leading to the other set of bedrooms, making sure it was clear. "What do you think he was trying to erase?"

"Not sure. Whatever it was, he definitely didn't want anyone to see it." Abe lifted his brows. "What kind of dumbass uses his work computer for something he doesn't want seen?"

"Maybe it's nothing then." Rico poured himself a cup of coffee. "If there was something terrible on it why wouldn't he have just taken it the first time he was there?"

Abe polished off his flavorless food before rinsing the bowl in the sink. "We would know if Pierce would have let Heidi handle it."

"That's not an option."

"I know." Abe sighed. "I just wish we could at least ask one of them."

"Vincent will work fast. If there's something there he'll find it. We deal with whatever it is then." He didn't like the thought of keeping this from Lennie, but as of right now all of this was simply suspicion. Looking for the fire in a room filled with smoke. There was no reason to cause Lennie or Elise additional stress over something that could be as simple as a man cheating on his wife.

Abe loaded his bowl into the dishwasher. "Sounds like a plan."

"You're making the plans now?" Elise came down the steps, her eyes staying far from Rico as she walked across the living room. "I thought I was the one in charge of this project."

"I'm gonna guess you're always the one in charge, Babe." Abe grabbed the keys from the counter and tossed them her way. "You're the kind of woman who likes to be in the driver's seat."

Elise caught the keys without blinking. "Don't pretend like you know me, Babe."

"Awe." Abe held his hands out. "I thought we were friends now. I shared my lunch with you."

"You thought wrong." Elise turned as Lennie came down the steps, carrying her empty plate and mug. "Are you ready?"

"Yup." Lennie's purse was over one shoulder as she came into the kitchen.

Abe stepped directly in her path. "I got those." He reached to take the dishes from her.

"You don't have to do that." She offered him a small smile.

"I really don't mind." Abe managed to get his hands on the items. "I like loading the dishwasher."

Elise stepped in, eyes narrowing. "Are you the kind of person who reloads a dishwasher because no one else does it right?"

Abe shot her a grin as he snagged the dishes out of Lennie's hands. "Don't pretend like you know me, Babe."

Elise scowled at Abe's back as he racked up the last of the breakfast mess and started the washer. "You're a pain in the ass."

Abe straightened. "Makes two of us then." He pointed toward the front door. "Aren't you upset we're behind schedule?"

She huffed out a breath, holding the glare she gave Abe a second longer before turning and stomping toward the door.

"Keep antagonizing her. See what happens." Rico shook his head as he walked past Abe. "You think you're doing one thing, but I can promise you it's not going to end up the way you think it will." He tipped his head toward the door as he reached Lennie's side. "Let's go make sure she hasn't left us."

Lennie's lips pressed out to hide the small smile teasing them. "She won't leave me."

"Then I will stick close." Rico rested one hand on her back.

"I thought you were giving me space?"

"My definition of space must be different from yours." He leaned into her ear. "Do you want physical space from me too, Lenore?"

He could back off emotionally. Control what he voiced.

Staying away from her physically would be infinitely more difficult, but he would give her that if she wished. Even if it killed him.

Lennie's dark eyes skimmed down his frame. "No."

"Good." Rico opened her door and kept his hand on her body until the last possible second.

He craved contact. Always had.

Physical touch was what soothed him from the time he was a child. When his friends were rushing from the house he was finding his mother. Seeking out the warmth of a goodbye hug before he left.

He'd sat on her lap until he was nearly a teenager. Kissed her on the lips until the day she left the world.

Changing his forever.

Rico took the other back seat, leaving Abe to deal with his own self-created issues. Elise moved the rearview mirror until she could look him in the eyes. "You're on my shit list too, butthole."

"I know mine wasn't the first asshole you've seen."

Elise snorted. "You're not wrong." She turned her glare onto Abe as he sat in the seat beside her. "I've been lucky enough to see plenty in my day." She pulled out of the u-shaped driveway and onto the road, heading for downtown.

Rico reached across the seat, finding Lennie's hand with his. He traced the tips of his fingers along her skin, stroking with a soft touch.

He didn't want to irritate her. Many women were overwhelmed by his desire to touch and be touched. Including the woman who walked away from the life they started, leaving him to deal with two devastating losses at once.

At the end of the day it wasn't something he could do. So he left his home. His country.

Thinking he could leave the pain along with it.

Lennie slowly turned her hand, resting it face-up between them. Her eyes followed as he continued his soft strokes, tracing the lines of her palm. The length of her fingers. The crease of her wrist.

He wanted to know all of her. Every inch. He wanted to touch it all.

Wanted her to touch all of him.

But he would start with this. Give her the time he promised to decide if she wanted the same thing.

The SUV slowed to a stop.

"Holy shit." Elise stared out the windshield at the office building in front of them.

Lennie's head snapped up and her eyes went wide. "Oh no." Her hand pulled from his and she jumped out of the SUV, leaving Rico to chase after her as she ran toward the crowd of people cluttering the parking lot.

Abe snagged Lennie's arm as she tried to rush past him, giving Rico time to race around the SUV. He got between her and the scene in front of them, leaning down until her eyes finally met his. "You and Elise stay here. We will go find out what happened."

Lennie's gaze drifted over his shoulder. "This is crazy."

"That's why I want you to stay here." He gently took her by the arm and eased her back toward Abe's open door. "Sit down. We'll be right back."

Elise was still in her seat, jaw slack as she stared at the billowing smoke coming from the building they were supposed to be inside.

Rico closed the door and turned to Abe. They shared a long look before heading toward the crowd kept at bay by the police spaced around the lot. Rico caught the eye of one of the cops who came the day before to remove Rob. He nudged Abe, tipping his head in the direction of the familiar face.

"Didn't expect to be here two days in a row did you?" Abe rested his hands on his hips as he scanned the building. "Any idea what happened?"

The billows of smoke were coming from one location in particular. The windows were blown out, letting the grey streaks push free of the very rooms they were supposed to be emptying.

"Looks like someone didn't want you to get your hands on what was in there." The cop sized Abe up. "We got a few phone calls about you last night. Your boss must be pretty powerful."

"He is." Abe scanned the line of cops. "What do you know?"

The cop shrugged. "Not much." He turned to eye the line of windows bleeding smoke. "We've got a call in to the owner of the security company that monitors the place. The surveillance was digital, so hopefully we will gain access to that soon."

The fire engine closest to the building lifted its ladder, stretching it toward the top floor.

"You think they'll be able to put it out?" Rico watched as a firefighter sprayed water into the broken windows.

"Should." The cop turned to watch. "The alarm and sprinkler system is functioning so as long as there's not—"

A sudden explosion sent Rico toward the ground, grabbing anyone around him as he went, shoving their heads into a more protected position as scraps of glass and metal spewed from the building. The cops did the same, yelling as they pushed the line of people back farther from the building.

Rico and Abe fell in line with them, moving the mass of gawkers as the grating sounds behind them grew louder and louder.

"It's going to come down." He glanced over his shoulder at the structure before turning to Abe. His eyes snapped to the SUV where Lennie and Elise were waiting. "Shit."

The Jeep was empty.

The cracking sound grew louder as Rico fought the crowd, pushing them back, hoping he was pushing Lennie at the same time.

Gaining enough distance to keep her safe.

"*Rico.*" His name in her voice was unmissable, even over the yelling and screaming happening around him.

He found her immediately, pushing her way toward him, fighting the wave of bodies headed in the opposite direction.

"*Go back to the car.*" He shoved a man in a suit who was dragging his feet, trying to look at the building as it continued to groan under the stress of whatever damage had been inflicted. "Get Elise and get in the fucking car." Rico shouldered another man out of the way.

Lennie wasn't listening. She was struggling in the mob as it tried to swallow her up.

Drag her under.

A crowd of panicked people was a dangerous thing. One that could cause unbelievable damage.

Lennie yelped as a woman crashed into her, knocking her off-balance. Her eyes held his as she started to go down, her body tipping as another person pushed against her, sealing her fate.

"Get her." Abe pointed Lennie's way as her head disappeared in the swell.

Rico no longer cared who else made it away from the building. Nothing mattered but getting to her.

Keeping her safe.

He pushed men down on each side, clearing a path to where he'd last seen Lennie's sweet face. His toe caught something and his stomach dropped. There was no way to pull her up. No way to fight the flow of the crowd fleeing the building as another explosion rocked it. All he could do was join her.

Cover her body with his.

Take the pain for her.

The sound was deafening. The crush of the throng punishing as feet kicked at his legs and ribs. Bodies tripped over them. Fell against him.

None of it mattered.

Because she was there.

Lennie was safe.

Even if he was not.

CHAPTER 17

SHE COULDN'T HEAR anything but the ringing in her ears and the screams of everyone around her.

Her head hurt. Her lungs hurt. She started to choke as the air around them thickened.

Clogged.

Rico's hand came to the side of her head, tucking her face closer to his, pressing it into his shoulder, their bodies taking another hit from the people she'd worked alongside for years as they tried to flee the collapsing building.

His body protected hers, absorbing the impact of the feet and legs that seemed to never end.

They needed to get up. Get off the ground before he was hurt.

Lennie struggled under him, trying to force her back away from the blacktop behind it.

But Rico didn't budge. His hands braced her head. His arms and weight pinned her in place.

She sucked in a breath, intending to tell him to let her up. Instead her lungs filled with dust and the smell of burning insulation, sending her into an immediate coughing fit.

Rico held her tighter.

A peek of sky appeared above them and a second later Rico was moving, hauling her along with him as he shoved his way to his feet. Hers weren't even on the ground before they were moving forward, away from the wreckage behind them and toward the outskirts of the parking lot.

His arm was tight around her as he all but carried her along, pushing through the people around them with the same mercy they showed them seconds ago.

None.

Suddenly they broke free from the crowd.

"I got her." Abe's graveled voice was unmistakable.

"No." Rico held her tighter.

"You're hurt, man." Abe's hand gripped Rico's shoulder, stopping their forward projection. "Just give her up for a second."

Lennie's attention went to Rico. His eye was split, the blood eking from it smeared against his tan skin. His cheek was red and scuffed, with a deep bruise forming under the skin. His breathing was shallow and sharp. She twisted in his hold, not to get away.

But to get closer.

She wrapped her arms around him, holding on as tight as she dared without knowing how much of him was damaged.

"For the love of—" Abe shook his head as he rested one hand on Rico's back and used it to push them along toward the farthest corner of the lot. Occasionally he reached out to knock anyone who got too close away and out of their path.

Elise stood outside the passenger's door of the SUV, gaze locked onto what was left of the building. One hand came to cover her mouth as she caught sight of them coming her way. "Lennie." She ran toward them, arms out. Her tall body hit Lennie's hard enough to bounce her into Rico.

He let out a low grunt and winced.

"Oh shit." Elise backed off immediately. "What in the hell happened?"

"Your friend isn't a very good listener." Rico rested one hand against the side of Lennie's face, pulling it to rest against his chest. "I thought I told you to stay in the car, Loba?"

"I couldn't see you anymore." She was fine when the building was just a little on fire.

But that first explosion sent her into a panic, and she might have made a bad decision because of it.

One Rico was paying for now.

"We need to take you to the hospital." Lennie leaned back, trying to get a better look at his face.

"There's nothing they can do for me there." Rico glanced Abe's way. "We need to call Pierce."

"I already did." Elise's eyes went from Rico to Abe. "He's booking a flight right now."

"There's nothing he can do here." Abe squinted at the building before turning back to Rico. "I need to make a phone call."

Rico tipped his head in a short nod as Abe moved away.

"Who's he calling?" Elise watched as Abe tucked his phone to his ear from a spot far enough from them that no one could hear the conversation.

"Didn't ask." Rico turned to the SUV. "We need to get you out of here." His dark eyes moved around the lot that was now packed with emergency vehicles. Police and firefighters were attempting to set up a new perimeter as more and more people from the office buildings around them filtered in, trying to get a look at the destruction.

"The windows of our office were all broken." Lennie didn't get a great look at the building before it went down, but she saw enough to identify where the initial problem seemed to be centered.

Rico was silent as he worked her toward the SUV.

"Right? It was the top floor windows on the south side. Those were our windows." She'd checked the direction twice to be sure. "None of the other windows were like that."

"We only saw one side of the building, Loba. There could have been more windows out."

While he wasn't wrong, Rico also didn't seem right.

"Someone did this on purpose."

"That is definitely true." Rico eased down into the back passenger's seat. "Buildings don't usually explode on their own." He reached for her. "Come here."

She eyed the ribs he'd been holding as he walked. "You're hurt."

"I will be less hurt with you close to me." His hand came closer. "Come."

"I'm the reason you're hurt."

"And you are the reason I don't care that I'm hurt." He shifted in the seat, pain lining his eyes with each movement. "I hurt less than I would if you were the one suffering right now."

Every bit of her wanted to be close to him. Relax into the heat of his body. Breathe in the smell of his skin. Use him to calm the rush of panic still making her legs weak and her hands shake.

"I need your touch, Loba." His fingers trailed over her arm. "It won't hurt me."

Lennie inched closer, trying to figure out how to squeeze in at his side, but the second she edged his way Rico took that choice away, snagging her and tugging her onto his lap.

She tried not to flail in surprise, knowing that would just hurt him more. "You are going to make everything worse."

"You are going to make everything better." His arms came around her as his face tucked close to her neck. "So it will be balanced."

"I'm sorry I didn't stay in the SUV. I'm not difficult, I promise."

"That's not a promise you have to make me, Loba." Rico's fingers moved over her skin with a soft touch, just like they had on the ride over. "You can be as difficult as you want to be." One hand slid down her thigh, smoothing over the skin not covered by the shorts she pulled on this morning, thinking they would be spending the day moving and sweating. "But there might be consequences." His fingers dipped under the ragged hem of the cutoffs, sliding around to the back of her leg and up to tease the crease where her thigh met her ass.

Lennie sat still, uncertain if he really meant what she thought he meant.

"Not into a little spanking, Lenore?"

The man was bleeding.

Bruised.

Possibly broken.

And talking about—

Her stomach clenched at the thought as heat crept over her skin.

Rico's lips pulled into a slow smile. "Seems like maybe you're open to the idea." The hand under her shorts kneaded her skin, his fingers working dangerously close to a more indecent spot.

Not that the spot they were already in was remotely decent.

"You were just trampled."

He nosed along her neck. "It would take more than that to keep me from wanting you, Loba." Rico's lips skimmed across her skin. "I could be half-dead and I would still drag myself to your bed one last time."

"That doesn't make any sense."

"It only has to make sense to me." Rico gripped her tighter, angling her legs into the SUV before pulling the door closed.

A second later Abe was shoving Elise into the passenger's seat. She smacked at him. "Stop it. You could have just asked me to get in."

"Don't act like you would have listened to me." Abe slammed the door shut and jogged around the car, starting the engine before his door was even closed.

"What's wrong?" Lennie looked from Rico to Abe then back again.

"Nothing's wrong." Abe glanced up at her in the rearview. "Unless we get pulled over. Then you're both getting a ticket."

"Not in Ohio." Elise crossed her arms. "In Ohio no one in the backseat over the age of sixteen has to wear a belt."

"Can they be piled up like that?"

"I'm hurt, man. You said it yourself."

"And having her stacked on top of you makes it better?" Abe leaned to one side. "I can't even see around her head. At least sit on the side."

Rico laughed but the sound was strained as he worked them away from the middle of the bench seat.

Lennie frowned at him. "I think we should take you to the hospital."

"I will let Eli check me out as soon as we get back home."

Elise sat up straight in her seat. "Does this mean we have to go back already?"

"Pierce wants us to fly back tonight."

Lennie's heart sank. "I haven't seen my sister yet."

It was one of the reasons she was most excited to come back to Cincinnati. To see her family. They were what got her on the plane.

Powered her through.

Abe caught Rico's eyes in the mirror. "I will see what we can do."

Lennie let out the breath stuck in her lungs. "Thank you." Her eyes went back to Rico. "Crap."

Staying to see her family meant Rico wouldn't be able to see Eli as soon.

Rico's smile was quick and easy. "Are you worried about me, Loba?"

"Someone has to be, because it doesn't seem like you are."

Rico reached up to smooth one hand through her hair. "This is nothing."

"I don't like the sound of that either." She'd dated a handful of guys. Usually office workers.

Definitely never a mercenary.

Rico would always be putting himself in danger.

Always be at risk.

"You look unhappy." Rico's fingers twisted in her hair, holding her tight as he pulled her ear to his lips. "I think I know how to make you forget your unhappiness."

This was another reason she might not be in a hurry to get back home. Here they were sharing a house with two other people.

In Alaska the walls were thick and the rooms were private.

If Rico was like this here what would he be like in Alaska?

232

She'd gotten a peek of it before they left. A glimpse into what it might be like to have Rico focus his attention on her.

And his attention was highly focused.

Blanketing.

It was something she might accidentally be able to get used to.

But it was still terrifying.

Abe glanced at the screen of his cell phone as they sat at a light. "Rico and I will drop you two off at the house. We need to go meet with the police."

"Shouldn't we go with you?" Elise was clearly as unhappy with the arrangement as Lennie was, but for a completely different reason. "We are the ones who worked there."

"Rico and I are the representatives of the current business owner." Abe turned the SUV onto the street where they were staying. "And we are the ones who dealt with Rob."

"What's *dealt with* mean?" Lennie watched Rico for any sign of what exactly Abe was talking about.

"It sounds like Rob is claiming we roughed him up." Abe's eyes went to Rico in the mirror. "One of us specifically."

Lennie stared at Rico. "Did you?"

"He put up a fight. Nothing I did was out of line."

"What if they arrest you?" The same panic she felt when the building exploded twisted her stomach.

"If they arrest me I won't stay there long." Rico found her hand and laced his fingers with hers. "Pierce will have me out before morning."

"*Morning*?" He would have to sleep there? With broken ribs?

"No." She shook her head. "I don't like this plan at all."

"It's not a plan, Loba. It's what has to be done. We aren't in Alaska. We have to play by different rules here, remember?"

"Let's just fly back then. We can go right now." She could see her sister some other time. Ohio would always be here.

"No, Loba." Rico rested his forehead against hers. "Everything will be fine." His thumb traced along her cheek as Abe parked in front of the house. "I will be back to you as soon as I can be."

"I don't like this."

"Good." Rico brushed his lips over hers as Abe opened the door beside them. He eased her off his lap and out onto the ground.

Were they all crazy? They had a freaking plane. They could just fly away.

For the first time in her life, flying in a plane seemed like a perfect idea. One she was happy and willing to do.

Hell, she'd even be the first one on the damn thing.

Elise grabbed Lennie, wrapping one arm around her shoulders. "Come on. It'll be fine. We'll watch some movies and eat some fantastic food and they'll be back before you know it."

Before she could argue any more Abe and Rico were closed into the SUV and pulling away.

"He didn't do anything wrong." Lennie rested one hand to her head, trying to calm the spinning there.

"That's why they have to go." Elise moved her toward the house. "If we leave and they issue an arrest warrant then Rico can't fly anymore. He's got to get this straightened out."

Lennie watched as the SUV disappeared from sight. "I hate this place."

It was where she'd always lived, but Ohio no longer felt like home.

It felt like a place that kept trying to force her back into her old self.

The one she let other people create.

And there might not be a huge difference between who she was now and who she was then, but at least now she was trying.

She was the one making the decisions on who she was going to be.

"I know." Elise punched in the code on the keypad and the deadbolt unlocked. "I'm not so sure I like it that much either."

"I thought you wanted to come back here?" Lennie dropped down to the sofa and let her head rest against the back.

Elise shrugged. "I guess I was remembering it better than it really is." She eased onto the sofa next to Lennie. "The food is good, though."

It was one thing she couldn't argue with. "The food is better here."

"Speaking of." Elise stood, grabbing her purse as she went. "What do you want for lunch?"

"I don't care. Surprise me." Eating didn't sound appealing at this point. Not when Rico was hurt and potentially about to be arrested for doing nothing wrong.

"You know that's my favorite answer." Elise pulled out her phone. "Are you really hungry or just kind of hungry?"

"I'm not hungry at all."

"So kind of hungry. Got it." She pressed the phone to her ear as she walked up the stairs and into her room.

Lennie jumped as her own purse began to vibrate on her lap. She reached in and fished out her ringing phone. The number was a familiar one.

She thought about ignoring it.

And then blocking it.

Instead she swiped across the screen and connected the call. "Hello."

"Holy shit, Lens. It's so good to hear your voice."

She wrinkled her nose. "Why are you calling me, Kyle?"

"Didn't you hear? The building exploded this morning. I was worried you might have been inside when it happened."

"No. I'm fine. Thanks for checking in." She didn't like his voice in her ear. Didn't like him acting like he was worried about her.

"I miss you, Lens."

"Why?" The question slid free easily. She'd always struggled to feel like she had a voice when it came to Kyle, but suddenly she wanted answers.

Real ones.

"I just do." He sounded almost whiny. "You were the perfect girlfriend. I should have kept you."

"Kept me? I didn't belong to you."

"That's not what I meant. I meant I shouldn't have done what I did."

It wasn't quite the apology she thought she wanted, and it made one thing perfectly clear.

She actually didn't care about Kyle or his apologies. She didn't care if he ever acknowledged what he did to her. All the things he said.

Because it no longer mattered.

Lennie smiled into the phone. "Goodbye, Kyle."

CHAPTER 18

"HE'S CLAIMING YOU broke his ribs." John, the cop they'd dealt with at Rob's arrest, sat across the desk from them. "His lawyer's pushing for an arrest."

"What are the charges?" Rico resisted the urge to wince as he accidentally took a deeper breath than he should have.

"What they're asking for is false imprisonment and assault." John let out a sigh. "I don't think it will stick, but his attorney is already throwing out terms like bias and police negligence."

"Then arrest me." He was willing to spend a night in jail if it meant that dickhead had less of a leg to stand on.

"Now wait a minute." Abe shook his head. "There's got to be another option."

"Let's just get it over with." Rico stood. "Call Charles. Have him start working on getting me out." Alaskan Security's in-house attorney was the best there was. Good enough Rico wasn't worried about any of this.

Abe raked one hand through his salt and pepper hair. "Goddammit. He's the one who broke into the fucking offices."

"I get it." John wiped both hands down his face. "But no one actually saw him break in. No one actually saw him trying to take anything."

"What?" Rico tilted his head. "There were security cameras all over that building."

"The one outside Investigative Resources was faulty."

"Faulty?" Rico glanced at Abe. "That's fuckin' convenient."

"We interviewed all the people who worked on that floor and none of them saw anyone come or go from the office after Investigative Resources shut down." John shook his head. "I don't know how in the hell he was able to get in there."

Rico met Abe's eyes, unspoken words passing between them. If he was going to be out of commission for the rest of the evening that left Abe to carry the burden of this whole shit show.

And it was getting messier by the second.

John stood up. "You gonna call your attorney?"

Abe thumbed across the screen of his phone. "Doing it now."

John grabbed a stack of papers off his desk. "I'll take my time. Drag it out as much as I can. You might not even make it past a holding cell."

Rico passed his wallet to Abe. "I'm not worried about it." The only part of this that bothered him was being away from Lennie.

He already itched with the need to be close to her.

It was why he worked so hard to stay detached, because when he was attached to a woman she was all he wanted. All he needed.

She was air.

And for some women it was too much.

It was for his ex-wife.

Smothering. That's what she called him.

So maybe a night in jail would be good for them.

Give Lennie a break from what might already be too much.

The phone on John's desk rang. He grabbed it. His eyes came to Rico as he listened. After a minute he dipped his head a nod the caller couldn't see. "Yes, sir."

He set the phone back in place and turned their way, looking from man to man. "I don't know who in the hell you guys are, but they pulled out the big guns to keep you out of trouble." He lifted his shoulders. "You're free to go."

There was only one man who could pull those kinds of strings that fast, and it was the same man Abe hadn't wanted involved.

John led Rico and Abe back to the front of the building, letting them out a passcode-protected door. Rico tipped his head the cop's way. "We'll be in touch."

He and Abe walked toward the SUV. When the door of the station clicked shut behind them Abe turned to glance back then scanned the empty lot around them. "Vincent must have found something."

"I'm sure we'll find out soon enough." Rico opened the passenger's door, doing his best to breathe through the pain slicing through his ribcage. It was worth every second of agony he had to suffer because Lennie came out of this morning unscathed.

Now he just had to keep it that way.

"Better be real damn soon. Shit's blowing up here. We don't have time to fuck around." Abe missed a gap in traffic Rico would have taken.

"You had plenty of room."

"I had what I had to have plus a half-second." Abe was a decent driver and had improved a lot in his time at Alaskan Security, but he was still too hesitant to be a main driver. The only reason he was driving now was because the bruising to Rico's ribs made any movement painful as hell, and the less he moved the faster it would improve.

"That's all you need." Rico checked his phone for anything that might have come through from Pierce or Intel while they were talking to John.

"We're not being pursued." Abe watched for another gap in traffic.

"There's always the chance we're being pursued." Rico took another slow scan of the space around them. He'd done it countless times already.

And would do it countless more.

"You have to always be ready. You have to always expect it, otherwise you're behind before you even start." His gaze rested on a sedan that seemed familiar. It eased into the line behind them at the stop sign.

Only the driver's seat was occupied, but the afternoon sun made it impossible to know if it was a man or a woman in the spot.

"Pull out when no one can make it out behind you." Rico snapped his attention up one side of the cross street and down the other. "Go after the Audi."

"There's not enough—"

"Just fucking go." Rico braced as Abe hit the gas and the SUV shot forward, jostling his body in the seat.

The line of cars behind them wouldn't be able to move for at least twenty more seconds which would buy them a huge amount of time.

"What the fuck was that about?" Abe shot Rico a narrow-eyed glance as he wove around the cars parked along the street.

"Beige sedan. Four cars back at the stop sign." He checked the side mirror for any sign of the car. "I've seen it somewhere before."

"There's probably a million beige sedans around here." Abe started to ease off the gas.

"If you slow down we're switching seats." Rico turned to look out through the back window, ignoring the stab of pain cutting into his chest. "Don't go near the house until I'm sure we're not being followed." Rico pressed his phone to his ear as he scanned the roads. Lennie picked up on the second ring.

"Rico?" Her voice was breathless and edged with something he would enjoy later.

Relief.

But right now he didn't have time for the distraction of what that meant. "I need you and Elise to pack up, Loba. As fast as you can."

"Why? What's going on?"

"Maybe nothing." The chances of that being a true statement were slim to none, but he didn't want her any more upset than she already was by this damn day. "But just to be safe we need to go somewhere else."

"Are we going home?"

The option was tempting as hell, but until Pierce gave them official orders they were stuck here. "Not yet. But probably soon."

"Okay." She didn't sound as upset as before that she might not be able to see her sister. "But you're okay? They didn't arrest you?"

"Not yet." Rico did another visual sweep as Abe took a turn fast enough to shove his chest into the seat's edge, stealing his breath.

"Rico?" A hint of fear hung in the way she said his name.

"I'm here, Loba." Rico fought through the pain stabbing into his sides. "We are on our way. Don't let anyone in. No one. Understand?"

"Yes." She was moving. He could hear the tap of her feet against the travertine tile. "We'll pack."

"Good. I will be there soon." He hung up, eyes moving along the windows in a steady sweep.

"We should have started with weaponry instead of driving." Abe raced across a street, barely making it between oncoming cars. "Then they'd at least be able to defend themselves."

"I wouldn't bet against them." It was the only thing that settled him right now, knowing Elise and Lennie were much more capable than most people knew.

And that was half the battle. Surprise was one of the most dangerous weapons there was.

Underestimating those two would be a huge mistake. One many men would make.

Hopefully that included the one behind whatever was going on now.

"Go to the house." There had been no sight of the sedan or any other car that had been behind them. "We need to get them out of there just in case."

"Elise drove to the house from the rental car place." Abe turned onto the street where they'd spent their last night. "But that was the day we got here. Before we found Rob in the office."

Chances were good no one was following them at that point, but until they knew the full scope of what was happening, staying at the house was not an option.

Abe pulled into the driveway.

"Shit." Rico had his door open before the SUV was at a full stop.

"What's wrong?" Abe was out and running toward the front door.

"The car's in a different spot. They went somewhere." Rico punched in the passcode, his heart racing as he waited for the lock to flip open.

"Damn it." Abe wiped one hand down his face. "What in the fuck were they thinking?"

"They're not trained in this. Don't expect them to automatically know protocol." That damn car would be the first thing to go.

Rico rushed inside to find Elise running around the house, grabbing items she'd left all over the place. Abe walked right past her. "Hurry up."

"We are hurrying." Elise grabbed a tablet from the coffee table and added it to the stack of stuff in her arms. "And you two still have to pack so don't act like we're the problem."

"We're already packed." Abe squinted out the blinds into the back yard.

"You knew we were leaving and didn't think it would be nice to tell us about it?" Elise's stress level was clearly escalating with every passing second.

"We are always packed." Abe turned from the window and strode toward his room. "We have to be ready for things like this, Babe."

"Don't lump me in with your universal we." Elise clutched her things to her chest. "I'm a fucking office manager. Not a damn," she waved one hand their way, "whatever you are."

"Where's Lennie?" Rico pushed past Elise. He didn't have time for her meltdown right now. He took the steps in two strides, the racing of his heart not slowing until he saw her.

"What's going on?" Lennie stood at the side of the bed they'd shared two nights in a row, shoving down the clothes haphazardly packed into her suitcase as she tried to work it closed.

Rico went to her side and pressed the two halves together, meeting the teeth of the zipper. "Where did you and Elise go?"

Lennie worked the tab along the tracks. "Elise went and picked up our lunch. Why?"

"I should have told you not to leave the house." Rico leaned to peek out the front window of Lennie's room. He grabbed her suitcase with one hand and Lennie's hand with the other. "Come on, Loba. We need to get out of here." He dropped her suitcase off in the living room before taking her along with him to get his own bag. The room was practically untouched outside of taking a shower or two in the small bathroom. He grabbed his bag and slung it over one shoulder.

"You ready?" Abe stood in the doorway holding his own bag.

"Yup." Rico held Lennie's hand tightly as they followed Abe out into the living room. Elise was frantically grabbing items from the kitchen and throwing them into a large paper shopping-style bag.

"Leave the rest." Abe snagged the bag on his way to the door.

"We can't just leave the house like this. Pierce will lose his deposit." Elise chased after Abe as he grabbed her stack of bags from where they sat next to Lennie's. "It's my responsibility to make sure this place is left the way we found it."

Abe turned quickly and Elise nearly bumped into him. "And it's my responsibility to make sure you don't end up dead." Abe lifted the handle on her bag. "Right now I'm more worried about that."

Elise's eyes stretched wide. "Dead?" She spun toward Lennie and Rico. "Why dead?"

"Come on, Babe." Abe pulled the door open, pausing to scan the front of the house before heading toward the SUV with quick steps. He pulled the rear passenger's door open as he passed. "Get in."

For the first time Elise didn't argue with him. She practically jumped in and immediately pulled the door closed, her body slouching down in the seat.

Rico opened the front door and used his hand in Lennie's to move her that direction. She didn't let go of him until the last possible second. Then she did exactly as Elise did and went straight in, closed the door and hunkered down, her head turned toward the back seat where her friend sat.

"Pierce had Heidi get us a hotel room with an untraceable name." Abe stacked Elise's bags into the back of the SUV. "It's got high-end security and twenty-four hour room service."

"Sounds like he's done keeping all this from Intel." Rico added his and Lennie's bags to the back before shutting the hatch and walking to the driver's door. He started the engine as Abe climbed in.

"What about my car?" Elise pointed to the rental. "I need to return it."

"We will come back for it." Abe didn't look up from the screen of his phone. "Right now you don't need it. You can't go anywhere without one of us."

"Oh my God." Elise pressed both her hands to her face, fingers spread. "This is freaking insane."

Rico moved quickly through the streets, taking turns and side streets in an effort to flush out anyone who might be trying to tail them.

The smaller the roads were the easier it was to spot a car following along.

He'd done this a hundred times. Enough it shouldn't have his shoulders bunched tight and his adrenaline spiking.

A soft touch almost made him jump.

Lennie's hand pulled back from where it inched across the edge of his thigh. He caught it before she could steal it away and pulled it to his lips, taking as much of a breath as he could manage as he held it there.

That's why this bothered him the way it did.

Because she was at risk.

If he fucked up Lennie could end up hurt.

It was one more layer of complication he would have to deal with later. When she was safe. Hidden from someone willing to destroy the building she should have been inside.

After fifteen minutes of driving he was confident there was no one successfully following their current path. "Where are we headed?"

Abe's phone came between the seats. "Here."

Lennie took it and scanned the screen. "Oh. Wow."

"Just tell me when to turn, Loba."

Lennie was a perfect navigator, giving him well-timed, clear directions as they moved closer to the opposite side of the river that ran just behind their rental. She leaned in as he pulled up in front of the hotel they would be staying in for the foreseeable future. "Holy cow. I can't believe we're actually staying here."

"Only because someone might try to kill us" Elise tipped her head to peek out the window. "They will charge Pierce so much money if they have to get our blood out of the carpets."

"No one will get in here." Abe sounded more certain than he was.

They both knew where there was a will there was a way.

The valet opened Rico's door as the doorman opened Lennie's. "Welcome to The Lytle Park Hotel." The valet was young but professional. "Will you be going out again this evening?"

"We will not." Rico left the keys in the car as he got out.

A set of men were already at the back loading their bags onto a luggage cart.

Abe tipped the valet as Rico went to snag Lennie and Elise, taking them straight inside the historic building.

"I wish I could enjoy being here." Elise's head dropped back as she took in their surroundings. "I've wanted to stay here since it opened up."

Abe caught up with them and went straight to the desk to check them in as Elise wandered to the grand piano next to the open bar just off the lobby.

Lennie inched a little closer. "How are your ribs?" She almost seemed to reach out to touch him, but like last time, she pulled back.

"Why do you think you can't touch me, Loba?"

Lennie pressed her palms together. "I don't know."

"You always say that." He studied her face. "But you always do."

She worked her lips to one side. Then the other. Her eyes dipped. "I guess I'm not sure when you would be okay with me touching you."

"Then I have an easy answer for you." He ignored the anger working in at whoever made Lennie think her touch would ever be unwanted. "I want you touching me always."

CHAPTER 19

IT WAS EASY to forget where they were.

Standing right in the middle of the lobby in the most exclusive hotel in Cincinnati, with any number of eyes on them.

Rico pulled her close. "But I won't make you touch me first, Loba."

She relaxed into him, eyes closing as his hand worked down the back of her head and over her hair, the tips of his fingers pressing into her scalp in slow circles. A soft sound slid from her lips.

A low rumble moved through Rico's chest. "You make me wild, Loba."

It was almost unbelievable to her. To be desired like Rico claimed.

To desire him back. Possibly with the same ferocity.

Part of her still struggled to believe it was true. That Rico really felt the way he claimed.

But the rest of her wanted to take it and run with it.

The freedom it brought was a temptation she didn't realize existed.

Being desired wasn't something she knew she craved until recently. Even then she thought it was simply about feeling wanted.

It was turning out to be so much more.

"I've got our room keys." Abe strode over and passed a card off to Rico. "We've got three side by side."

"Three?" Lennie's phone dinged in her purse, signaling a text message. She fished around for it as Elise came their way.

"One King suite and a set of Queen rooms with a shared door." Abe handed a key to Elise.

Lennie finally found her phone and pulled it free, reading the text from Heidi.

You're welcome.

"I figured I knew who the King room belonged to." Abe shot Rico a grin. "Unless you want to switch and give me the King room?"

"Not a chance." Rico kept her close, one hand curved against her hip as they followed the bellmen to the fourth floor. Their rooms were at the end of the hall, the doors separated by an inside corner. They waited as the bellmen dropped off their bags. As soon as they were tipped and gone Lennie peeked into the room.

"Holy shit." Elise came in behind her. "This is even nicer than I expected." She walked to the line of windows overlooking historic Hyde Park. "Maybe potential death is worth getting to stay here."

"We're not going to die." Lennie went to stand at her side. "Rico and Abe won't let it happen."

"You only think that because Rico is rocking your honey pot." Elise eyed her as she crossed her arms. "You okay with sharing a room? I can be the bitch and tell the boys they get the queen rooms and we can stay here if you want."

Lennie leaned her head on Elise's shoulder. "You are never a bitch, you know that, right?"

Elise frowned as she looked back out over the gardens. "I've recently been told otherwise."

"That's because Rob is an asshole." It was common knowledge in the office, even before this recent incident. "And creepy as shit."

"Right?" Elise's head came her way. "He had a certain ick factor." She shook her head. "Chandler's the one who hired him. That shit wouldn't have flown if he hadn't been there."

The former co-owner of Investigative Resources was also an asshole. More so than any of them actually realized, but the fact that he was dead because of it made that slightly more palatable. "I wonder what Mona and Eva could have done with the company if Chandler hadn't been there to drag them down."

"Doesn't really matter now." Elise's lips almost lifted into a smile. "It worked out well for us in the end."

"Except for the part where we're hiding in a hotel because someone might want to kill us." Lennie tipped her head from side to side. "Again."

"You wanted excitement." Elise wiggled her brows. "You're getting it."

"Be careful what you wish for I guess."

"I'll keep that in mind." Elise glanced toward the door where Rico and Abe were talking in hushed tones. "You sleeping with me or Rico the Freako?"

"Definitely him." She lifted one shoulder. "No offense."

"At least one of us is getting visits from the orgasm fairy." Elise sighed. "Have one for me."

"That sounds—"

"Like something a good friend would do." Elise grinned. "And not gross in any way." She pointed Lennie's way as she backed toward the door. "You should also say that when it happens, 'this one's for Elise'. It won't be weird at all."

"I'm sure it won't." Lennie couldn't stop the smile on her face. "You're my favorite."

Elise paused, her grin turning to a genuine smile. "There's no one else I would rather be potentially killed with."

"Same." Her smile held as Elise left. When she was gone, Lennie turned to the small sitting area along the windows. She ran one hand along the fabric of the sofa as she turned toward the bed.

And stopped.

Rico stood at the closed door to the room, his eyes on her. "You like the room."

"I do." Lennie bit off the rest of the words that wanted to come out. Held them back out of fear.

Fear she was no longer letting hold her back.

"I like that I'm sharing it with you more." It didn't come out easily, but she managed to say it anyway.

Rico was silent, his eyes never moving as her words hung in the air between them.

"Come to me, Loba."

She only hesitated for a heartbeat. Only considered it for a moment.

Then she pushed back the awkward way it felt to cross the room while he watched her, and slowly moved his way. With each step her focus moved farther from how she felt, and closer to the look in his eyes.

Because the look in his eyes made her feel like something she'd never been before.

A wanted woman.

A woman who knew she was wanted.

And part of her thought there might be power in that. In knowing you were wanted so desperately by a man you wanted back.

She stopped right in front of him and waited. Mostly because she wasn't sure what to do next.

"You are beautiful, Lenore." Rico's eyes moved over her face as his fingers came to trace her cheek. "So beautiful." His touch trailed down the side of her neck. "So sexy." His body came close, barely brushing against hers. "I want to touch you all the time."

She closed her eyes as his hands warmed her skin. "You can touch me all you want."

"It will be too much for you, Loba, if I touch you all I want."

Her lids lifted to find his eyes on hers. "But I like when you touch me." She leaned into the hand on her face. "It makes me feel better." She almost winced at the neediness the statement insinuated.

Almost tried to take it back.

But she'd spent her life thinking she'd never feel this way about a man. Thinking she was destined to surface-level relationships with nothing more than a feeling of fondness on her end.

And maybe she'd done it to herself. Maybe the fears she harbored held her back more than she realized.

Or maybe she simply hadn't met her person yet.

Maybe it took that person to bring out these feelings in her. Maybe her desire was tied to more than biology.

"I like it when you touch me too."

She wanted to touch him. So much. But a lifetime was difficult to overcome in a few days. "You still scare me."

Rico shook his head. "I don't scare you, Lenore." His hand found hers and he lifted it to his face, curving her hand against the square line of his jaw. "What we could have is what scares you."

Her stomach tightened at the accuracy of his words. "Why do you think that?"

"I don't think. I know." His hand pinned hers in place, holding it tight to his skin. "Because it is what scared me." The back of the fingers on his free hand skimmed across her cheek. "I didn't want this again, Loba. I didn't want the risk."

The admission was a stab to her gut. "Oh."

His lips curved in a slow smile. "I like the disappointment on your face." The hand holding hers in place dropped. "But there's no reason for you to be disappointed." His hands both came to her face, resting along her jaw and neck, warm and solid. "You hunted me, Loba."

"I didn't."

"You did." He leaned closer. "And I hunted you back."

It was a revelation of sorts. The real reason she was always passed over by men.

She passed over as much as they did.

She wasn't really interested in any of them. They probably saw it. Knew she was exactly what she'd been called.

Cold.

Detached.

Frigid.

Because she was. To them.

None of those men knew her.

She didn't know any of them. Why would she want them? Their attention.

But she'd watched Rico from afar for months. Gotten to know him without the danger of having to let him know her back.

She saw how he treated his friends. The men at his side.

The women at hers.

He was a man worthy of her interest. Her attention.

Her desire.

"Loba," Rico's hold on her face lost some of its weight, "I don't like that look in your eyes."

"You put it there." The words were breathless with an excitement she'd never known.

A power she didn't know existed, let alone that she would one day hold it.

Power over a man.

Sexual power.

Lennie reached out to rest one palm in the center of his chest, slowly dragging it down.

"Lenore—"

"Ricardo." She pressed against the solid plane of Rico's stomach, pushing him toward the sofa at his back.

The dark brown shade of his eyes went almost black. "I don't think you know what you're doing."

She definitely did not.

She was going to do it anyway.

No uncertainty.

No doubt.

No fear.

Lennie pushed a little harder as his steps slowed, the heady feeling swimming around her insides a drug that she wanted more of.

This was why women flirted.

Tossed their heads back when they laughed.

Bit their bottom lip.

She'd watched it countless times, wondering what purpose any of it served.

This was the purpose.

Rico bumped into the sofa and she gave him one more little shove, being careful not to bump his ribs too hard as she knocked him to the plush cushions.

He stared up at her looking a little uncertain. A little off-balance.

A little scared.

"Now what, Loba?" His voice was husky. Rough.

Too bad she didn't really have an answer for him. She was flying by the seat of her pants on this one.

Maybe that was a good place to start.

Lennie grabbed the hem of her shirt and lifted it up, pulling the soft jersey printed with Alaskan Security's logo over her head before tossing it to one side.

As she reached to unhook her bra his nostrils flared, stoking this newfound sense of sexuality she possessed.

Because he brought it to her.

The bra went along with the shirt, hitting the ground with a soft sound that was hidden by the drag of air Rico sucked in.

She paused, expecting him to reach for her, try to touch her, pull her closer.

Instead Rico sat perfectly still, the silent intensity that drew her to him burning in the darkness of his eyes. It emboldened her. Spurred her on.

Made her brave.

Lennie hooked her thumb into the waistband of her shorts and worked the button loose before dragging down the zipper. The cut of the shorts required a wiggle to work them over the fullness of her hips.

"*Dios mío.*" Rico wiped one hand down his face in a move that sent her pulse racing with the excitement she'd been chasing.

Looking for in all the wrong places.

Because maybe the only excitement she needed was right in front of her.

She kicked her shorts away and stood in front of him. Naked. Unafraid.

Empowered.

Rico still didn't reach for her. The only bit of him that moved was his chest as it rose and fell in short, sharp sweeps.

So she kept going.

Lennie slowly eased down, lowering toward the floor.

"Loba." His tone held a hint of warning.

And it didn't scare her in the least.

Lennie rested her palms on his legs, skimming them up the width of his muscular thighs as she dropped to the plush carpet.

To her knees.

A position of submission that was anything but.

She held his heated gaze as her hands continued their path, moving up to the waistband of the tactical pants he always wore. Her breath stopped as she reached the button and zipper. She'd never been this forward in her life.

Never wanted to be.

Sex was a necessary activity.

It was fine. Palatable.

Nothing she ever sought out on her own.

Not until this minute with this man.

She wanted to pursue him. Wanted to be forward. Wanted all the things she never really did before.

She just wanted him.

Rico didn't stop her as she unfastened his pants, but he watched every move she made like he might grab her at any time.

Put an end to this moment.

The line of his dick was pressed against his stomach by the constraints of the pants, but the second that impediment was removed it bobbed free.

She should be ashamed of looking at it the way she was, but there was something oddly beautiful about the stretch of his skin. The soft smoothness covering something so rigid.

Lennie crawled her fingers closer, wanting to touch him the way he'd touched himself that night in the shower. She'd memorized the squeeze of his fingers. The pull of his fist.

Replayed it more times than she should have.

Imagined what it might be like to be the one doing it.

But now she didn't have to imagine anymore.

Rico sucked in a breath but she didn't even pause. Didn't hesitate.

His skin was hot as she ran her palm down his length in a long stroke before pulling it back free. She fisted him again, working her way to the base before once again sliding back, eyes never leaving the sight of where she touched him.

A drop of moisture beaded at the slit, tempting her to push herself more.

To take what she wanted.

To own what she could be.

Lennie dropped her head, lips parting as they slid against him. Over him. Tongue sliding over the tip of him before she pulled him deeper.

"Fuck." Rico's hands came to the sides of her head, not pushing or pulling, but tangling in her hair, winding it back. His head fell back as she swallowed him down again, eyes closing as her name fell from his lips. "Lenore."

She'd never even considered the thought this act could be pleasurable for a woman. Never once thought it might be something she'd ever enjoy.

But seeing what she could do, the power she held over this man, it was a high she might never want to give up.

Suddenly Rico's hold on her tightened, stopping her. He scooted forward and eased his ass to the floor pushing her back a little in the process.

She grabbed his shoulders to avoid falling over. "What are you doing?"

"You didn't think you would be the only one having their fun tonight, did you?" His head tipped back to lie against the cushion where he just sat. "On your knees, Loba. I want to taste you."

Lennie didn't move. Mostly because she wasn't one-hundred percent sure what he meant.

Rico straightened, his face coming close to hers. "I want your pussy on my face, Loba."

"Now?" It squeaked out.

She was thinking they'd be easing into all the things. All the adventures.

"Not now, Loba." Rico's lips curved into a slow smile. "Always."

CHAPTER 20

"YOU WON'T BE able to breathe."

"Then I will die happy." Rico let his head fall back again. "Bring it to me, Loba."

Lennie hesitated. She wasn't used to this. Wasn't used to being comfortable with a man.

With what they did together.

Her eyes moved over the sofa.

"I can wait all night." Rico scooted his ass away from the sofa a little more, easing the strain on his neck just in case he had to make good on that offer.

"What if I don't like it?"

The question sent a rush of anger through his veins. Knowing there was a reason she asked it.

And that reason was most definitely a man.

"If *you* don't like something then *I* don't like it." Rico straightened. "This is about finding what we both like." He carefully pushed up from the ground, catching her around the waist as he moved, doing his best not to aggravate his injured ribs. "Then we do more of it."

Lennie seemed to relax as he stood. "I don't know what I like."

Once they were on their feet Rico pushed her toward the bed. "Then we will be busy." When her thighs bumped the mattress he pulled her against him, lifting her up, ignoring the stab in his lungs as he did. He would welcome pain anytime it was for her.

Lennie tipped back and he let her fall, head to pillows, body to sheets.

He tugged his shirt off, being careful not to overextend, trying to avoid making the injuries to his ribs steal the breath from his lungs.

Rico shoved his open pants to the floor, climbing onto the bed as soon as they'd cleared his feet.

Maybe pushing her wasn't the best way to start. Maybe the best way to start was in comfortable territory. Use that to tease Lennie along the path she wanted to take.

He grabbed the covers and pulled them up, letting the sheets fall over them. He might be perfectly comfortable with his naked body, but that didn't mean Lennie was as relaxed about hers.

And he wanted her relaxed right now. Worrying about nothing but what felt good.

And what didn't.

Rico wrapped around her, needing to be closer. He slid his hands through her hair. Over her face.

He'd been chasing the high of sex for years. Using it as a drug to carry him past the suffering of loss.

It didn't work. The pain was still there, festering like a neglected wound.

Sex was a band-aid on a broken bone. It fixed nothing.

And now here he was. Still broken.

But no longer wishing things were different.

"I want to be yours, Loba." Rico ran one finger down the center of her forehead and along the slope of her nose. "I want to be who you can't wait to come home to." He traced along her lips. "The one you tell your secrets." Rico followed the line of her jaw. "The one you trust more than anyone else."

Lennie's lashes lifted and her eyes fixed on him. "You already know my secrets."

Rico smiled. "Not all of them." He leaned in to run his nose along the side of hers. "I don't know your favorite way to come."

The soft intake of her breath shot straight to his dick.

"I love when you gasp, Loba."

Lennie's lower lip slid between her teeth.

"Talk to me." Rico found one hand, lacing her fingers with his. "Tell me what you're thinking."

The line of her teeth pressed deeper into her lip. Finally it slid free and she took a slow breath. "I was just thinking I might like it if we had sex like this." She hesitated just a heartbeat. "Face to face."

She could have asked him for anything and he would have given it to her.

But this—

This would test his limits. His ability to restrain the side of him she called to.

Lured from where it hid out of self-preservation.

"We don't have to." Lennie tried to move away.

Steal her closeness.

Rico pulled her back to him. He rolled onto her, the tip of his nose meeting the tip of hers. "If I have you like this then we won't be fucking, Lenore." His knee caught one of her thighs and pushed it out, making room for his hips to settle between them. "Are you ready for something more than fucking?"

"You mean am I ready for you to be mine?"

He tucked his chin in a small nod. "*Si*."

Her lip went between her teeth again, but this time it was only for a second. The breath before she spoke was shorter and sharper. "I kind of thought you already were."

It was what held him back. The reason he tried to keep his head.

Thinking she was unsure. Still expecting this to be the fun, fast, rush she'd claimed to be in search of.

It was what he'd hoped to give her at first, but Lennie quickly dug into him with claws he should have seen coming.

Because she was every bit the wolf he called her.

And he would let her shred him every day.

And every night.

Rico caught her mouth with his, holding it hostage the way she held him. Owning it the way she owned him.

Her arms came around his neck, holding tight as he fought the need driving him. The need to be hers. To give her everything he had.

Everything he was.

The second he was sheathed he sank into her body, his forehead meeting hers as he seated fully. He couldn't stop touching her. Holding her face. Her hands. Eyes locked together as he rocked into her, trying to steal as many seconds from this moment as he could.

Because this was a moment he would remember forever.

The moment he came full-circle.

The moment the man he was met the man he became.

And the woman they would love.

Because he would love Lennie. There was no question in that.

If he didn't already.

Her soft hands gripped his shoulders, fingertips digging in as her skin flushed, the perfect pink creeping across her face and neck.

"Are you thinking about what we're doing, Lenore? Is that why your skin is pink?" Rico caught both her hands and twined his fingers with hers, holding them to the mattress at each side of her head. "Are you thinking about all the other things we will do?"

The flush got deeper.

"I will do everything to you, Loba. I will let you do everything to me." His jaw was tight making it hard to fight any words free.

But he wanted to talk to her.

Always.

To touch her.

Always.

To be like this with her.

Always.

"Tell me I belong to you." He needed to hear it. Needed to know she wanted to possess him the way he wanted to possess her.

"You belong to me." It was quiet and soft and fucking perfect.

"Say you own me."

"I own you." It was a little louder. A little more sure.

And it was hell on his ability to restrain himself. Rico fought one hand loose from hers and shoved it between their bodies. "Then take what you want from me, Loba." He found her swollen clit.

Her head tipped back and her eyes rolled closed.

"Look at me, Loba." He wanted her to see him.

She might be the only one who really did.

Her lids lifted, slow and heavy as her lips parted. She pulled him down, chest to chest, mouth to mouth.

Her thighs gripped his hips, making it harder to move, harder to not move.

Her hands pressed into the skin of his face, holding tight as her body went rigid under his.

Eyes locked onto his as she came.

Watching as he joined her.

Rico fell into her, face buried in the soft pile of her hair, forcing him to fight for every breath he managed.

But he'd give up air to be close to her.

To be hers.

And he was.

He was hers and whether she was ready to say it or not, she was his.

****

"IT LOOKS DESERTED." Rico peered through the binoculars at the two-story house in an upscale subdivision just outside of the city. "The lawn looks high."

"This seems like the kind of place that checks that shit with a ruler." Abe sat perfectly still in the passenger seat of their newly-rented SUV. "Which also means it's the kind of place that will notice two men camped out on the curb."

"I think we should go in." Rico set the binoculars down as a car approached. It slowed as it went past them and he made a show of looking at his cell, hoping they looked lost instead of suspicious.

"This isn't Alaska, man. We can't just go around doing whatever the fuck we want knowing someone will be there to clean the mess up." Abe's eyes stayed on the car as it slowly rolled down the street.

"That's why we can't make a mess." Rico set his phone down and shifted the SUV into gear. They'd barely been there ten minutes and already clearly aroused suspicion, which meant it was time to get moving.

"Why couldn't he live someplace a little less…" Abe tipped his head and smiled at a man out getting his mail. "Neighborhood watchy?"

"To be even more of a pain in the ass."

Vincent called Abe early this morning to let him know what they'd been able to find on the computer Rob was trying to take with him.

And it wasn't pretty.

Rico scanned the house Rob owned as they drove past it. "Maybe we'll get lucky and he'll be there when we go in."

"That's exactly what I'm talking about when I say we can't go around making messes." Abe huffed out a breath. "I know you want to kill him. I want to fucking kill him too, but we can't."

"Maybe we should invite him to Alaska." Rico watched the house in the side mirror, looking for anything that might give them a clue where Rob was now. "All expenses paid."

"Maybe we don't have to kill him." Abe watched the roads as they pulled out of the subdivision. "Maybe he's in the pile of the building he most likely blew up and they just haven't found him yet."

It was one of their working theories. That Rob was responsible for the explosion at Investigative Resources.

Rico turned out of the neighborhood as he brought up another of the possibilities. "Or maybe someone else was trying to clean up the mess he made."

"Vincent's working on finding the other men involved. He said it might take another day." He dropped back in his seat, frowning. "Too bad we can't just have Heidi fucking do it."

Rico turned into a small strip mall and parked. "This isn't our jurisdiction."

Abe shifted in his seat, stretching his long legs out in the floorboards. "Technically it's not GHOST's jurisdiction either."

They'd sent the laptop to Vincent, thinking the team at GHOST would be the least invested and best equipped to find whatever might be hidden on the hard drive.

And maybe they were. Maybe Heidi wouldn't have been any faster at digging through everything Rob tried to obliterate.

Rico tapped his fingers against the wheel. "What else do you think he had in that office?"

That was the information they could really use. Knowing the reason the building was taken down.

"Maybe nothing." Abe dropped his head to the rest. "At this point we don't know who did what. Maybe Rob's not connected to the explosion at all."

"Maybe Rob's dead." Rico glanced Abe's way. "We should check in with John. See if he's heard anything from Rob or his attorney."

Abe straightened. "That's a good fucking idea." He pointed at Rico. "Why in the hell didn't we think of that sooner?"

"Because this whole thing is a shit show." Rico pulled out of their spot, resisting the urge to make another pass at Rob's house. "I can't wait to fucking fly home and forget this whole damn trip."

"Hopefully that's what happens." Abe pulled out his phone and thumbed through the screens. "Hell, if Rob's disappeared then there's no one to keep pushing for your arrest and we can leave as soon as Pierce gives us the go-ahead."

Rico split his focus between Abe's call with John and the roads around them as he worked his way back toward the hotel where Lennie and Elise were holed up. He carefully moved through traffic, taking a path that would make a tail obvious.

So far no one was following them, which eased the tension making every muscle in his body ache.

Abe ended the call but immediately made another one. Pierce's voice was audible even across the car.

Probably because he sounded pissed as hell.

He must have heard from Vincent too.

Abe's answers were short and sharp and in less than a minute he was off the phone again, this time setting it in the console between them.

"Pierce find out about the videos?"

Abe tipped his head in a nod. "Yup."

"He coming here to try to kill him?"

"He's sending reinforcements. We're staying until we find Rob and bring him to Alaska." Abe shook his head. "Not sure what Pierce is going to do when he finds out Rob clearly wasn't alone in his business venture."

"How did so many fucked-up people work at the same damn place?" He'd been trying not to think about it. Trying not to let the violation crawl too deep.

Because Abe was right.

He'd kill Rob with his bare hands if he had the chance.

"I'm going to go out on a limb and say it might have all gone back to one single fuck-up." Abe dragged one hand down the outside of his arm. "Chandler was a psychopath. Willing to do whatever it took to get where he wanted."

"And filming women like that was what could get him what he wanted?" The temperature in Rico's body started to climb as he thought of all the women that had been violated. Women who worked at Investigative Resources. Women who came there looking for help. Women Rob managed to lure to that nice house they were just looking at. Women they had yet to identify the location on.

There were hundreds of videos on a site connected to Rob, and it all started with a handful of uploads he tried to delete from the laptop Abe was smart enough to keep his hands on.

"Who's he sending?" Rico turned into the short drive that ran along the entrance of the hotel.

"Tyson, Reed, and Jameson." Abe grabbed his phone and tucked it into the pocket of his jeans as they climbed out of the SUV.

"When will they be here?" The tightness in Rico's chest eased a little knowing there would be more protection here for Lennie and Elise.

"They're flying out first thing in the morning. Should be here before dinner."

"I think we should consider flying the girls home." Rico's steps sped as he moved through the hotel

"I agree." Abe punched the fourth floor button as they waited for the elevator doors to close. "There's no benefit to having them here."

"I don't know that I'd say that." Being apart from Lennie wasn't anything he was excited about, but it was better than the alternative. "But there's no reason to risk them getting caught up in this."

Rico snapped the key card into the reader outside the room he shared with Lennie and pushed the door open. The air left his lungs on a swift exhale at the sight inside.

Lennie smiled at him from where she sat in the center of the bed they shared last night. Hopefully one night of many.

"You're back." She pressed her lips together as her eyes dipped to the plates circling where she and Elise were camped out, enjoying all that room-service had to offer. "We weren't sure how long you would be gone."

"I'll just head back to my room." Elise grabbed a plate with each hand.

"No." Rico crossed to the side of the bed closest to Lennie. "You stay. Abe and I need to make a few calls." He held Lennie's gaze. "I just wanted to make sure you were okay."

Her head tipped in a little nod, lips holding a soft smile. "We're okay."

"Good." Rico leaned one hand onto the mattress and caught her face with the other. He

274

pressed a kiss to her temple. "I will be back very soon."

She gave him a soft smile. "Good."

CHAPTER 21

"WHEN WERE YOU going to tell us you were planning to ship us back alone?" Elise stood in the center of Abe's hotel room, hands on her hips as she stared him down.

"We aren't shipping you back alone." Abe stood in front of the windows. "Rico is flying you back."

Elise eyed Abe. "What are you doing then?"

Lennie was equally irritated, but so far Elise was handling the situation perfectly so she was just going to let her have at it.

"I'm staying here with Tyson, Jameson, and Reed. GHOST has requested Rogue's assistance in dealing with what's being labeled a terrorist attack."

Elise snorted. "It wasn't a terrorist attack."

"A building was taken down by an unknown assailant. That is classified as a possible act of terrorism." Abe walked toward Elise. "Add in that the office targeted had a history of investigating some of the most powerful people in the country, and the possibility only increases."

Elise's brows lifted. "Some of the most powerful people in the country?" She snorted. "We should have had you write the copy for our ads."

"There's no telling how this will play out." Abe crossed his arms like it would make Elise less apt to argue with him. "You will be safer in Alaska."

It made sense. There was no reason for her and Elise to stay here.

But leaving didn't make her happy.

"What if we just stay here in the hotel?" Lennie took over where Elise left off. "We can stay in our rooms until this is all over and go back then." She hesitated just a second. "Together."

Rico studied her for long enough she almost squirmed under his dark stare. Finally he let out a breath and came her way, wrapping one arm around her. "Come on, Loba. Let's go talk." He held her close as they walked through the halls of the hotel, making their way out to the enclosed patio area. A bench sat along the wall surrounding the space, tucked into a tiny gazebo covered with climbing pink roses.

Rico sat on the bench and immediately pulled her down beside him, angling her upper body across his before wrapping both arms around her. "I don't want you away from me, Loba. Not at all."

Lennie stretched her legs across the unoccupied side of the bench and rested her head against Rico's chest. "Are you going to at least tell me what's happening?"

"I can't tell you all of what's going on right now." His hand smoothed down her hair, fingers tracing along her skin.

She tipped her head back to meet his eyes. "Why?"

"Because I don't know enough. Right now telling you what I know will not help you." He inhaled and let it back out. "It will only upset you for no reason."

"Or maybe it will upset me for a very good reason." Lennie scoffed. "I work for the same company you do. Why do you get to know everything and I don't?"

"This isn't about Alaskan Security, Loba. Right now this is about something else."

"Does anyone at Intel know what's going on?"

Rico shook his head.

"So we're not involved at all?"

"Right now this is Vincent's investigation."

The head of GHOST was just beginning to step from the shadows, and even then it was only because he realized Alaskan Security was worth just as much to him as he was to them.

"Then why isn't Shadow coming to handle this?" Shadow served as the go-between for Alaskan Security and GHOST up until very recently. "Isn't that their job? To do Vincent's bidding?"

"Shadow is unavailable."

Lennie's throat tightened. "So when Shadow is busy Rogue is going to step in?"

What Rico did before was scary enough.

But working for a division of the government that didn't actually exist was terrifying.

278

"This is what I do, Loba. What I'm good at." Rico's touch continued on, moving over her arms and back. "It saved me when I lost everything." He pulled her closer, going quiet for a minute. When he continued his voice was softer, his words slower. "My mother was sick when Paola left. She knew how difficult it was for me. I think knowing she couldn't fix the pain I was in was too much. It broke her heart." His chin rested on her head. "When she died I had nothing left to lose."

Lennie's stomach clenched and her eyes watered.

"Talk to me, Loba. Tell me what you are thinking. I need to know."

She shook her head, holding back emotions that were too strong too soon.

Admitting them would be as stupid as having them felt.

"Lenore." Rico's voice made her jump a little. "Please." An edge of desperation tinged the last word.

Lennie cleared her throat, trying to ease the tightness there. "I just don't like thinking about that."

"Why?"

"I just don't."

Rico's finger pressed under her chin, forcing her eyes his way again. "Tell me why."

She pressed her lips together, holding back like she knew she had to.

Rico was different than the men she'd known before, but there were limits, even for him.

"Why don't you trust what I tell you, Loba?" He leaned closer until his lips were just above hers. "I want all that you keep from me. I want all of you, Lenore. The good. The bad. All of it."

"I know." He'd made it very clear to her, but she still struggled to believe Rico really meant what he said.

"Then why don't you give it to me?"

"Because I'm scared." That was a truth she could give him.

"What are you scared of? Are you scared of me?" His eyes held hers. "Or are you scared of what might happen if I mean what I say to you?"

The complete accuracy of what he said made her suck in a breath.

She'd tried to hide from the fear. Tried to pretend it didn't exist.

Because who was scared of that? Of something real?

Of something that might be everything you've ever wanted but didn't believe could exist.

Rico's lips pulled into a slow smile. "That is what I thought." He laced the fingers of one hand with hers. "Tomorrow I have to take you home to Alaska."

"But—"

His expression sharpened and one black brow lifted. "This is not an option. Abe is right. There is nothing to gain and everything to lose by having you and Elise here." Rico's thumb dragged across the skin of her hand as he continued on. "You will have plenty of time to think about what you want while I'm gone." He lifted her hand to his lips, running them along the back of her palm. "But there is no halfway with me, Loba. Not where you're concerned." His mouth stayed on her skin. "I want all of you. Body. Mind. Soul. I want to give you all of me."

Her eyes wouldn't blink. All she could do was stare at him in disbelief.

Was he saying what it sounded like he was saying?

"I want you in my bed every night." Rico lifted his lips from her hand and leaned close to trace them along her neck. "I want you to be mine in every way. I want to be yours in every way." His voice was low in her ear. "I want it all and I want it now."

She'd spent years holding back. Always keeping a safe distance between her and anyone she was with.

It was why she'd been called all the things she had.

But it wasn't out of awkwardness or insecurity. Not really.

It was out of fear.

That's what it always came back to for her.

Fear.

And wasn't that why she moved to Alaska? To take on the fear that held her back in ways she could admit.

And ways she was only just beginning to accept.

"Rico, I—"

"Shh." His thumb came to brush across her lips, cutting off what she was about to say. "I have a surprise for you before I take you home."

"You two ready?" Abe's rough voice stole her attention.

He and Elise stood just outside the doors leading to the hotel.

"Where are we going?" Panic brewed in her belly. "I thought we weren't leaving until tomorrow?"

"That's right." Rico eased her up, wincing a little as he stood.

An idea caught in her mind. One that would stop the upset taking over her insides. "You should stay with us." Her eyes went to the ribs he'd clearly been favoring. "You're hurt."

He smiled. "That's not how it works, Loba. You know that."

Lennie didn't resist the frown twisting her mouth.

"You should be careful making that face at me, Lenore." He pulled her against his side and leaned into her ear as they walked toward Abe and Elise. "It makes me want to prove I can take it away."

The ache in her stomach bloomed into butterflies almost immediately.

Rico laughed low in his chest. "That look is even worse."

Abe turned and started walking toward the front of the hotel.

Lennie looked at Elise as they followed Abe through the halls, hoping her friend would clue her in about where they were going. Elise lifted her shoulders in a shrug. "I tried to put on my going-out dress and he shut me down."

"I saw that dress." Abe stepped through the automatic door, his eyes scanning the space just outside. "And I don't feel like beating men off you with a damn stick." He reached for Elise. "Come on. Stay close to me."

Elise's eyes went wide as Abe wrapped one arm around her and moved them across the drive to where the SUV was idling. The valet jumped out and tipped his head their way. Abe immediately opened the back door and tucked Elise inside before closing it and once again scanning the space.

"Why are we going somewhere?" Lennie tried to get more information out of Rico as he opened the passenger's door and pressed her toward it.

"Because we are." He glanced down at her feet. "All the way in, Loba."

She pulled her legs inside and a second later her door was closed too.

"So much for a fun trip." Elise huffed out a breath. "We didn't get to go out once."

"At least we got to eat everywhere you wanted." Lennie watched Rico through the windshield as he slowly rounded the front of the SUV, his dark eyes missing nothing of their surroundings.

"That doesn't make me feel any better." Elise slumped down in her seat. "This whole thing has been a shit show."

Abe opened his door and eased into the space that barely fit his tall body. "That's a hell of a pout on your face, Babe."

"I'm not pouting." Elise turned her face toward the window, angling her whole body away from Abe.

"Good." Abe hooked one arm across the back of his seat, his attention split between the front of the SUV and the back as Rico drove them through the streets of Cincinnati like he'd lived there his whole life.

"Am I still going to learn how to drive?" Lennie wanted to touch him, but their conversation earlier had her feeling a little unbalanced.

Not uncertain.

Just unsure.

"The first thing you're both going to learn is weaponry." Abe ducked his head to peer out Elise's window. "Then we'll go from there."

Elise tipped her head to peek at him over one shoulder. "What kind of weapons?"

"Guns." Abe's attention went out his window. "I'd feel a hell of a lot better right now if you were armed too."

"Too?" Elise leaned away from him. "Do you have a gun right now?"

"I always have a gun, Babe." Abe shot her a wink. "Or two."

Elise's eyes widened. "But that hotel said no guns." Her gaze moved over Abe's long frame. "There was a big sticker right on the door."

"I saw it." Abe's gaze settled on Elise. "I ignored it."

Lennie clasped her hands in her lap as she fought the urge to touch Rico.

He always touched her. It was calming. Grounding.

To feel like someone was there with you. Holding you down in the best possible way.

So why couldn't she just tell him the truth? End this oddness she felt.

Take the step she so desperately wanted to take.

Rico merged onto 75 northbound and quickly cut across traffic, moving into the left-most lane. Almost immediately he was cut off by someone driving ten miles an hour slower than they were.

"What in the—" He jumped into the next lane over and tried to get around the car that cut him off.

The car sped up.

"Are you kidding me right now?" Rico was forced to slow down as he closed in on the truck in front of him.

"I tried to tell you traffic here was bad." Lennie smiled a little. "That's why I didn't know Luca was there. Everyone here drives like that."

"This is stupid." Rico slid into the slow lane, taking every bit of the space available to pass an aging sedan before hopping back toward the center. "The left lane is the passing lane. He's not fucking passing anyone."

"They don't really follow that rule here in Ohio." Elise leaned forward. "The little old men love the left lane. They think they own it."

Rico scoffed as another car changed lanes, cutting off his path to a gap in the faster lane.

Lennie reached across the console without really meaning to, and definitely without thinking about it. Her hand was on Rico's thigh before she knew she'd done it.

And then it was too late to snap it back.

Rico's hand twisted where it held the wheel, squeezing a second before relaxing. His shoulder lowered as his free hand came to grab hers, his warm fingers sliding between hers.

The ride was quiet as they moved away from the city, Rico and Abe both silent as their eyes constantly moved.

After about twenty minutes Rico took an exit for a newly built-up area where an Ikea was erected less than ten years ago. He passed the road leading to the superstore and turned into a place she actually knew pretty well.

It was the one restaurant she'd really looked forward to eating at while they were here. It wasn't anything fancy. It was actually a chain, but there wasn't a single one anywhere in Alaska.

"Damn, Lennie." Elise leaned forward as Rico parked. "He brought you to Mellow Mushroom."

Her love of the pizza place was well known in the office. She frequently came in Monday mornings with leftovers for her lunch.

Elise wiggled her brows at Rico. "Better watch yourself, Slick. She'll end up falling in love with you."

Rico looked Elise right in the eye. "That's the plan."

Rico and Abe got out and closed their doors.

Elise peeked around the seat at Lennie. "I am so freaking jealous of you right now."

"You don't want to be in love." Lennie eyed her friend, trying to move the conversation along. "You just want someone to sex you."

"I definitely want someone to sex me, and because of freaking Rob I'm not going to get any of that while I'm here either."

Their doors opened at the same time.

Rico held his hand out for Lennie. She gave him a little smile and immediately grabbed on in spite of the fear telling her to pull back. The minute her palm hit his the fear was forgotten.

Or maybe gone.

"Come, Loba. Let's make sure you enjoy your last night in town."

She let him pull her out of the seat. Abe and Rico moved them into the restaurant with a speed that indicated just how big of a deal this venture out into the world was.

Lennie hesitated in the vestibule. "Are you sure we should be here?"

Rico's arm was banded tight across her back and he was as close as was possible to be in decent company. "Everything is fine, Loba. I wouldn't have brought you out here if I wasn't positive you would be safe."

She eyed the door leading into the restaurant.

Surely no one would do anything inside a crowded establishment.

If anyone was trying to do anything to her at all.

This could all be for nothing.

Lennie dipped her head in a little nod. "Okay."

Rico smiled wide. "Okay." He pulled open the door and led her inside.

The smell was so familiar it hit her like a ton of bricks, taking her back to a time when her life looked very different.

But the smells coming from the kitchen weren't the only thing that was familiar.

Lennie leaned, looking toward the room that ran along the front of the building as a voice she knew well carried out between the open brick arches.

Her sister's head popped into view, her mouth splitting into a wide smile. "Lennie Bear!" She rushed in, grabbing Lennie in a tight hug that squeezed the breath from her lungs.

Or maybe it was the man at her side, watching with an almost-there smile, who made it hard to breathe.

CHAPTER 22

THIS WAS WORTH whatever they had to do to make it happen.

The look on Lennie's face.

The clear happiness shining in her eyes.

A set of kids came running, squealing as they collided with Lennie's legs, latching onto her and holding tight.

Lennie dropped to her knees. "I've missed you." She scooped up their wiggling bodies and rocked them from side to side.

"We surprise you." The smallest of the group was a little girl with light hair and dark eyes. She clapped as she skipped in place. "We having a party."

"We are?" Lennie's smile hadn't dimmed at all since she realized what was going on. "That is so exciting." She stood as the two little boys each grabbed a hand and pulled her toward the room where the rest of her family was waiting for her.

Far enough from downtown he could be sure no one would be in any danger.

Lennie's sister gave Elise a hug before taking her to where the rest of the group was already seated and sipping their drinks. Lennie was passed around the room, hugging and laughing her way through the group. The last one in line was a giant of a man with warm eyes and a bald head.

"Hey, Baby." He held her the way only a father could, hanging on longer than anyone else had.

This was the right thing to do.

And not just for Lennie.

Lennie beamed at her dad, smiling so wide her cheeks had to hurt. Her eyes slowly came Rico's way.

Her father eyed him with a gaze that probably made most potential matches shrink down.

Lennie reached up to tuck a bit of her hair behind one ear. She dropped the hand to her side.

Then it slowly came his way.

Reaching.

Rico edged the crowd, making his way to where Lennie stood with her father. The man who loved her more than any other ever would.

Including him.

Her hand slid into his and she gently pulled him closer. "Dad, this is Ricardo." Her eyes stayed on Rico's face. "We—" She cleared her throat. "He's—"

"Rico. I'm the pilot for Alaskan Security." Rico reached his free hand out.

Her father gripped it in a tight shake that lasted long enough to say more than any words ever could. "Tim." His gaze was unrelenting as he continued to squeeze Rico's palm. Finally he dropped the shake. "How long you been flying?"

"Over ten years." He took a glass of water the waitress handed him with a nod and a 'thank you' before focusing back on Tim. "I was in the Colombian Air Force."

Lennie's father's brows lifted. "How'd you end up in Alaska?"

"My mother passed away and there was nothing keeping me in Colombia. The owner of the company made me an offer I couldn't refuse."

Tim almost nodded. "He seems to do that a lot."

Rico smiled. "Pierce is willing to pay for the people he wants on his team."

Lennie's father huffed out a breath. "He's willing to make an offer a young girl can't refuse."

"Dad. We talked about this." Lennie's tone was gentle but strong. "I needed a change."

"You needed the hell away from that prick Kyle." Tim's skin started to get red where it peeked out the collar of his shirt. "That asshole was so full of bullshit he might as well have been a sewer."

Lennie's eyes dropped.

"I'm sorry." Her father reached for her, wrapping her in another hug. "I'm glad you realized he didn't deserve you."

Lennie peeked Rico's way. "Me too."

A second later her sister was wrangling her kids into seats and the ordering process started. Enough pizzas were picked to feed an army, along with a few appetizers that ended up getting passed around the tables.

Rico sat at Lennie's side, across from her sister and brother-in-law, who turned out to be a pretty interesting guy. He worked in graphic design for a local company, making commercials for a few of the area colleges and sports teams.

Her parents sat at the end of the table, one of Tim's arms wrapped around his wife's shoulders, keeping her close at his side. JoAnn, her mother, was quiet and calm.

Just like Lennie.

Her sister leaned more toward their father's temperament. A little louder. A little bolder, but still kind and friendly, smiling often as they spoke about work and family.

Lennie whispered in his ear as the conversation carried on without them. "Thank you."

Rico smiled. "Are you happy, Loba?"

She tipped her head in a little nod. "Mostly."

"Mostly?"

Her smile faded. "I'm not happy that you'll be here and I'll be in Alaska."

Rico draped one arm across the back of her chair and rested his lips against her forehead, pressing a kiss to her skin. "I will be home to you soon. I promise."

It was an odd thing to say.

He hadn't called anywhere his home in years.

Because home wasn't a place. It was where the people you love were.

And he had no home.

Lennie's hand found his. "Good."

Her hand stayed in his the rest of the night, holding tight while she told her family about Alaska. What her job entailed.

As the conversation lulled her brother in law tossed his napkin over his empty plate and leaned back. "Was that building that had the explosion near where you used to work?"

"Um." Lennie reached for her glass. "It was." She swallowed down a few gulps of water.

"A building exploded?" Her sister looked from her husband to her father. "How did I not hear about that?"

Her husband shrugged. "I only heard about it from someone who works down there and actually saw it happen." He shook his head. "I don't think I saw anything about it in the news."

Her sister's brow wrinkled. "That's weird." She shrugged. "It must not have been that bad."

Rico glanced across the table to where Abe sat at Lennie's brother-in-law's side.

Abe held his gaze long enough it was clear they were both thinking the same thing.

Maybe Vincent had even more power than they realized.

Once the leftover pizza was boxed up, everyone started packing up to clear out. Lennie's sister caught one of her boys and started fighting a wet wipe across his sauce-stained mouth as she carried on a conversation with Lennie. "When are you going back?"

"Tomorrow." Lennie picked up her niece and snuggled her close. "But I'm getting better at flying. Maybe I can come back soon."

Her sister let the little boy go and he immediately ran for where his grandmother was passing homemade cookies out of a plastic storage container. "I'm so proud of you, Lennie." She reached across the table to grab Lennie's free hand. "You are doing so much that I never would have been brave enough to do."

Lennie's eyes came Rico's way a second before going back to her sister. "I was just tired of not doing things because they scared me."

"Some of the best things are the scariest." Her sister pointed to where her kids were circling the cookies. "Look at them. They're terrifying."

Lennie's head fell back on a long, loud laugh.

As they filed toward the door her sister grabbed Rico's arm. "Bring her back sometimes, will you?" She gave him a quick side hug. "And thanks for this. We've been missing her."

"I can understand that completely."

Her sister's eyes moved over his face. "I bet you can." She gave Lennie one last hug before loading her kids into their van and pulling away, waving through the window as her husband drove.

"So maybe I'm going to stop giving you shit about how much you love that place." Elise had one hand on her stomach as she fell into her seat. "The curry chicken pizza was freaking amazing."

"I told you." Lennie climbed into the SUV. "You're not the only one who knows what's good to eat."

Elise pulled her wallet out of her purse. "Fine. You can pick where we eat when we come back." She pointed her wallet toward the coffee shop right next door. "Can we get some Starbucks? My ass is dragging."

"I would say that has more to do with the fact that you're filled with carbs than a lack of caffeine." Abe leaned closer as Elise started digging through her purse frantically. "What's wrong?"

"I can't find my damn debit card." She started stacking the contents on her lap as she emptied the bag. "It has to be in here somewhere."

Abe fished out his wallet. "I got it."

Elise paused, her movements stalling out as she peeked Abe's way. "That's nice of you, but I still need to find my card."

Lennie turned toward the back seat. "Maybe it's at the hotel."

"I haven't had it out since—" Her eyes squinted a little. "Damn it." Elise reached over to shove at Abe's shoulder. "This is your fault."

"My fault? How is this my fault?"

"Because you rushed me." She slammed everything back into her purse. "You made me hurry to pack and I left my card on the counter."

Abe dodged another push. "Why was your card on the counter?"

"Because I ordered food." Elise's head fell against the seat at her back. "I have all my bills set to auto pay on that damn card." She reached for Abe's shoulder again but he caught her hand.

"You can't just shove someone when you're frustrated. You're not a fucking child."

Elise's head slowly turned his way. "Don't come at me because you only ate salad for dinner and you're still hungry."

"I'm not still hungry." Abe let her hand go. "And you're the one who started it."

"Who's being a fucking child now, Abraham?" Elise leaned as far from Abe as she could manage.

"Let's just take her to get her card." Rico drove past the coffee shop and headed toward the interstate. "It'll take two seconds."

They needed to check on the house anyway. It would tell them just how much they were up against. If there was any sign someone had been there then it would be clear Rob was probably still around and possibly more skilled than they guessed.

If nothing was bothered then maybe it meant Rob was as gone as his house indicated he was.

"Thank you, Rico." Elise crossed her arms. "That would be amazing."

"It'll be something." Abe eyed him in the rearview mirror. "Better make a list of anything else you forgot because we're not doing this again."

The drive to the house was quiet with Elise ignoring Abe and Lennie silently staring out the windshield.

He wanted to tell her so much. Ask her so much.

To know what she was thinking.

If she'd decided what she wanted from him. For them.

But it would have to wait. Possibly weeks, while he stayed here and cleaned up a mess he hoped she never knew the complete truth of.

Vincent managed to pull the site down, but the full extent of its reach spanned oceans and years.

Rico wove his way through the streets leading to the house, every turn bringing them closer to the river they'd stayed on each side of. When he was sure no one was staking out the house he pulled down the street, passing it once before circling back and finally pulling into the drive.

The little car Elise rented was still in the driveway, looking as fine as it did when they left.

The SUV was barely stopped when Elise grabbed the handle to her door, ready to bolt.

Abe grabbed her. "If you think you get to go in there you're fucking crazy." He hefted her away from the door. "You two are staying in here until we're positive the place is clear."

Rico opened his door and rested one leg on the ground outside. "Come on, Loba. Climb across."

Lennie's brows came together in confusion.

Rico motioned for her to climb across the console and into his seat. "You're in the driver's seat. If anything happens I want your foot on that gas, understand?"

"You want me to just leave you here?"

"*Si.*" Rico surveyed the yard as he fully exited the vehicle. "Come on, Loba. We can't be here long."

Lennie was across the seat in a heartbeat. "I'm not leaving you here."

"You will if you hear anything." Rico leaned down, aligning his eyes with hers. "Promise me. I can't do what I need to do if I'm worried about you being safe."

Her lips pulled into a tight purse that bordered on a frown. "I don't like this."

"You don't have to like it." He pressed a quick kiss to her lips. "You just have to do it."

Abe already had his pistol out of its holster. "Come on. Let's get this damn card so Elise can pay her fucking bills."

"Stop acting like you're doing me a favor." Elise tried to scoot out but Abe shut the door on her. She leaned forward to yell at him out Elise's open door. "I'll go in there all by myself if that's how you're going to be."

"Over my dead body." Abe wasn't even looking at her as he spoke. He tucked close to the side of the SUV, slowly working his way toward the back.

Rico met Lennie's eyes. "Promise me, Loba."

She huffed out a breath. "I promise." Lennie pointed toward where Abe was creeping toward the door. "Go. Hurry."

Rico closed her door and tucked down, moving low and fast on his way to where Abe was almost at the front of the house.

They stood on each side of the front door and waited, listening for any sign that someone was inside.

Abe reached out and pressed the doorbell.

Again they listened.

Silence.

There was no sign of movement anywhere in or around the house.

Even the girls were stock still in the SUV.

Abe punched in the code for the door. The deadbolt flipped open and a second later they were inside, one across the entry and the other right behind, moving as a single unit as they crept into the quiet house.

The scent of takeout still lingered in the air from the meal that brought them here now. Abe tipped his head toward the right and the rooms they'd occupied.

Rico nodded and they were moving again, crossing the large central space, working toward the short row of stairs leading to one set of bedrooms and bathrooms. Abe went first, clearing one room and then the next while Rico stood in the hall. Once those rooms were done they moved on, back across the main living room to the side Lennie and Elise claimed. This time Rico went in, checking rooms and closets for any sign someone was lying in wait. But this area was just as untouched as the rest.

Abe straightened, tucking his gun into the holster at the back of his pants. "Maybe Rob really is gone and this is all going to blow over."

"Good." Rico holstered his own weapon as they went toward the kitchen to retrieve Elise's forgotten card.

As they passed the open door a flash of color caught Rico's eye.

A second later an engine revved and tires screamed for traction.

"What the fuck?" Abe turned toward the front of the house as Rico started to run.

He took the stairs leading to the door in one jump. As he hit the porch the car he'd seen following them the day before raced from the driveway, cutting across the grass at the corner of the asphalt as it took the turn fast enough to make one thing very clear.

They were in pursuit.

And there was only one vehicle they could be chasing.

CHAPTER 23

"WHAT THE ACTUAL fuck is going on?" Elise gripped the front seats as she leaned forward, her eyes snapping from the back window to where Lennie sat, doing her damndest to keep the SUV as far from the car behind them as possible.

"That was freaking Rob." She'd seen him the second he jumped out of the car and started running their way.

A gun in his hand.

And all she could think of was to do exactly what Rico told her to do.

Get the hell away from there.

And take Rob with her.

"I know." Elise shimmied between the front seats, worming her way into the passenger's seat. "But what in the hell is he doing?"

"Well," Lennie glanced in the rearview mirror, "it looks like he and his friend are trying to chase us down." She took a breath as panic tried to take over her brain. "Possibly so he can shoot us for messing up whatever he was planning to do."

"This isn't worth a few damn clients." Elise turned in her seat to peer out the back. "Oh God. They're catching up to us."

"I know." Lennie checked the speedometer.

This was a residential area. There could be kids outside. Little old men walking their dogs.

"You've gotta go faster, Lennie." Elise was going to give herself whiplash looking back and forth. "They're getting closer."

"What if I kill someone?" Lennie gripped the wheel as she came up on a light. "The light's red." She rocked a little in her seat. "The freaking light's red."

"You've gotta go through it." Elise spun in her seat. "What's that sound?" She grabbed for Lennie's purse. "It's your phone. It's probably Rico. He can tell us what the fuck to do." She turned the purse over, spilling it everywhere as she rushed to get to the phone.

By some miracle the light they approached flipped to green a second before Lennie crossed the intersection.

Elise held the phone up, her face twisting into an awful expression. "What the fuck?" She turned the screen Lennie's away.

"I'm a little busy right now." Lennie checked her side mirror instead of the phone screen, easily catching sight of the car that was not backing down.

And also didn't seem as concerned with murdering an innocent pedestrian as she was.

"It's Kyle."

"Kyle?" Lennie caught his name across the screen from the corner of her eye. "Ignore him."

"I can't believe you haven't blocked him."

"*Elise*." Lennie couldn't unclench her teeth. "Can you call someone who can help us figure out what in the fuck we should do?"

"I need your code to use your phone."

Lennie rattled off her code.

"Jesus Christ." Elise stabbed at the screen. "Take a hint, Kyle."

"Is he calling again?" Lennie glanced in her mirrors, checking to make sure she was managing to stay at least a little ahead of Rob.

"I ignored it." Elise swiped across the phone. "Where's Rico's number?"

The phone started buzzing again in her hand.

"Goddammit, Kyle." Elise's finger was poised over the screen, ready to send him straight to voicemail once more.

Lennie slapped at her hands. "Wait." She looked in the mirror again. "Answer it."

The timing was too suspicious.

Too perfect.

Elise lifted her brows and connected the call. "Sorry, Kyle. Lennie can't talk. She's busy." Her eyes widened and her jaw dropped a second before setting in a tight line. "Who the fuck do you think you are?"

Lennie grabbed the phone and pressed it to her ear. "What do you want, Kyle?"

"Pull the car over, Lennie."

"No thank you." She pushed the pedal a little closer to the floor, anger taking up more and more of the space fear occupied in her stomach.

"Fine." Kyle's words were clipped. "I'll go back to the house and visit with your boyfriend."

Lennie's stomach dropped as the car chasing them hit the brakes, stopping in the middle of the street before making a U-turn and heading in the opposite direction.

Lennie slammed on the brakes, slowing the SUV just enough to keep from rolling before cranking the wheel hard to the left.

Elise's body lurched against the door as she fumbled the phone she'd retrieved from her own purse. "What are you doing?"

"Leave him alone, Kyle." Lennie ignored Elise as her friend continued ranting beside her. "What do you want?"

"I want the computer."

The computer? "What computer?"

"The computer you took from Rob. The one you didn't give to the cops."

Lennie was stunned into momentary silence. "We don't have any computers. They were all in the building."

"It wasn't in the building, Lennie. I checked before—"

"Before what?" Lennie pressed the phone tighter to her ear. "Before what, Kyle?"

"If you don't have the computer then I guess I should definitely go find your boyfriend. Maybe he's the one who stole it."

Lennie scoffed. "Rob was the one trying to steal it. It belongs to Investigative Resources."

"Stupid bitch. You don't fucking know anything. Never did."

"I know who owns that damn computer, and it's sure as hell not Rob." A calm washed over her. She wasn't far behind them. There was no way they'd even get close to Rico.

She'd run them over first.

She spent so long thinking she was the issue when it came to her relationship with Kyle.

Obviously she'd been wrong as hell.

Because this guy was a lunatic.

"And no one has the damn thing anyway, because it went down with the building you blew up." Lennie pressed the gas harder, her earlier concerns all but forgotten.

Turned out it was easier to chase someone than it was to run from them.

"Lennie." Elise pressed back into her seat as they raced up on Rob and his passenger.

Who she was now pretty sure was Kyle.

"You called me frigid." Lennie pushed the gas as hard as it would go, taking the front fender of the SUV almost to the bumper of the sedan. "You said I wasn't good enough for you."

"Give me the fucking computer, Lennie."

The car in front of them suddenly braked, wheels screaming as they locked up in an attempt to force Lennie to hit them.

Instead she whipped into the other lane, flying around them, not touching her brakes once as she darted in front of an oncoming pickup before jerking back into the right lane. "I think I know who has your computer, Kyle."

"What are you doing, Lennie?" Elise had her phone to her ear, skin pale as she crawled around in her seat, trying to look behind them.

"I'd love to introduce you to him." She smiled. "His name's Vincent. I'm sure he's excited to meet you too."

Whatever was on that computer was clearly something Rob and Kyle didn't want anyone seeing. Maybe knowing it was already too late would scare them off. Send them into hiding.

Like the worms they were.

"You're lying, Lens. I can hear it in your voice." Kyle sounded deadly calm. "You forget I know you. Intimately."

She nearly gagged at the reminder.

She'd spent all her adult life picking men she knew she wouldn't really want, all in an effort to stay safe. Stay in a no-risk bubble.

And look where it landed her.

"You don't know me, Kyle. Not at all."

He thought she would go along with whatever he said because she always did. It was easy that way. Kept her from being too invested in anything. Too attached.

Not that she would have ever ended up attached to Kyle.

But holding back wasn't just something she did with men.

Lennie turned to Elise. "I love you."

Elise's eyes moved from one side to the other. "What?"

Lennie dropped her phone. She didn't have anything else to say to Kyle. She reached for Elise. "I love you. You are one of my favorite people in the world."

"That's super nice, but right now we have other things going on." Elise glanced out the windshield. She pointed up the street. "Is that my car?"

The small two-door raced toward them.

"No." Elise was on her knees, watching as the car sped past so fast it was impossible to see who was inside.

Not that Lennie needed to.

"*No.*" Elsie crawled between the seats like she could stop them as they headed straight for the sedan. "No, no, no, no, no." Her hands went to her face. "That's a fucking rental."

Lennie cut the wheel hard to the left for the second time, managing to get turned around just as the little car Elise rented jerked, spinning almost in place as the sedan closed in. The rear end of the little car came into direct contact with the front end of the sedan, shoving it nose first toward the shoulder. Momentum carried both cars off the road and into the ditch less than ten yards away.

The doors to the little car were open before it came to a full stop. Abe and Rico jumped free in long, smooth steps, like they weren't exiting a still-moving vehicle, guns drawn as they ran straight toward the sedan.

Lennie's heart stopped as the passenger's door opened on the sedan and Kyle leaned out, holding a gun of his own.

A gun he was pointing right at Rico.

"Do something, Lennie." Elise leaned forward, both hands pressed against the dash. "We have to do something."

She only had one option.

One weapon, and even then, she didn't have very much to work with.

Lennie shoved her foot to the floor, hoping she could work up enough speed in the short distance to at least buy Rico a little time. The sound of the large engine stole Kyle's attention, dragging his eyes her way.

Along with the barrel of his gun.

"Duck." Lennie reached out to grab Elise by the hair, pulling her head down as the first shot split the windshield.

Their bodies jerked forward as the SUV hit the driver's side of the sedan, shoving it a few more feet before coming to a stop. Everything was quiet for a second.

Then all hell broke loose.

Tires screeched against the roadway and suddenly there were men everywhere. All dressed in black tactical gear with guns pulled and pointed at the sedan rocked up on one side.

Lennie and Elise peeked over the dashboard as the men reached into the destroyed car and pulled Kyle and Rob free of the wreckage, dragging them out and across the ground.

A black car with tinted windows pulled up to the scene. The passenger's door opened.

"Holy shit." Elise sat up, a thin split on her forehead seeping a tiny line of blood. "It's Vincent."

Lennie stared at the head of GHOST as he walked up to one of the men. "What in the hell were Rob and Kyle doing?"

"Something bad." Elise shook her head. "Something real bad."

Lennie watched as Kyle kicked at the huge man hefting him across the ground toward a waiting van. "He's a freaking idiot."

"I knew that the minute he dumped you."

"Yeah, but now I've been dumped by a guy who ended up arrested by GHOST." Lennie wrinkled her nose.

"Pretty sure this isn't considered an arrest." Elise sat lower as the man dragged Kyle toward the open back of the van. "You might want to get a good look at him because this will probably be the last time you ever see his dumb face."

"You think?" She wasn't stupid. She knew what GHOST was.

They dealt with international cyber security and they tended to use a heavy hand with anyone they discovered was behaving badly.

"They weren't just trying to steal client names." Lennie jumped a little as the man dragging Kyle picked him up by the back of his pants and shirt and basically threw him into the back of the van.

"No shit."

Lennie sat up a little more as she caught sight of Rico, pushing his way through the men crowding the area around the cars. He came straight to her door and yanked it open.

"I—" Her explanation was cut short as Rico grabbed her and pulled her from the SUV, holding her so tightly she could barely breathe.

"Are you okay?" He cradled her head, pinning her to him. "What in the hell were you thinking?"

"He was going to shoot you." Lennie blinked at the reminder. "He had a gun pointed right at you."

"Abe would have taken him out the second he did."

"That doesn't help you." She pushed at him. "You would have still been shot and I don't know what—" It was so easy to bite it off. Stop the confession.

She always had. She always pumped the brakes on any sort of emotions she had, holding back to stay in her bubble of safety.

Only now it didn't make her feel safe. Now it made her ache. It left her longing for what might be, if only she was brave enough to take that chance.

"I can't wait, Loba." Rico's hands came to her face, holding it in place as he stared into her eyes. "I need to know what you want. I can't go on like this."

She'd lived her whole life carefully avoiding anything that made her scared or pushed her out of her comfort zone.

Flying. Friendships. Relationships. Love.

She'd never loved a man. Never let herself get to that point. Love was the ultimate risk, and if something involved risk she walked away, preferring to be bored and safe over any possible happiness she had to put herself on the line to earn.

Not anymore.

Lennie smiled in spite of the fear still trying to drag her down into the trenches. Trying to make her duck and cover. It was still there.

It just wouldn't win anymore.

"I love you."

Love was supposed to take time. Supposed to be a carefully walked path where she always stayed one step behind.

It was not supposed to be like this. Fast and scary and unavoidable.

But there it was. Standing right in front of her.

"I don't want to go home without you." The second confession was easier than the first. "I want to be together."

Rico was silent.

He didn't move.

"Please say something." She tried to fight the fear, but it was being bolstered by regret. Trying to make her wish she could take her words back.

But it wasn't going to happen. No matter what Rico said back.

He pulled her in again, crushing her body to his.

She tucked her face into the crook of his neck and breathed deep, letting the warmth of him ease the fear. Hold it at bay.

"You are never what I expect, Loba." Rico stroked down her hair. "I think I know what you will do, and then you prove I am wrong."

"Don't feel bad." She closed her eyes, trying to relax the twisting in her belly. "Half the time I don't know what I'm going to do."

His laugh was low and soft. Rico still held a smile as his head lifted, dark eyes on hers. "*Te amo.*"

Lennie smiled a little. "*Bueno.*"

Rico's thumb moved along her cheek. "We will have to work on your Spanish, Loba." He leaned in to rest his forehead against hers. "Because I want my *ninos* to speak Spanish too."

Lennie couldn't hide her smile. "That escalated quickly."

"That's the way it is with me, Loba." He pulled her closer. "I have passion for the things I want."

She should be terrified. Scared out of her mind over everything. Ready to run in the opposite direction.

And she was scared. Maybe even terrified.

She just wasn't running. Not from Rico.

"Rico." Abe's distinctive voice pulled Rico's eyes from hers.

Abe stood with Vincent, surveying the scene.

Rico eased her toward the open door of the SUV. "Stay here." He closed the door and made his way to where Abe and Vincent were.

"What do you think they're talking about?" Elise watched the men.

"With Vincent, who knows." Lennie didn't know a lot about the leader of GHOST, but she knew enough to realize that he put his own team first. No matter what.

Vincent tipped his head at Rico and Abe and walked back to the car he'd exited mere minutes before. As quickly as they arrived, Vincent and the men with him were gone again, leaving nothing but a tow truck to collect the sedan.

"Pierce is going to kill me." Elise shook her head. "He's going to fire me."

"Why?" Lennie glanced at her friend.

Elise pointed to the small sports car. "Both the cars I rented are wrecked." Her head fell back against the seat. "How is that even possible?"

Lennie shrugged as she looked Elise's way. "On the plus side you get to go out now."

CHAPTER 24

RICO LAID IN the center of the bed, one arm propped behind his head as Lennie inspected the contents of the breakfast cart just delivered to their room. "Is there something missing, Loba?"

"I don't think this is ours." She lifted the lid on one of the plates. "It's egg whites and fruit."

There was only one person he knew who ate like that. "Sounds like Abe's breakfast."

"I don't want it." Lennie set the silver lid back in place. "I can't believe he wants it either."

Rico tossed the blankets covering his body to the side.

Lennie's eyes slowly worked down his frame, the flush that drove him wild creeping over her skin.

He shook his head at her. "None of that until you've had breakfast."

Lennie pressed her lips together. Her first instinct was always to hold back. Keep her thoughts to herself. He wanted to change that.

"Give it to me, Lenore." Rico walked her way. "Tell me what's in that perfect mind of yours."

"Remember the time I watched you..." Her eyes fixed on his dick. "You..."

"I remember." He reached down to stroke the part of him that was already interested in offering her a repeat performance. "Is that something you want again?"

"No." Her eyes came to his a little wider than normal. "I mean, yes. But..." The pink on her cheeks deepened. "I would maybe feel bad if you were the only one who did that."

Once again, she surprised him. "Are you offering me a show, Loba?"

She lifted one shoulder in a little shrug. "I didn't know if it was something you would want."

"I want what you want." He eased in closer to her. "Anything you want from me I will give you."

"What about what you want?"

"I want it all, Loba." He eased one hand up the outside of her thigh. "I want to do everything that's ever been done to you. I want you to do everything that's ever been done to me." He traced the crease where the fullness of her ass met her thigh. "That's why you are the one in charge. Because if I was in charge I would be tied to the bed begging you to let me come."

She sucked in a breath. "You would let me do that?"

"*Beg*, Loba. The word is beg. I would beg you to do that." He backed away from her. "But you get nothing from me until you eat." Rico snagged a towel from the bathroom and tied it around his waist.

Lennie's lips curved in a sly little smile. "That didn't end well last time you tried that."

"I'm not worried about Abe seeing my asshole." Rico pushed the cart toward the door and out into the hall. He knocked on Abe's door and waited.

Abe yanked it open, his hair dripping wet, wearing a matching white towel around his own waist.

"They brought us your breakfast." Rico pushed past his friend and into the still-dark room. "Got a headache this morning?" They'd stayed out late last night, taking the girls drinking and dancing before their planned flight home today.

The pile of blankets on one of the queen beds shifted.

Rico stopped as a form sat up straight, long hair a tangled mess, hands swiping at the strands.

"Morning, sunshine." Abe snagged the carafe of coffee off the tray Rico brought in and poured a stream into one of the cups. "How ya feelin'?"

Elise blinked, wiping at a smear of black smudged down one cheek. Her head snapped from side to side. "What's—" Her eyes went to where Abe stood, holding out the coffee he'd just poured. "Oh no." She scooted toward the headboard, the dress she wore last night coming into view as the covers fell down. "No." Elise covered her mouth with one hand. "Oh, God." She jumped off the bed, snagging her shoes as she ran to the door connecting their two rooms, pulling it open and racing through, slamming it behind her.

"Ouch." Rico grabbed the cart meant for him and Lennie, ready to escape the room.

"Nothing happened." Abe sipped at the coffee he'd poured for Elise.

"Sure." Rico kept going.

"Seriously." Abe followed him. "She slept in that bed. I slept in the other one. I just didn't want to leave her alone in case she got sick."

"She seemed pretty upset over a night of nothing."

"I had to carry her up from the uber after she threw up in the bushes. I'm sure she's thrilled there was a witness."

It made sense. Elise didn't seem like the kind of woman who appreciated someone having something to hang over her head.

Luckily Abe wasn't that kind of a guy.

"Should be a fun plane ride home." Rico pushed the cart with Lennie's breakfast out into the hall. "We'll be ready to head out in a couple hours."

"A couple hours?"

"You heard me." Rico shot Abe a wink. "Some of us have things to take care of this morning."

"And you look happy as shit about it."

"That I am." Rico tapped on the door.

Lennie peeked out a tiny crack before opening it wide.

"Were you worried it was someone else?" He pulled the cart into the room, tossing his towel on the bathroom floor as he passed.

Lennie glanced toward the door. "Have you heard anything else from Vincent?"

317

"There's no one else here that will cause problems for us, Loba." Rico lifted the lid on one of the plates, revealing French toast topped with a scattering of fresh fruit and whipped cream. He lifted his brows in question.

"That one's mine."

"What did you choose for me?" He lifted the lid on the other plate. It was a serving of scrambled eggs, a slice of ham, and a serving of shredded fried potatoes with a biscuit on the side.

"Technically I picked that one for me too." Lennie chewed her lip.

"Taking a play from the book of Elise are you?" He grabbed both plates and crawled onto the bed. "You're using me to get everything you want?"

"And then some." Her eyes darted his way and he could see the fear still lingering there.

It's why she was his wolf. She didn't back down. Even from her own fear.

She pushed through. Fighting for what she wanted.

"I plan to give you more than you ever ask me for, Lenore." He settled against the headboard. "Come here."

"Are you going to eat naked?" Her eyes skimmed across his bare chest.

"Is that a problem?"

"It's just distracting." Lennie rested one knee on the mattress. "It's hard not to keep looking."

"Then keep looking, Loba." Rico relaxed back. "I'm not going to stop you." He held the plate of toast out. "But remember, you will get nothing from me until you've eaten."

"You keep saying that." She took the plate and lowered into the spot right next to him.

"Because I mean it." He stabbed his fork into one of the fluffy curds of egg and held it out to her.

She took the bite, chewing slowly.

"What's wrong?" Lennie's emotions were much easier to read than her thoughts, which was a double-edged sword for him. It was easy to tell when she was upset, but it was also easy to tell when she was other things.

Things which were distracting as hell.

"What do you think Vincent's going to do with Rob and Kyle?"

"He will try to get as much information out of them as possible." Rico lifted one shoulder. "If they realize they should make themselves valuable then they will live."

"What information does he want from them?"

He and Abe had offered Lennie and Elise the bare minimum yesterday, giving them time to come to terms with what happened.

But he wouldn't keep the whole story from her any longer. "Rob and Kyle were supplying a product to a shell company being used to filter money out of the US."

"They were laundering money?"

"Si." Rico took a breath, waiting for the question that would be the most difficult to answer.

"To where?"

Rico shook his head. "That is information I was not given."

"From where?"

More information he didn't have. "I don't know."

"Does Vincent know?"

"I would assume he at least has suspicions." Rico waited, knowing it was coming.

"What were they supplying?"

This was the part he knew she would struggle with.

He certainly was. "There were cameras in the bathrooms at Investigative Resources, Loba. They were recording all the women and running a website charging to watch the videos."

Lennie stared at him, a forkful of French toast hovering in front of her open mouth. "They were charging people to watch women pee?"

"They were charging people to watch women do whatever women do in the bathroom."

"Ew." Lennie's nose wrinkled. "Ew."

"Most of the transactions were not done by real people. A system was created to continuously run charges, moving huge amounts of money every hour."

"Most?" Lennie's fork went back to the plate. "But not all?"

"Not all."

Lennie rested her plate on her lap as she went quiet. Finally one hand went to her head. "You can't tell Pierce. He'll break into GHOST headquarters and kill Rob and Kyle."

"Mona isn't the only woman who was recorded, Loba." He had to make sure she understood. She had the right to know what was out there.

Lennie's head bobbed in a little nod. "I figured." She poked at her food. "You know he tried to make me feel bad for not trusting him." She snorted out a little laugh. "But I never could make myself." Lennie stabbed the bite she'd dropped. "Now I know why." She shoved the bread into her mouth, chewing a second before her head snapped up his way. "Does Elise know?"

"Not yet." They'd agreed to tell Lennie first, hoping she would be the one to handle it the best.

And so far she hadn't disappointed him.

Not that she ever could.

"I should be the one to tell her." Lennie leaned into his side, resting her head on his shoulder. "Maybe we should wait until we're back home so I can tell everyone at once."

Home.

He loved the sound of that word coming from her mouth. "I think you know them better than anyone else. You know what will be best."

Lennie dropped her head back to look up at him. "Heidi will help Pierce break into GHOST to find them."

Rico shook his head. "That is not our problem to handle, Loba."

Lennie's eyes held his. "What is our problem to handle?"

"We only have one problem." He reached out to slide one finger across her face. "You have to decide where we will make our home."

****

"I'M GOING TO kill him." Eva's upper lip was twisted into a snarl as she stared at Lennie and Elise.

"No." Mona sat next to her best friend, arms crossed over her chest, a matching snarl twisting her own lips. "You're pregnant. I'll kill him."

Lennie glanced at where Heidi sat, looking way more relaxed than she'd anticipated.

Of all her former coworkers, she'd expected Heidi to freak out the most. Instead, she appeared calm and collected.

Maybe even relaxed as she stared down at her phone, typing out a text message.

Eva turned to where Heidi sat. "Did you hear what they said? Rob was recording us in the bathroom."

"I heard." Heidi didn't look up from her phone.

Mona leaned forward, eyeing their friend. "That's all you have to say?"

"What else am I going to say?" Heidi set the phone on her desk and finally looked up.

"We expected you to want to kill him even more than Mona and Eva." Elise turned Lennie's way. "I thought she would be halfway there already."

Heidi's blue gaze met Elise's. "I don't have to be there to kill him."

"Damn." Elise shook her head. "You are scary as shit." She slowly smiled. "That's why you're my best friend."

Heidi leaned back in her seat, running one hand over the curve of her growing belly. "Unfortunately, the problem we have doesn't end with Kyle and Rob."

Lennie's stomach clenched tight. She was getting better at pushing through fear when it tried to hold her back, but right now the fear wasn't for herself.

It was for her friends.

For the company she felt oddly protective of.

"What do you mean?" The danger to Alaskan Security was supposed to be over. Ended when Mona killed the man who tried to take them down.

"I mean we should get used to the fact that things might never be normal here." Heidi shrugged. "We go around pissing powerful people off and they're going to retaliate."

"But Rob and Kyle weren't powerful." Elise's hands gripped her knees. "And GHOST has them. They're done."

"*They* are done." Heidi slid her laptop closer. "But they were just the sludge on the floor of the bottom-feeder pond." She tapped keys as she continued to talk. "Vincent sent me what they found and it's pretty interesting."

"Interesting?" The word made her hopeful. Interesting didn't sound too bad.

"Maybe interesting was the wrong word." Heidi's eyes slid to one side. "Maybe I meant pretty terrible."

Mona's clear blue eyes were sharp. "Explain."

"So it's clear someone else we know was involved in this too. It's the only way Rob would feel comfortable doing what he did on his work computer. He wasn't worried about getting caught."

"Fuck." Eva pressed the heels of her hands into her eyes. "Chandler." She let out a long, gurgley groan. "That asshole's going to haunt us forever."

"It's my fault." Mona's spine was straight in her seat. "I'm the reason he had the power he did at Investigative Resources."

While Mona was now the strong, confident wife of the owner of Alaskan Security, it wasn't long ago that she and Lennie had quite a bit in common.

It was one of the reasons Lennie knew she could be different. Because Mona did it.

"But he's super dead now, so it doesn't really matter anymore." Lennie wasn't going to argue with Mona. She knew owning your mistakes had power.

But she also wasn't going to let her dwell on it.

"So then this should all be done, right?" Eva looked toward Heidi. "If Chandler's dead and Kyle and Rob are probably not far behind him then what's the problem?"

"The problem is Chandler was pretty much a bottom feeder too." Heidi snorted. "If he wasn't dead already he'd be dead now. The guys he was dealing with on this whole thing are bad news."

"How bad?"

"Bad." Heidi glanced at her computer screen. "Funneling millions through that website, bad."

Elise crossed her arms and smiled. "Not anymore they're not."

"Yeah." Heidi pursed her lips. "That's probably not going to make them real happy. They were laundering money for a reason and we fucked it all up."

"Vincent fucked it all up." Lennie sat a little straighter in her seat. "He's the one who has Rob and Kyle. Not us."

"Vincent is invisible, Lennie." Heidi almost sounded apologetic. "He's exactly what his team is. A ghost."

"That's not right." Lennie scooted to the end of her seat, any warm feelings she might have had for Vincent evaporating in the blink of an eye. "He can't leave us on the hook for this."

"It's part of the deal, Ms. Bates." Pierce strode into their office, tall and perfectly poised.

Like always.

He went straight to his wife's desk and leaned against it.

Like always.

"GHOST offers options that wouldn't be available to us any other way." Pierce crossed his arms. "Without them we are simply another security company."

"With them we're on the shit list of anyone they piss off." Elise stuck right with her, facing down the owner of the company. "And I would guess Vincent loves to piss people off."

"Vincent keeps humanity from being taken over by the Chandlers of the world. He is what stands between men who are only out for themselves and innocent people."

"But he stands behind us." Lennie glanced at Heidi's phone. No doubt there was a direct line to the head of GHOST in the contacts. Heidi would probably even give it to her. Just for fun.

"He stands *with* us, Ms. Bates." Pierce shook his head. "Just because something isn't seen, doesn't mean it's not there."

The room fell silent as the women stared at Pierce.

He cleared his throat, slowly rising from his wife's desk and walking toward the door. "On that note, I'm here to give you your next assignment." He turned to face them.

"I need you to find the men Rob and Kyle were working for." He paused taking a slow breath. "And it's in everyone's best interest that you do it quickly."

EPILOGUE

"WHAT DO YOU think, Loba?"

Lennie looked around the townhouse, trying to come up with the words to explain how she felt about the beautiful, but clearly expensive, condo. "It's gorgeous."

That was actually a huge understatement.

The place was stunning. Wide-plank wood floors in a warm tone that perfectly complemented the cabinets in the large open kitchen. Marble countertops. A high-end gas stove that rivaled the one in–

Lennie turned to Rico. "Who's the seller?"

Rico's lips lifted in a slow smile. "I told him you would figure it out."

The line of three-story condos were erected in the most scenic section of Fairbanks. They were close to downtown, but also a short drive from headquarters.

Perfectly situated for anyone working at Alaskan Security.

"Pierce built all these?" Lennie walked to the kitchen, reaching out to slide one palm across the smooth marble surface of the counter. "Why?"

"Because we're his family, Loba."

Her throat tightened.

Pierce was a level of intimidating few people could manage to interact with, let alone deal with on a daily basis.

She'd seen his soft side enough times to know there was more to the owner of Alaskan Security, but this was a whole new level of more.

"This had to cost hundreds of thousands of dollars."

"Over a million." Rico followed her as she made her way down the hall. "But he will recoup the cost as they sell."

They would certainly sell.

Each townhouse had a basement that included a two-car garage, a bonus room, and a bathroom. The main level consisted of a living room, dining room, and the kitchen she'd been admiring, along with a laundry room and–

"Oh." Lennie stopped at the open door to the master bedroom. She took a few steps in and peeked toward the attached bathroom. "Oh my."

Rico's gaze darkened as they watched her walk into the space. "You should watch what you say here, Lenore. Especially if you don't want this to be our home. I'd hate for someone else to buy a bedroom we've already made use of."

It was odd to think of it that way.

As something that would be theirs.

Their home.

She ignored the suggestion in his words, trying to keep her line of focus on the task at hand. "Do you like it? I'm not the only one who has to like it."

"You are, though."

Lennie crossed to the large window that looked out over the row of small, but tidy fenced-in yards spanning the back of the building. "I want you to like it. It will be your home too."

"You are my home, Loba. Not a building. My home is wherever you are."

She turned to face him. "You're making this difficult."

Rico gave her a slow smile. "I'm making this easy. You choose what makes you happy and it will make me happy too."

"It just seems so expensive." She should talk herself out of this. It wasn't practical. It had marble and carpet that felt like the padding was made of freaking pillows.

"Pierce didn't build these to make money. He built these so the men and women he owes his company to would have nice homes." Rico slowly came her way. "Room to raise their children."

She rested one hand on her head. "I'm not ready to even think about having children. I think Eva and Bess ruined me." Lennie had seen enough vomit in the past six months to last her a lifetime. Both women were so sick it made her question whether she would ever want to be pregnant herself.

"There are many different ways to have children, Lenore." Rico's gaze was steady as he watched her.

The moment was surreal.

They were standing in what might be their future home in the room where they may one day conceive their future children. Based on the life she lived before coming here, she should be terrified. Panic stricken.

At the very least considering passing out.

Possibly fleeing.

But Lennie wanted to do none of those things.

She always tried to take relationships slow, thinking that would help her find the feelings other women seemed to come by so easily. But those feelings never came.

Then she met this man.

And no one would ever call Rico slow. When it came to love, and any of the affections that came with it, Rico moved as fast as he drove.

Maybe as fast as he flew.

And she was right there beside him.

Sometimes it still scared her. Still made her want to retreat back into her old self.

But Rico made her want to be brave. Made her want to be better.

Not just for him, but for herself too. For the future they talked about every day.

And even for the children she wasn't quite sure she was ready to have.

"Are any of the other townhomes sold?" The condo they were in was an end unit with windows not just on the front and back, but also up one side. That meant it got more light than the interior units, but also wouldn't be buffered against the cold Alaskan winters like they would.

"Half of the units are already sold." Rico wrapped his arms around her, pulling her close. "Does that mean you're interested in making this one ours?"

"I'm just surprised no one took the end unit." She loved plants, and honestly the end unit was the best option to make use of the limited Alaskan sunlight. There would be plenty of places for her houseplants, including the fiddle leaf fig Rico helped her choose when she first came to Alaskan security.

"This unit may have been set aside just for you."

Lennie tipped her head back to look up at him. "When did Pierce start building these?"

"The plans began right after he found out Bess was pregnant again." Rico paused. "Then the construction was expedited once Heidi and Eva announced their pregnancies."

"We weren't even dating then." There was no way he could've reserved a unit for them that long ago.

"I am not the only one who loves you here, Loba." Rico's voice was low and soft. "You have many friends who want you to be happy."

Her throat suddenly became tight and her eyes burned. She had friends before coming to Alaska. But they were as casual as the rest of her relationships.

"Who else bought units here?"

The thought of living side-by-side with the people she'd grown so close to made Lennie's belly warm. Her whole life she'd only been close to her family. It was part of what made her so confused about how she ended up.

Her family was wonderful. Her parents had a great relationship. She grew up seeing a healthy happy marriage.

And she still spent so much of her life terrified of relationships.

"Talk to me, Loba." Rico rested his lips on her forehead. "Why are you sad?"

"I feel like I wasted so much time." Most of the women she was friends with now had been in her life for years. Years she spent keeping her distance, worried they would reject her. Years worried she wouldn't be good enough for them.

Years missing out on what she had now.

"You have time left." Rico stroked one hand down the back of her head. "You should make the most of it."

"Is that your way of trying to get me to have babies?" She smiled up at him.

"I told you. I like what you like. I am happy when you're happy. If you want babies, we have babies. If you don't, we have each other." Rico's eyes darkened. "And without the distraction of babies I will have more time to think of creative ways to take up your nights."

Just the thought made her skin hot.

"What do you think, Loba?" Rico pushed against her, his big body forcing them toward the wall. "Is this the room where you want to spend your nights with me?"

She pressed her lips together, the temptation to resist putting herself out there still something she had to work to overcome. "I wasn't thinking about the nights." Her back bumped the freshly-painted drywall.

A low rumble moved through Rico's chest where it pressed against hers. His lips brushed against her jawline on their way to her ear. "I would never limit you to only my nights, Loba." His hand ran up the outside of her thigh, catching the hem of her dress and lifting it as he went. "I want you to fill every second of my day."

Her heart raced as she pushed out words that still weren't easy to say. "I want you to fill me every second of the day."

"*Dios mío.*" Rico's fingers gripped the side of her panties, yanking them down until they tangled at her knees. "You will kill me with words like that."

Her heart sped as he turned her away from him, her back to his front.

"I will cry when it is too cold for you to wear these dresses." The cool air of the room suddenly met her bare ass. Rico's hands slid over her belly as he pressed into her, the solid line of his dick, making her gasp as anticipation fisted her stomach.

"Technically it's too cold to wear them now."

Rico's lips ran along the side of her neck as he pushed her against the wall. "Then why did you wear this dress?"

"Because I like it." The truth was still sometimes difficult to admit. Even when she wanted to.

"Not because you wanted to tempt me?" Rico's hand slid between her legs, his fingers stroking along her slit. "Not because you were hoping I would find a way to make you come?"

He was a sneaky man, and it landed her in positions like this almost every day.

In the utility closets.

In the bathrooms.

In the conference rooms. Anywhere they had a few minutes alone together, Rico took advantage.

"Is that what you want now?" Rico found her clit and began to work it in slow circles. "For me to make you come?"

"Yes." Her answer was more air than sound.

"Then ask me for it." Rico's fingers left her clit to slide into her body with a slow glide. "Ask for your pleasure, Lenore."

This was new.

Which was not new.

In the three months since coming back from Cincinnati, Rico had broadened her horizons in ways she didn't even know existed.

He suggested things she didn't know were possible.

And certainly didn't expect to enjoy.

But she always did. "Make me come."

"Beg me for it." The roughness in his voice made her pussy clench tight around his fingers.

"You like when I make you beg?" His lips rested against the shell of her ear. "Maybe I will make you beg me again tonight." His fingers flattened against her. "Maybe I will lick your pussy until you almost come and then I will stop and make you beg me to finish."

Her knees nearly buckled.

Rico wasn't asking for anything he hadn't already offered her. Begging for release was something he definitely enjoyed. More than a few times he spent an evening restrained while she did anything she wanted to him.

And Rico made it clear she was not to let him finish easily.

Until now, Lennie had only really been on one side of the act.

But this.

This made her wish she'd requested the favor be returned.

"We can do that now." It didn't sound particularly sexy or particularly suggestive, but she learned early on that Rico didn't expect her to sound like either of those. He just wanted to know what she was thinking. So she tried to tell him.

"Not now, Loba." Rico's fingers worked faster. "I am not taking you to Pierce's office looking like a woman who needs to come." The pressure of his touch was perfect, the pace exactly what she needed, when she needed it. "But tonight," his lips pressed to her ear, "you will beg."

That was all it took to end what he'd started. Lennie's head dropped back to his shoulder as she did her best to keep her feet under her as his palm ground against her, dragging the orgasm out until her body went limp.

Rico caught the waistband of her panties and pulled them back into place with one hand while the other arm stayed banded around her waist.

The hem of her dress dropped into place. "What will it be, Loba? Is this our home?"

Her eyes were closed, head still resting against the man behind her.

Rico was right.

She was home.

It just had nothing to do with where they were standing.

BONUS BITS ONE

"HOW'S SHE DOING?" Brock's voice was low as his eyes drifted into the hospital room at Wade's back.

"She's good. Tired, but good." Wade turned, giving Bessie's sleeping form one final look before heading out into the hall.

Pushing the hospital-issued bassinet holding his daughter in front of him.

Brock hooked one hand on the edge of the clear plastic bin containing the newest member of the Alaskan Security family. "She's a pretty little thing, isn't she?"

"She looks like her mama, thank God. Bess threatened my life if this one came out looking like me too." Wade eased the rollered cart down the hall toward the dimly-lit family waiting area where his mother spent most of the previous evening pacing the floor.

It'd been a long night for everyone. Bess was in labor almost 12 hours and she was exhausted. She'd stayed awake long enough to eat and feed the baby, and now that she was finally asleep, he wanted to give her a little time to rest before Ruby woke up ready to eat again. "How's everything going at headquarters?"

"Busy." Brock followed him into the small area that held a number of comfortable chairs, a coffee station, and an array of snacks.

Wade went straight for the coffee, pouring two cups out and passing one to Brock. "I think it's going to be that way for a while."

Things were changing at Alaskan security, and not just as far as the business was concerned.

The men around him were moving from being lifelong bachelors to husbands.

And more than a couple were already expanding their families.

Wade snagged his own coffee and took a long draw. "How is Eva doing?"

"The same." Brock stared into his cup. "It's hard. Even harder than I expected it to be."

That was saying something. No doubt Brock knew this would be one of the scariest times of his life.

"She's going to be fine." Wade said it with confidence. Statistics were on his side.

Not that he expected that to help Brock any.

His sister-in-law had died following a c-section. Her life cut short by a blood clot no one saw coming.

It was an incident that ultimately took his brother's life too.

"I know." The lines around Brock's eyes said differently. "I just hate that she feels so bad and it's my fault."

"Wait till she goes into labor. She'll remind you it's your fault." Bess was the sweetest woman Wade had ever met. Her gentle nature and quiet strength were only a small part of the reasons he'd struggled to go on after they went their separate ways.

But that sweetness evaporated when she was in labor. "She threatened to divorce me."

That got a small chuckle out of Brock. "At least you got to be with her this time." He shook his head. "I can't imagine not being able to be there for Eva right now."

It was something Wade tried not to dwell on. All he'd missed out on because of his own fears.

But it was hard.

Harder now that he'd seen firsthand exactly what Bess had to do without him. "Watching what they go through makes you look at them differently."

He knew Bessie was strong. He knew she was a force.

But watching her bring new life into the world—

That took his admiration for her to an entirely new level.

"I don't think I could handle this as well as Eva has." Brock eased down into one of the waiting room chairs. "She's sick around the clock. Nothing ever sounds good. Nothing ever tastes good. She's already lost almost 10 pounds."

The worry on his best friend's face was clear. It was why Brock had been single for so long. Loving a woman is what killed his brother. A life without her ended up being impossible to face.

And now Brock was staring down his ultimate fear.

"So what you're saying is this baby is going to be an only child?" He'd been friends with Brock for years.

Long enough to know his best bet was to try to lighten the mood. Try to get Brock out of his funk.

"I feel guilty."

"This isn't just your fault, man." Wade lowered into the seat next to his friend. "She had a part in this too."

Brock shook his head. "That's not what I feel bad about." His eyes lifted to Wade's. "Some days I wish we hadn't done this."

"I think that's normal."

"It's normal to wish your baby didn't exist?"

"It's normal to want the woman you love to feel healthy. You're not wishing the baby didn't exist. You're wishing Eva wasn't suffering. Those are two different things."

"Are they though?" Brock ran both hands down his face, fingers digging into his tired-looking eyes. "Because you can't have one without the other." He leaned back, letting his head tip against the wall behind them. "How am I going to be a good dad when I wish my baby didn't exist?"

These were the things no one really talked about.

Everyone focused on the mother. Rightly so.

She was the one who dealt with the physical effects of pregnancy.

She was the one whose whole life changed in an instant.

340

Whose body was taken over, hijacked by a tiny invader.

Who then had to suffer to release the small squatter into the world.

It was important to focus on the mother.

Unfortunately, many fathers were left to struggle with their own emotions and fears, guilt keeping them silent.

Because how did they have the right to complain?

"It's okay to be scared. It's okay to feel guilty. It's okay to not be okay." Wade had many difficult days during Bessie's pregnancy. Days where he worked hard to hide how he felt from the woman he loved.

But another woman he loved helped him through.

"Maybe you should talk to my mom sometime." Talking to her was what helped him understand it was okay for him to struggle with this transition as well.

Brock sighed. "I'll be fine. I just need to push through it."

Wade shook his head. "Why would you push through it? It's hard and it's okay to admit it's hard."

"I'm supposed to be fine. Eva needs me to be fine so I can take care of her."

It was a fact Wade struggled with himself. Feeling like he didn't have the right to be scared. Like he didn't have the right to not be okay. "Maybe she will feel better knowing she's not the only one struggling."

Brock stared at him.

"I know it doesn't make sense, but maybe Eva will feel less alone knowing you are having a hard time too."

"I'm supposed to take care of her. I'm supposed to be the one who can make it better. How can I make it better if I'm not fine?"

Wade had asked his mother that exact question. "Eva isn't with you because she thinks you're perfect. She isn't with you because she expects you to always take care of her. She's with you because she wants to be on your team."

"She's with me because she likes my gravy."

Wade snorted out a little laugh. "Not right now she doesn't."

Brock's lips almost lifted into a smile. "I've made everything I can think of trying to get her to eat. Nothing ever sounds good."

"Just wait. After she has the baby she'll want to eat everything. As soon as they're done delivering they are starving. You'll get to make up for lost time."

He'd ordered dinner for Bess and himself after Ruby's birth. She ate all of it. Hers and his. Then he hit up the snack bar and brought her back a pack of Doritos and a set of chocolate-frosted cupcakes. She'd scarfed those down and then promptly passed out.

"That's another thing that worries me." Brock shook his head. "How am I going to handle seeing her in pain? I can't even deal with seeing her nauseous."

"You'd be surprised what you can handle." Wade reached up to rest one hand on Ruby as she stirred in her swaddle. Unfortunately, the hand he gave wasn't enough to keep her settled. She blinked a few times, kicking her feet as she started to fuss. Wade stood up and scooped her from the bassinet. He immediately held the tiny bundle Brock's way. "Here you go, Uncle Broccoli."

Brock leaned away. "No thanks."

"You're not scared to hold a baby are you?"

Brock crossed his arms tight over his chest. "I've held plenty of babies, but that one's yours. I know you want to hold her."

Brock was right. He would have given Ruby up, but only because this was his best friend.

Wade cuddled his daughter against his chest. "It is different when it's your baby."

"Really?" Brock leaned in, reaching one hand toward Ruby. His expression softened when a little hand immediately latched onto his finger. "What if it's not?"

It was difficult to really connect with an unborn baby, even when it was yours. Wade had watched as Bessie's belly grew. He'd felt his daughter kick.

But on some level it still didn't seem real. Not like it had with Parker.

He'd immediately bonded with the son he hadn't known existed. He'd expected to bond with this baby the instant he knew she was there.

It didn't happen that way.

"It's hard to explain, but the second you see their little face it just happens. You immediately fall in love." Wade stared down at the second angel

343

his wife had given him. "It's a love I just can't put into words." He turned to his friend. "But I can promise it will be there for you too."

BONUS BITS TWO

"SIR?"

The voice at his door was quiet. Hesitant.

Like every voice that came before it.

Vincent took another sip of the whiskey he'd been nursing since finally escaping the main floor for a moment of peace. He didn't turn to see who drew the short end of the stick this time. "What is it?"

"There's an issue."

There always was.

"I'll be in." He stared out the single window in the building. One that was put in at his request.

A reminder there was a world outside this place. One he was once a part of.

Many years ago.

At one time he would have hurried from his chair. Rushed to take on whatever threat loomed.

Take down whoever dared go up against him.

But the shine was gone. Tarnished after years of wear.

Years of seeing the worst there was in the world.

Finding out for every one he took down, there were ten more in line.

Waiting.

Vincent drained the last of his drink, setting the empty glass next to the bottle he would visit again before the night was over.

If it was ever over.

They all bled together. One feeding into the next in a never-ending loop of evil and depravity.

"Sir?" This time the voice was soft, but not hesitant. "You should hurry."

"Should I?" Vincent slowly stood, straightening out the weariness he never seemed to be able to shed. "I'm sure no one is going anywhere."

The urgency was gone. Had been for too long.

Long enough he was questioning his own purpose here.

If he was still the man who should be sitting at that desk.

"It's him."

There were few things in this world that made his heart race. Even fewer still that he looked forward to. This was one of them.

Vincent immediately focused on the young man at his door. "What has he done now?"

"At first we thought it was Heidi."

Of course they did. The hacker at Alaskan Security was always finding her way into their system. Her abilities would be a valuable asset for GHOST, and he'd tried at one point to lure her into his world.

She declined the offer.

Smart woman.

Heidi's IP address was allowed certain liberties in GHOST's system. An agreement he'd made with the owner of Alaskan Security.

Of course she always tried to push past the limits of those liberties. A fact he enjoyed immensely.

Vincent crossed the room, all his attention on the game of cat and mouse they'd been playing with someone who might actually be more skilled than Heidi was. "How far did he make it this time?"

"I'm not sure." Elias, a newer recruit, kept pace with his long strides. "But he made it past the firewall."

Vincent stopped. "What?"

"The firewall. He made it past the firewall." The man's skin paled. "He was in before there was any sign it was happening."

His pulse picked up and he began to walk again, this time faster. "Where did he go from there?"

"That's the strange thing." Elias grabbed the door to the main floor and pulled it open. "Nowhere."

Every eye in the room landed on him as he walked in. Vincent headed straight to the main desk at the center of the barely-lit room. He leaned down, one hand resting against the cool surface as he scanned the screens lining the area. "Show me where you first saw evidence he was here."

Elias swiped across the largest of the screens with one finger, pulling up lines of code. He pointed to a single line. "Here."

It was impossible. "There's no way anyone should be able to get into this system."

And yet this man had done it, and done it without being seen.

"Print it off." He walked to the printer and stood, knowing he wouldn't have to wait long.

Vincent snagged the paper as soon as it slid free of the jet. "There's nowhere else he went?"

"Not that we can find." Elias shook his head. "We don't know what the purpose was."

"I do." Vincent turned and walked toward the door. "Double-check everything and make sure the firewall is still intact."

He didn't stop walking until he was back in his office. This time he closed his door.

He'd been disappointed when Heidi chose Alaskan Security over GHOST. Her abilities were unparalleled.

At least he'd thought they were.

Vincent went to his desk and pushed the bottle he visited each night to one side, pulling his computer into its place as he slipped on his readers and scanned the page in front of him.

Tucked neatly into the lines of code was a set of numbers that was out of place. The indication his people found that their repeat visitor was back.

And this time he managed to breach their system.

Normally this would result in the entire lockdown of GHOST. A complete scrub of all their systems and the design of a new, improved firewall.

But this man wasn't trying to cause harm. He'd been inside their system and the only thing he left was this single breadcrumb, inserted in a way that it was completely benign.

Vincent moved through the screens on his computer until he found the one he was searching for.

He entered the series of numbers.

The IP address he'd been given.

In a few short breaths he had a location. A narrowed idea of where their uninvited visitor was located.

Vincent typed in the coordinates, ready to scan the area he would be visiting at his earliest ability.

Before the map could populate the screen his computer went black.

"Damn it." He shoved back from the desk to check the cord he'd most likely kicked free of its plug.

The computer was plugged in.

His eyes slowly lifted to the screen.

A pinpoint of light started at the center, slowly growing until it consumed the entire space.

Then it went black again.

The soft sound of an open audio line was the only sign the computer was still active.

"Hello, Vincent."

His eyes snapped to where the camera was located at the top of the screen.

A light and lyrical laugh carried through the open line. "Worried I can see you?"

He'd been wrong.

Their visitor was not a man.

It was a woman.

"It seems unfair that you can see me but I can't see you."

"Life is unfair, Vincent."

"I won't argue that point." He leaned back in his chair, putting on the same show that got him through the past thirty years. He retrieved the glass he'd rejected not long ago and poured himself a few fingers.

But not for the same reasons as the ones that came before.

"What can I do for you?"

"I would like a job."

"We're not hiring." He sipped the whiskey, taking down very little.

"You're always hiring the right people."

Her knowledge was slightly unnerving.

And also slightly exciting. "Is that what this was about? Proving to me that you're one of those people?"

"I'm not so interested in proving anything to you, Vincent."

Her voice was as smooth as the whiskey rolling across his tongue. Rich and full with a bite he felt in places he shouldn't. "If this wasn't about proving your skill then what was it about?"

"I didn't say it wasn't about proving my skill. I just said it wasn't about proving it to *you*." The edge of her voice pulled him closer.

350

"What's your name?"

"If I tell you then you will come find me."

"Who said I wasn't coming to find you anyway?"

"It will be hard when you don't know where to look." Her words carried a hint of amusement. "I would assume you're smart enough to know that if I can find my way into your system then I can make sure my IP address doesn't lead you straight to me."

"What's your plan then, Miss—"

"It doesn't seem like a good idea to give you my name, Vincent."

"You know where my team is located. You've been inside our system. You have my name and you've seen my face." He snorted as he reached for the edge of his laptop, ready to close it in spite of his desire not to.

He wanted to keep talking to her. He wanted to hear a little more of that silky voice as it said his name.

"*Wait.*" For the first time she sounded on edge.

He cocked his head. "I'm a busy man. I don't have time to waste on people who won't put their own ass on the line."

"Does that mean you would consider hiring me if I did?"

"I can't hire someone I can't identify, so unless you're willing to—"

The screen flashed to life.

What he saw there stole the air from his lungs.

He was expecting...

Not this.

Wide brown eyes stared back at him, deep and soulful. Lined with lashes as dark and thick as the cascade of curls framing the face of a grown woman.

Not a young woman, ready to start a life and a family.

A peer. A woman who'd seen many of the same days he had. Maybe not all.

But most.

Her lips were full and her softly-rounded cheeks pinked across the rise of the bones beneath them. A scatter of freckles dotted her nose, giving her an air of innocence.

Her chin lifted a tiny bit as those soulful eyes locked onto his. "My name is Julieanne Marello." Her shoulders squared. "And I would like to work for GHOST."

****

Printed in Great Britain
by Amazon